★ THE SONS OF ★
LIBERTY

CREATED AND WRITTEN BY **ALEXANDER LAGOS** AND **JOSEPH LAGOS**

ART BY **STEVE WALKER**   COLOR BY **OREN KRAMEK**

LETTERS BY **CHRIS DICKEY**

Random House 🏠 **New York**

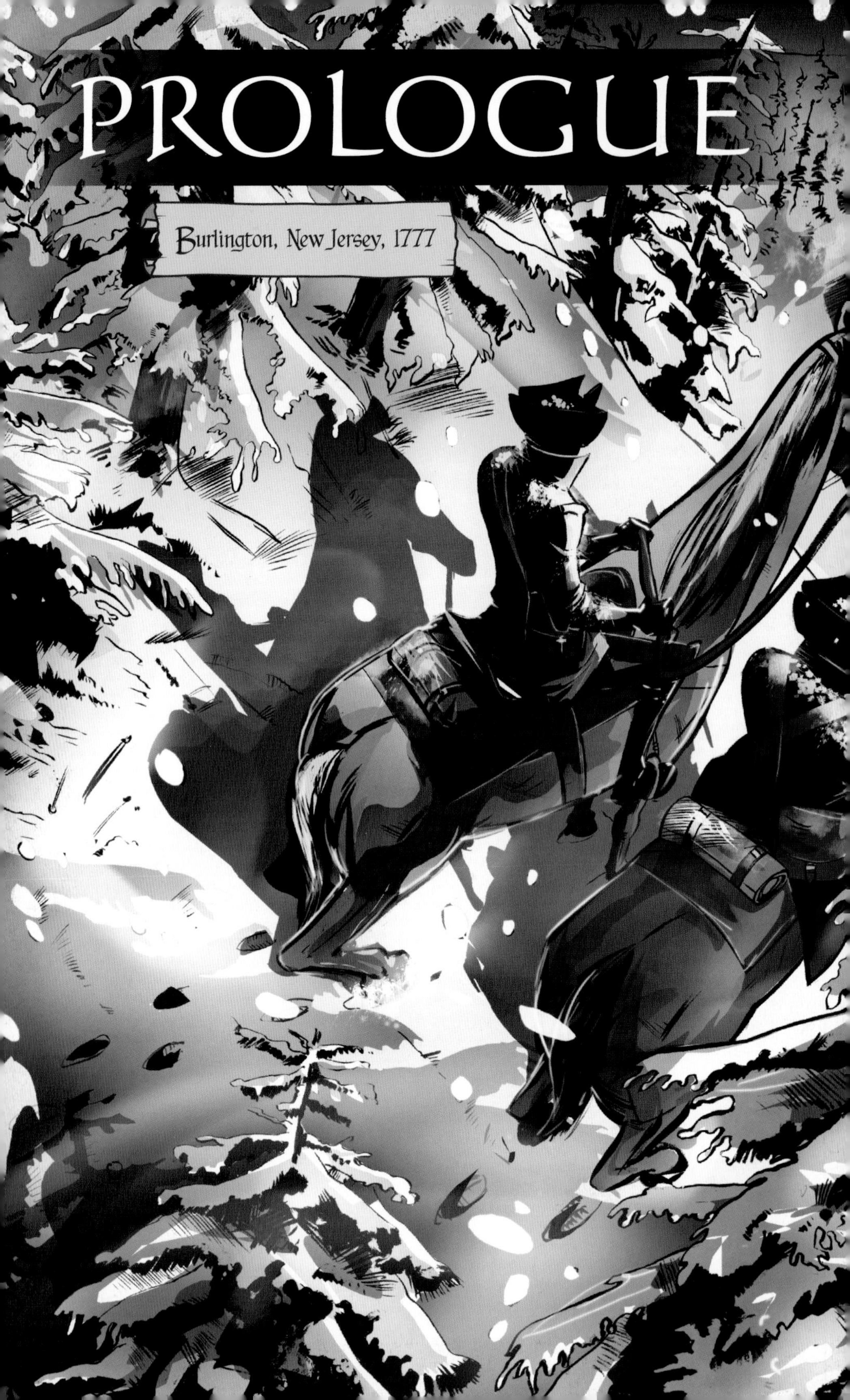
PROLOGUE
Burlington, New Jersey, 1777

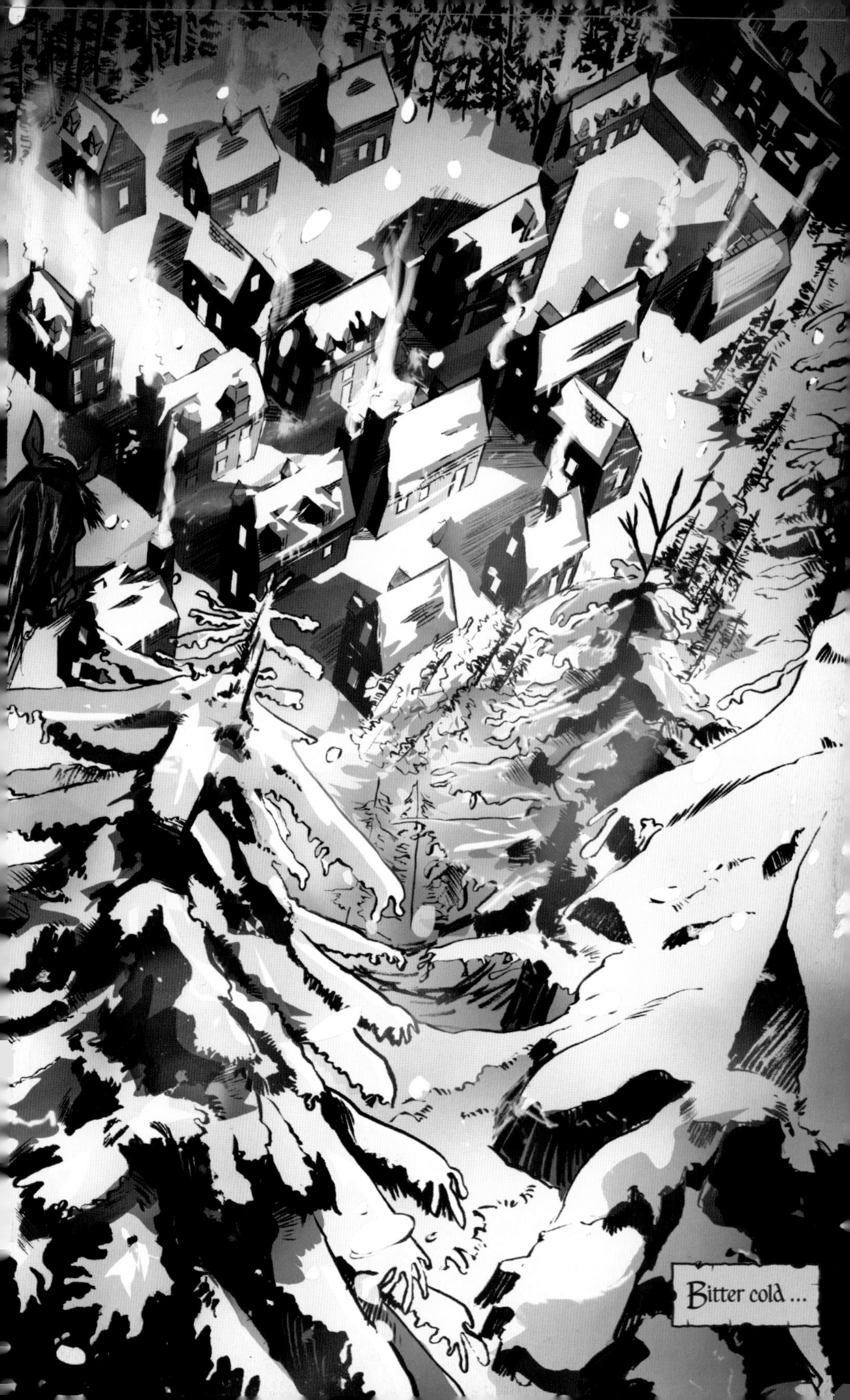
Bitter cold ...

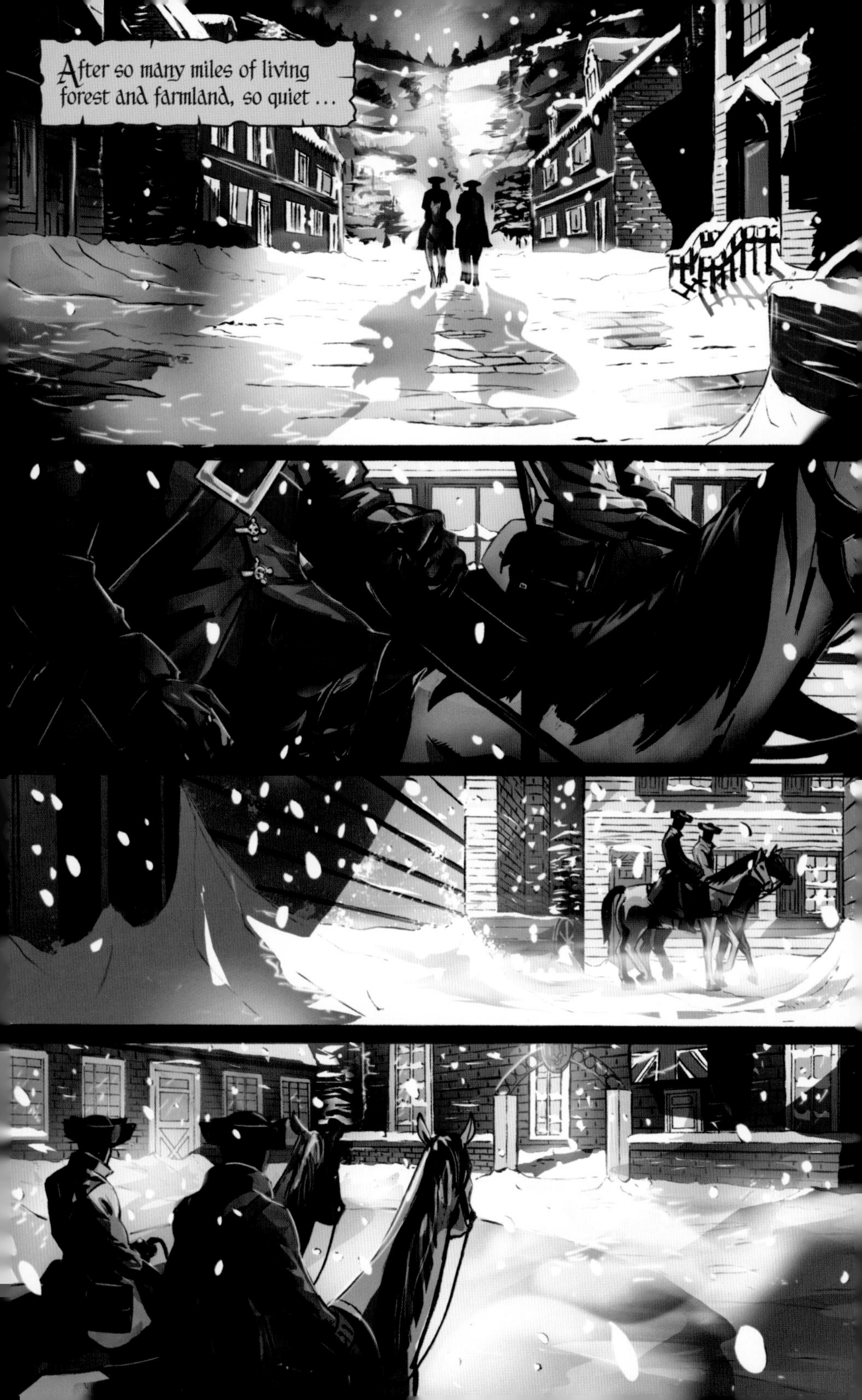
After so many miles of living forest and farmland, so quiet . . .

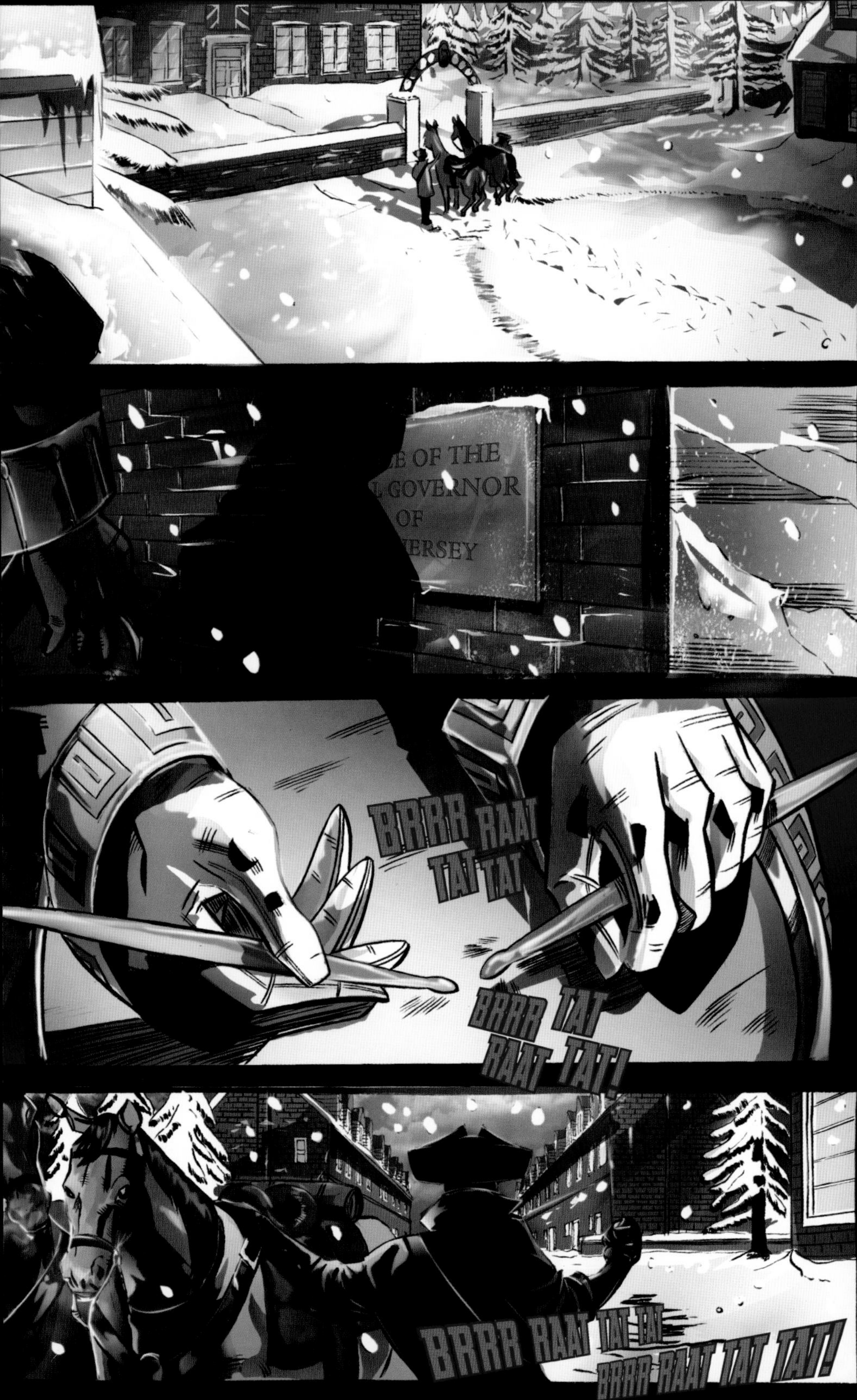
OF THE
GOVERNOR
OF
BRRR RAAT
TAT TAT
BRRR TAT
RAAT TAT!
BRRR RAAT TAT TAT
BRRR RAAT TAT TAT!

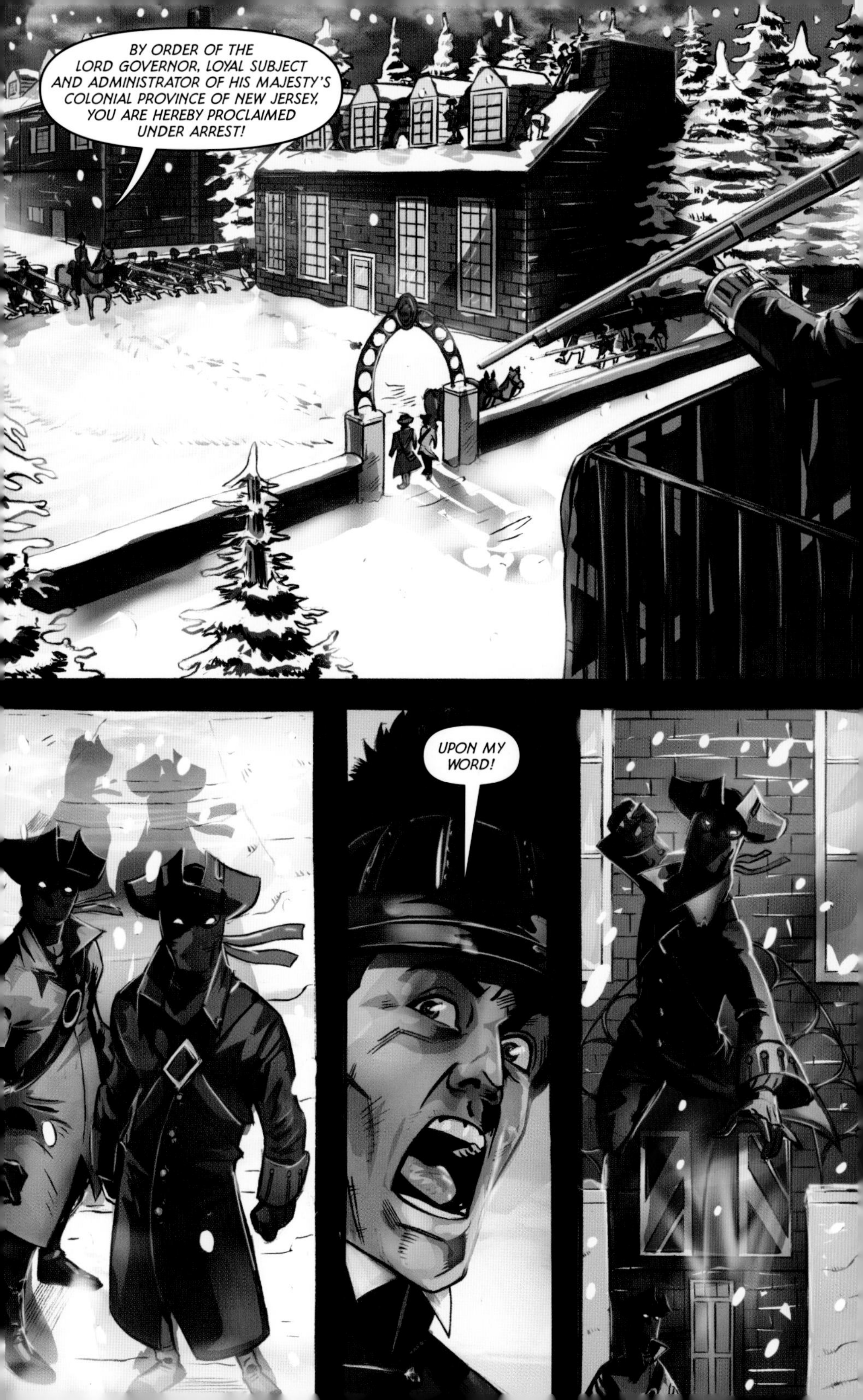
BY ORDER OF THE LORD GOVERNOR, LOYAL SUBJECT AND ADMINISTRATOR OF HIS MAJESTY'S COLONIAL PROVINCE OF NEW JERSEY, YOU ARE HEREBY PROCLAIMED UNDER ARREST!
UPON MY WORD!

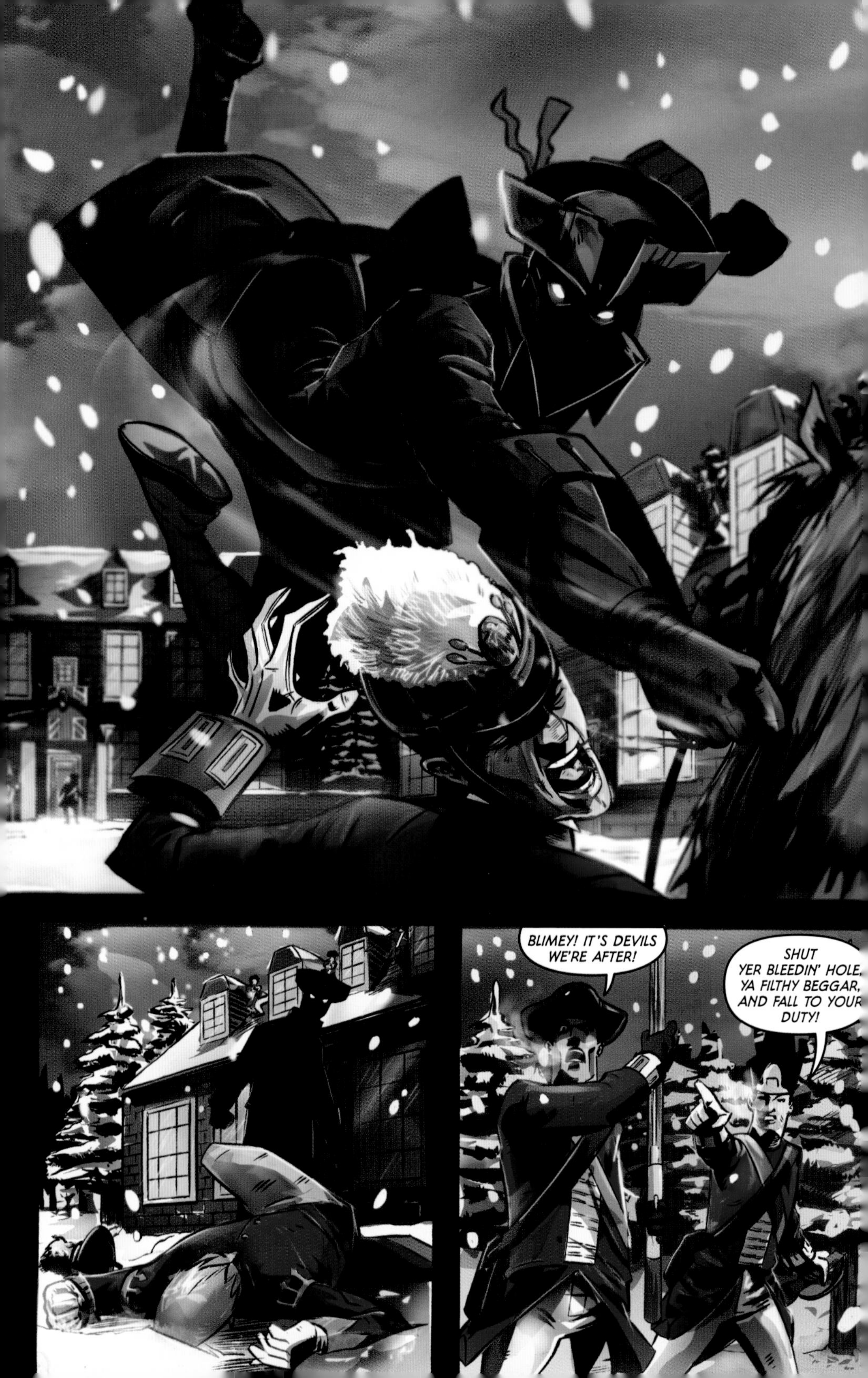
BLIMEY! IT'S DEVILS WE'RE AFTER!
SHUT YER BLEEDIN' HOLE, YA FILTHY BEGGAR, AND FALL TO YOUR DUTY!

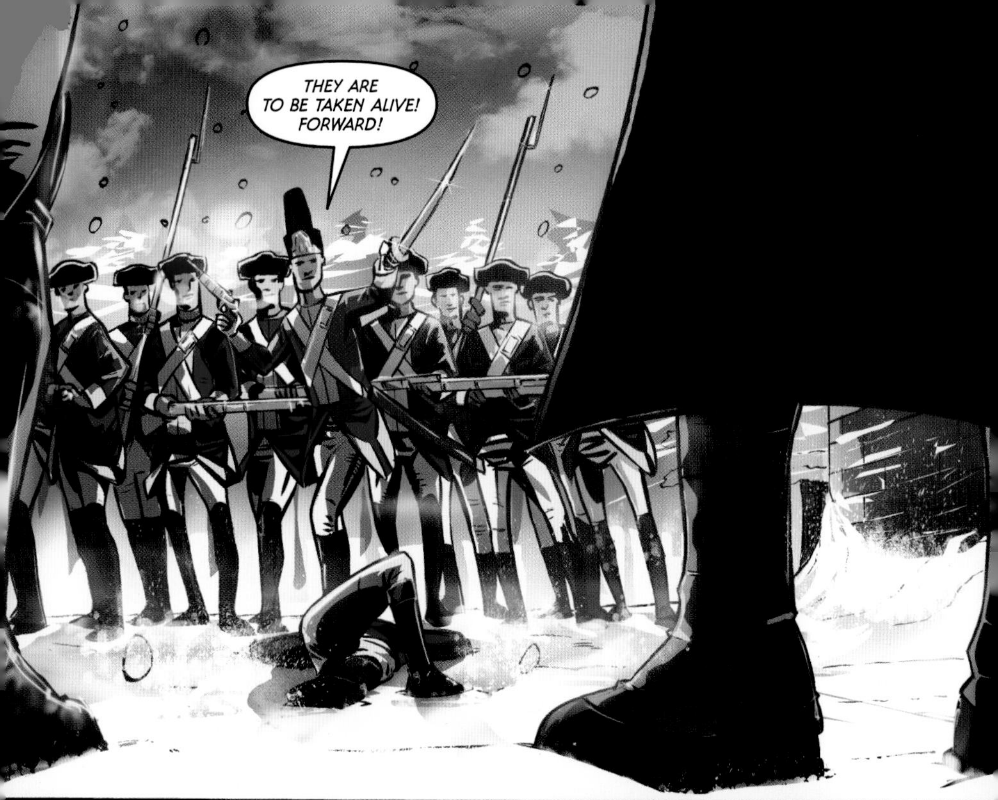
THEY ARE
TO BE TAKEN ALIVE!
FORWARD!

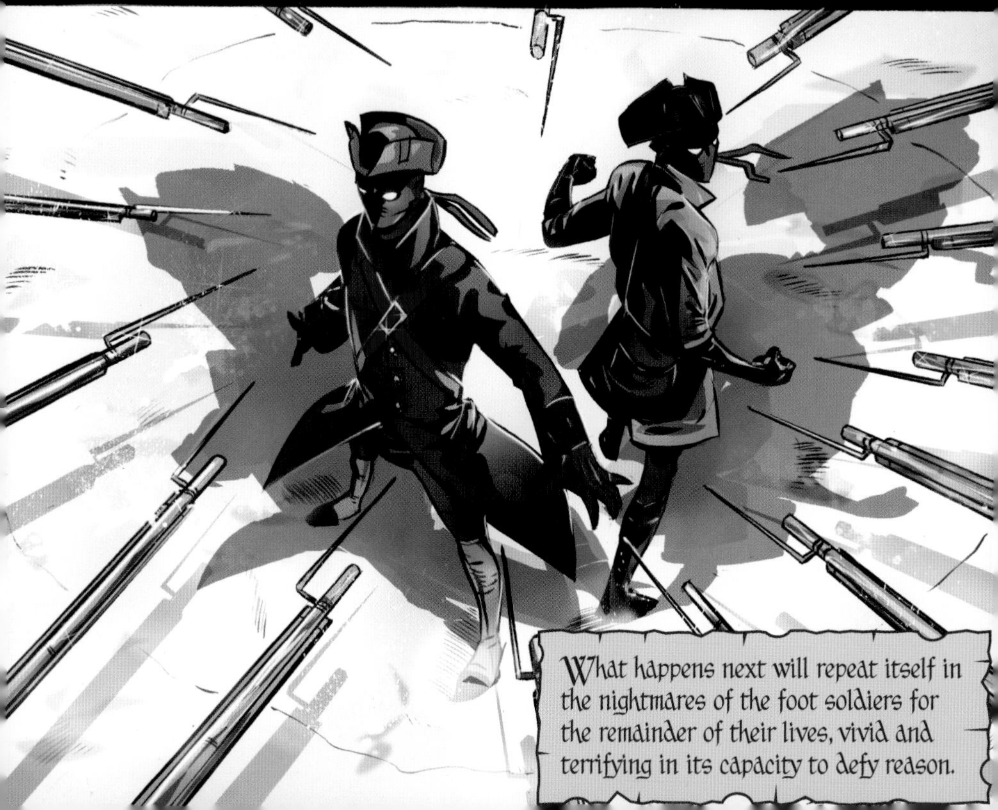
What happens next will repeat itself in the nightmares of the foot soldiers for the remainder of their lives, vivid and terrifying in its capacity to defy reason.

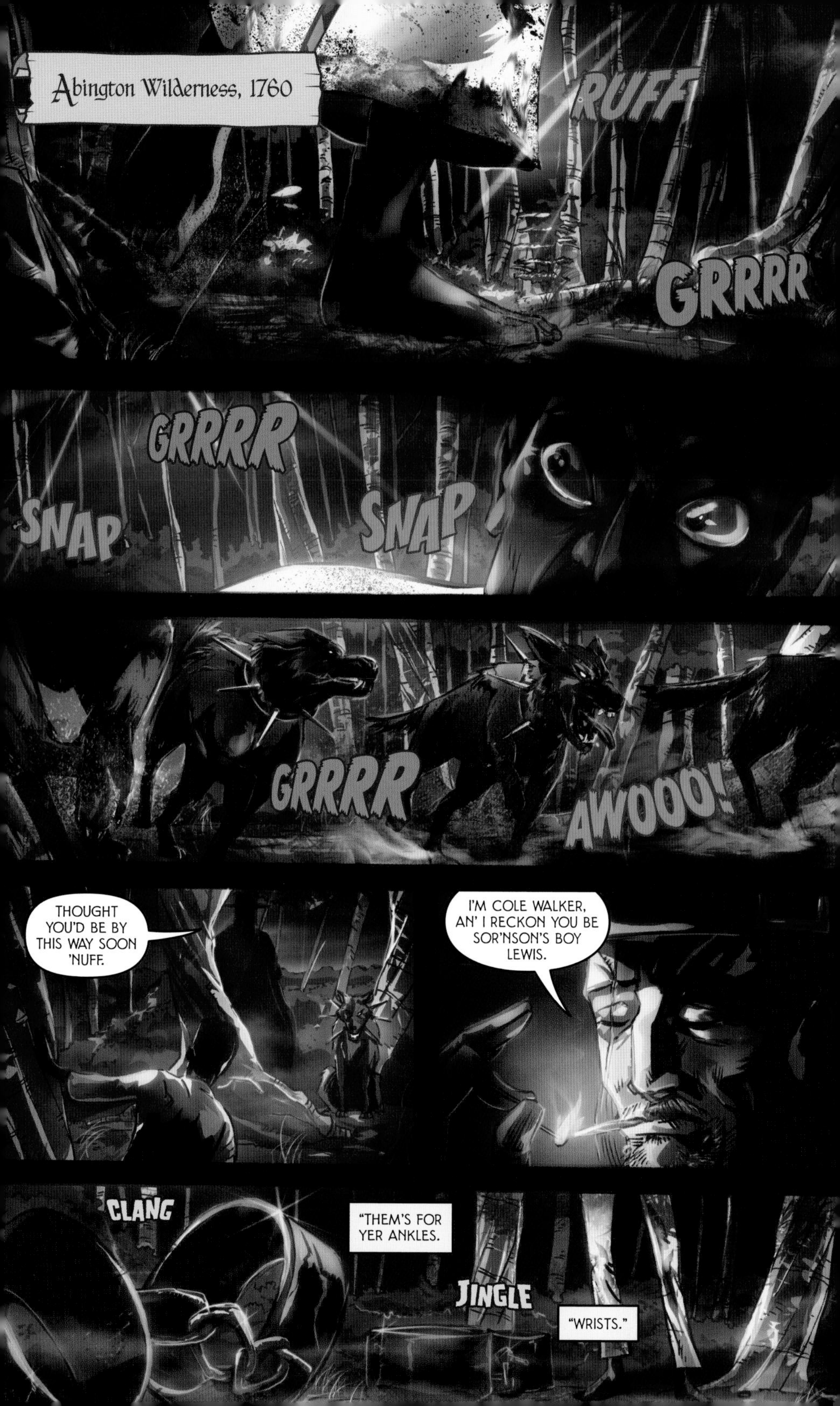

Abington Wilderness, 1760
RUFF
GRRRR
GRRRR
SNAP
SNAP
GRRRR
AWOOO!
THOUGHT YOU'D BE BY THIS WAY SOON 'NUFF.
I'M COLE WALKER, AN' I RECKON YOU BE SOR'NSON'S BOY LEWIS.
CLANG
"THEM'S FOR YER ANKLES.
JINGLE
"WRISTS."

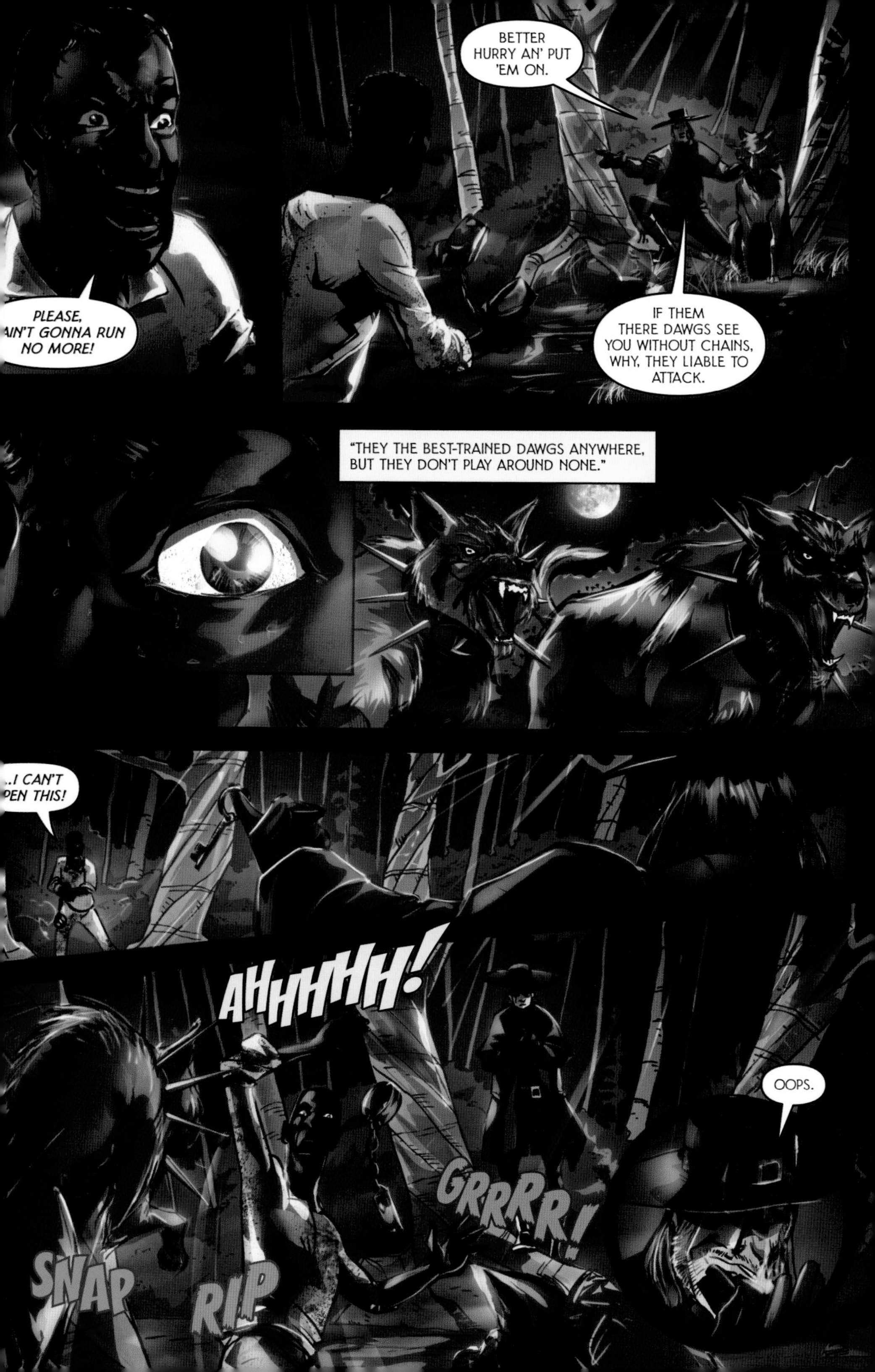
PLEASE, AIN'T GONNA RUN NO MORE!
BETTER HURRY AN' PUT 'EM ON.
IF THEM THERE DAWGS SEE YOU WITHOUT CHAINS, WHY, THEY LIABLE TO ATTACK.
"THEY THE BEST-TRAINED DAWGS ANYWHERE, BUT THEY DON'T PLAY AROUND NONE."
..I CAN'T PEN THIS!
AHHHHH!
OOPS.
GRRRR!
SNAP
RIP

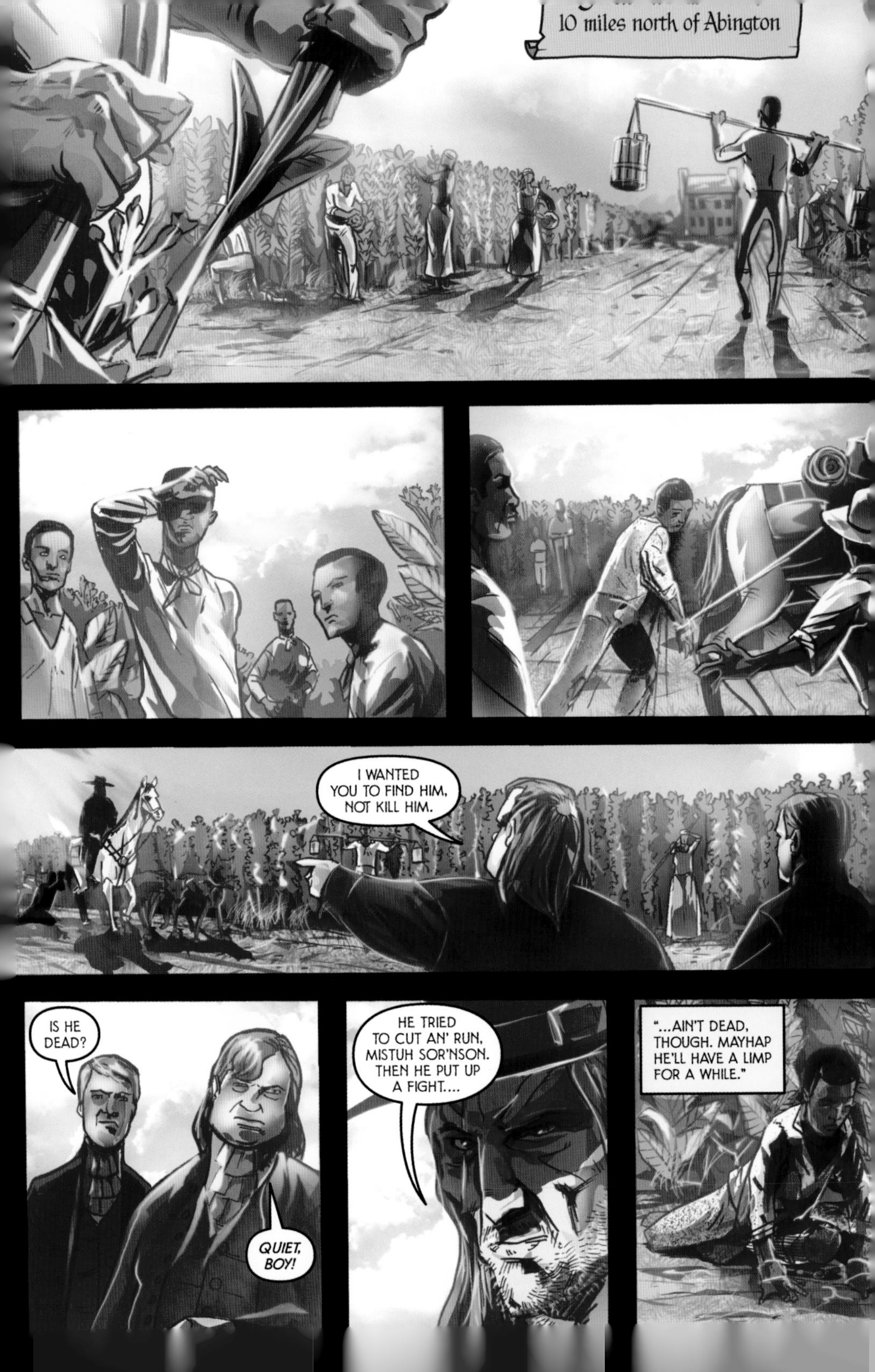
10 miles north of Abington
I WANTED YOU TO FIND HIM, NOT KILL HIM.
IS HE DEAD?
QUIET, BOY!
HE TRIED TO CUT AN' RUN, MISTUH SOR'NSON. THEN HE PUT UP A FIGHT....
"...AIN'T DEAD, THOUGH. MAYHAP HE'LL HAVE A LIMP FOR A WHILE."

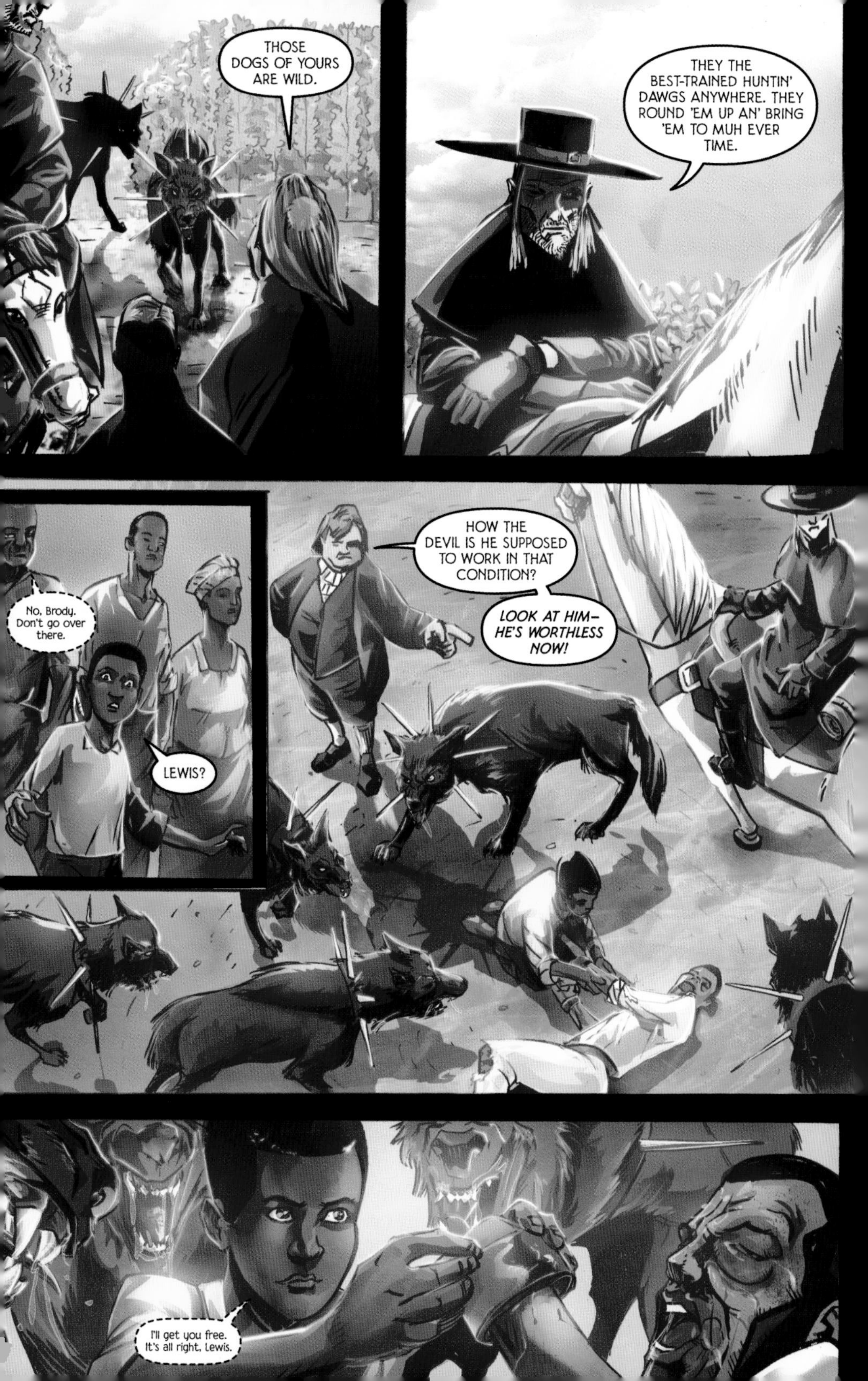
THOSE DOGS OF YOURS ARE WILD.
THEY THE BEST-TRAINED HUNTIN' DAWGS ANYWHERE. THEY ROUND 'EM UP AN' BRING 'EM TO MUH EVER TIME.
No, Brody. Don't go over there.
LEWIS?
HOW THE DEVIL IS HE SUPPOSED TO WORK IN THAT CONDITION?
LOOK AT HIM— HE'S WORTHLESS NOW!
I'll get you free. It's all right, Lewis.

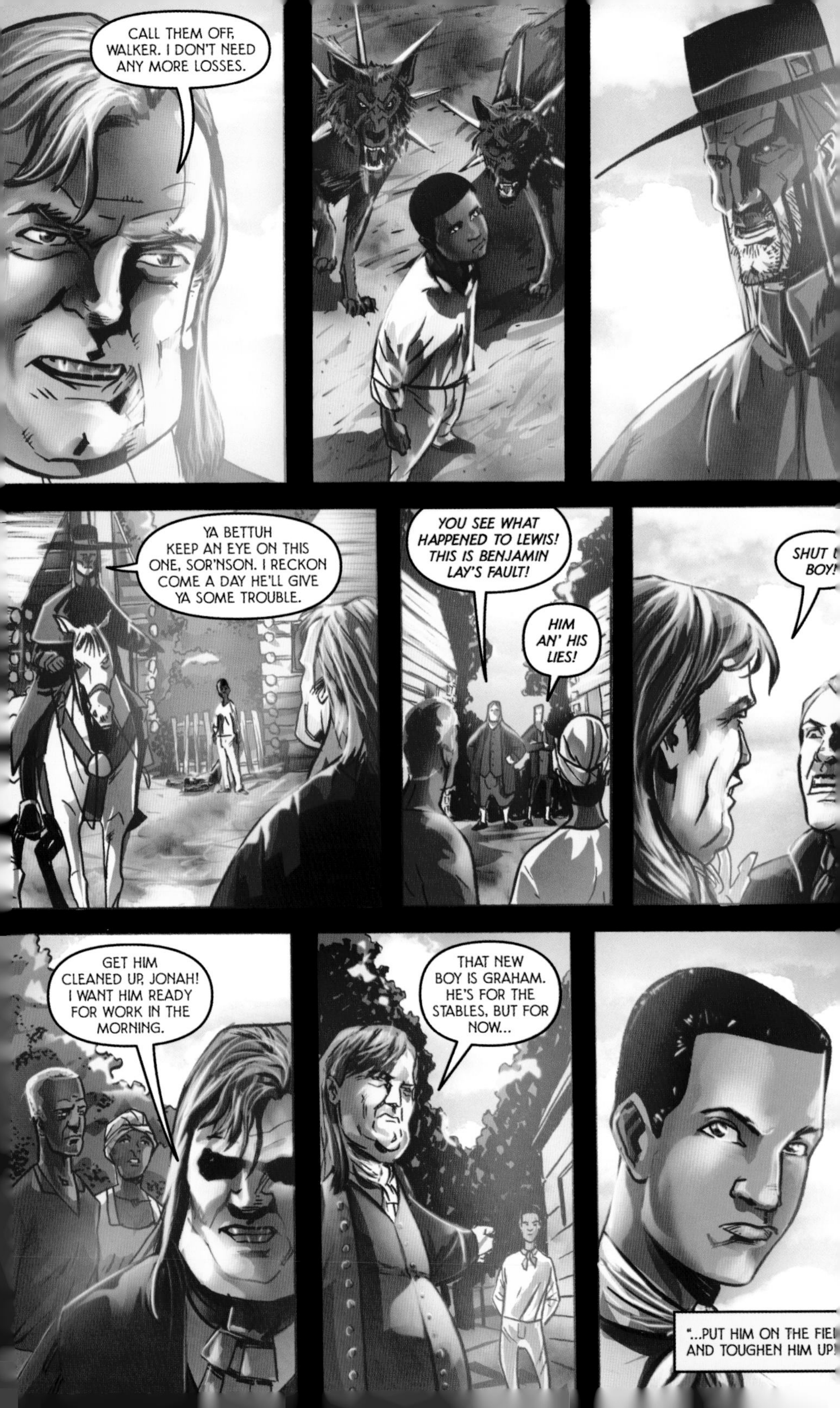
CALL THEM OFF, WALKER. I DON'T NEED ANY MORE LOSSES.
YA BETTUH KEEP AN EYE ON THIS ONE, SOR'NSON. I RECKON COME A DAY HE'LL GIVE YA SOME TROUBLE.
YOU SEE WHAT HAPPENED TO LEWIS! THIS IS BENJAMIN LAY'S FAULT!
HIM AN' HIS LIES!
GET HIM CLEANED UP, JONAH! I WANT HIM READY FOR WORK IN THE MORNING.
THAT NEW BOY IS GRAHAM. HE'S FOR THE STABLES, BUT FOR NOW...

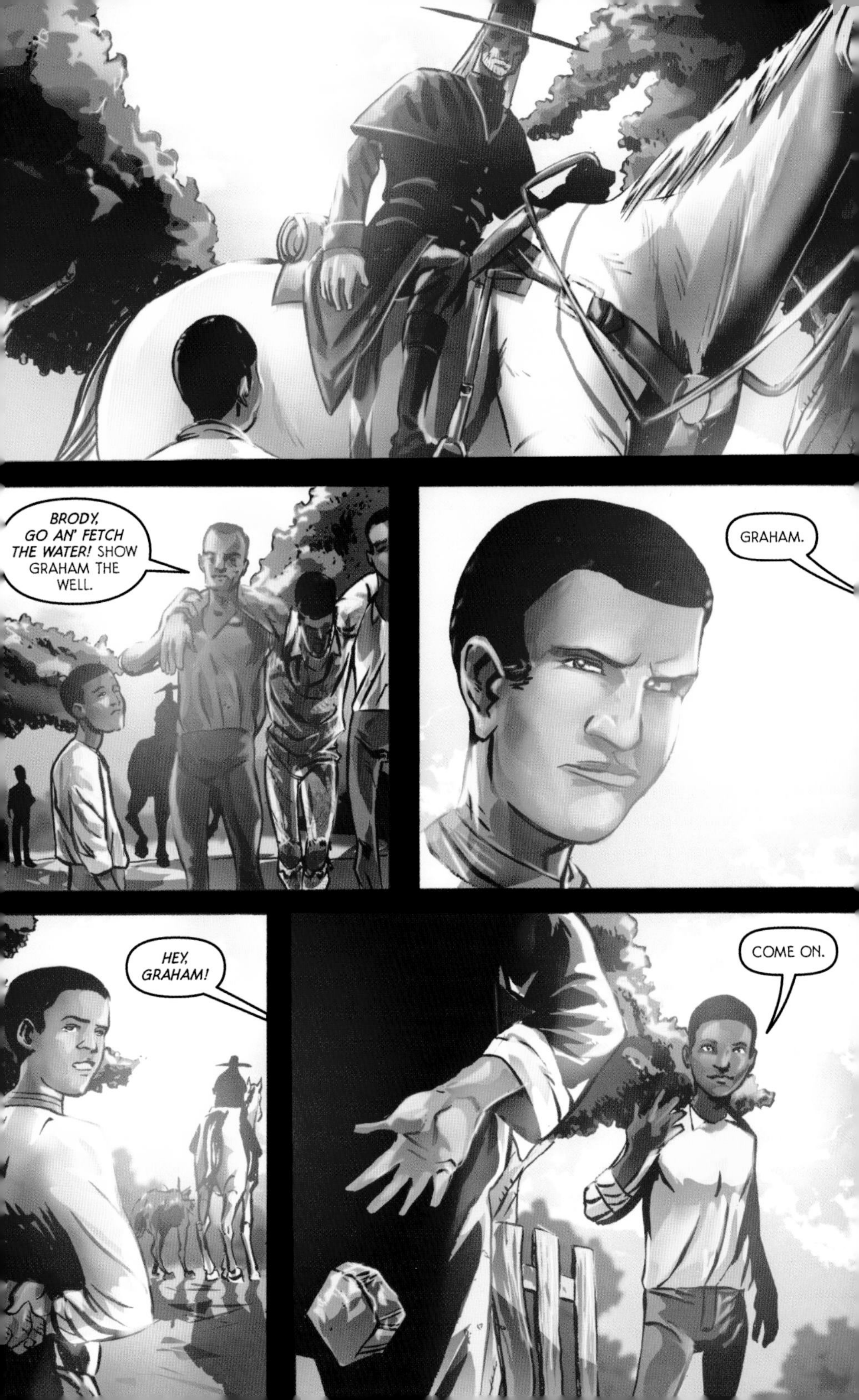
BRODY, GO AN' FETCH THE WATER! SHOW GRAHAM THE WELL.
GRAHAM.
HEY, GRAHAM!
COME ON.

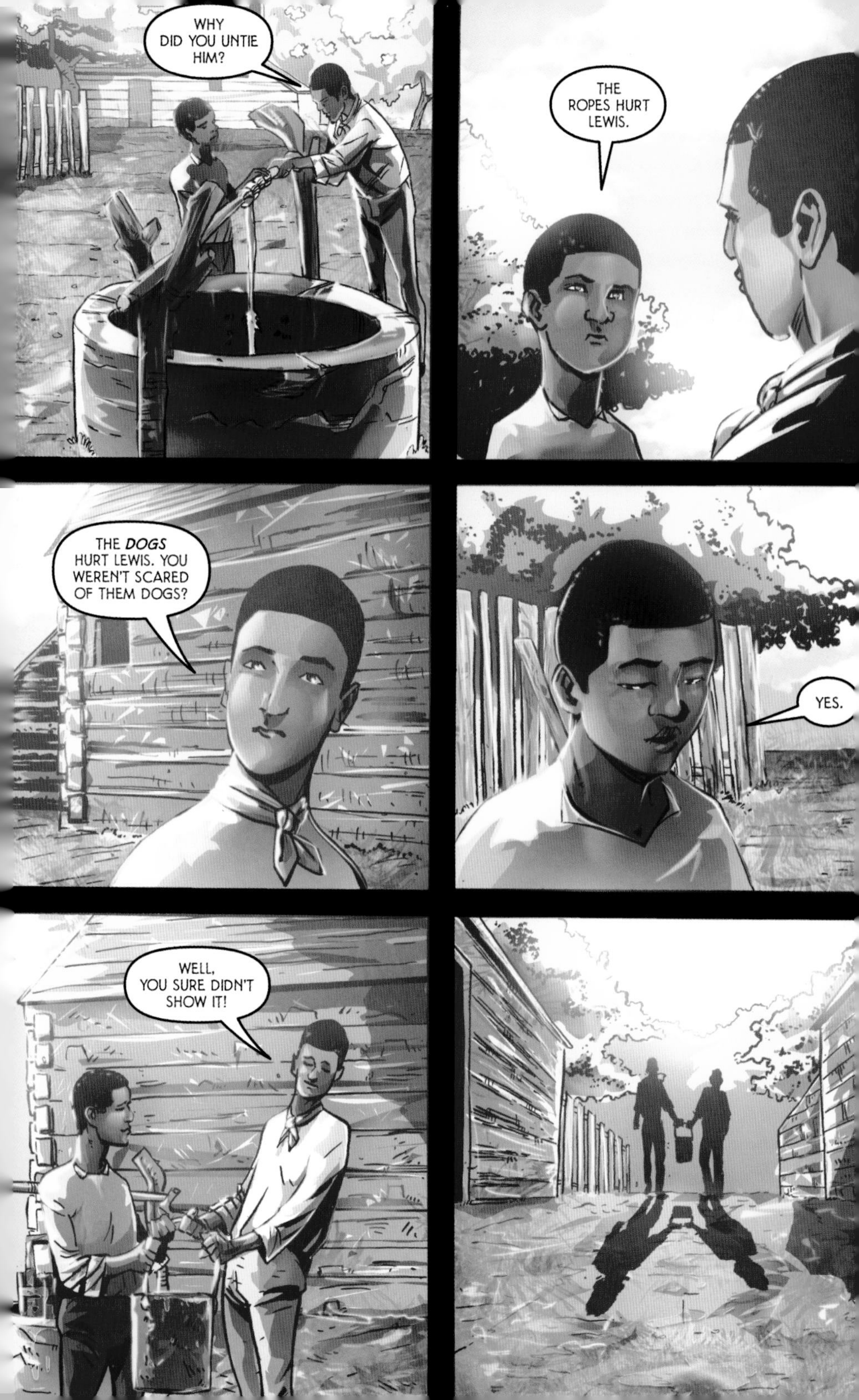
WHY DID YOU UNTIE HIM?
THE ROPES HURT LEWIS.
THE *DOGS* HURT LEWIS. YOU WEREN'T SCARED OF THEM DOGS?
YES.
WELL, YOU SURE DIDN'T SHOW IT!

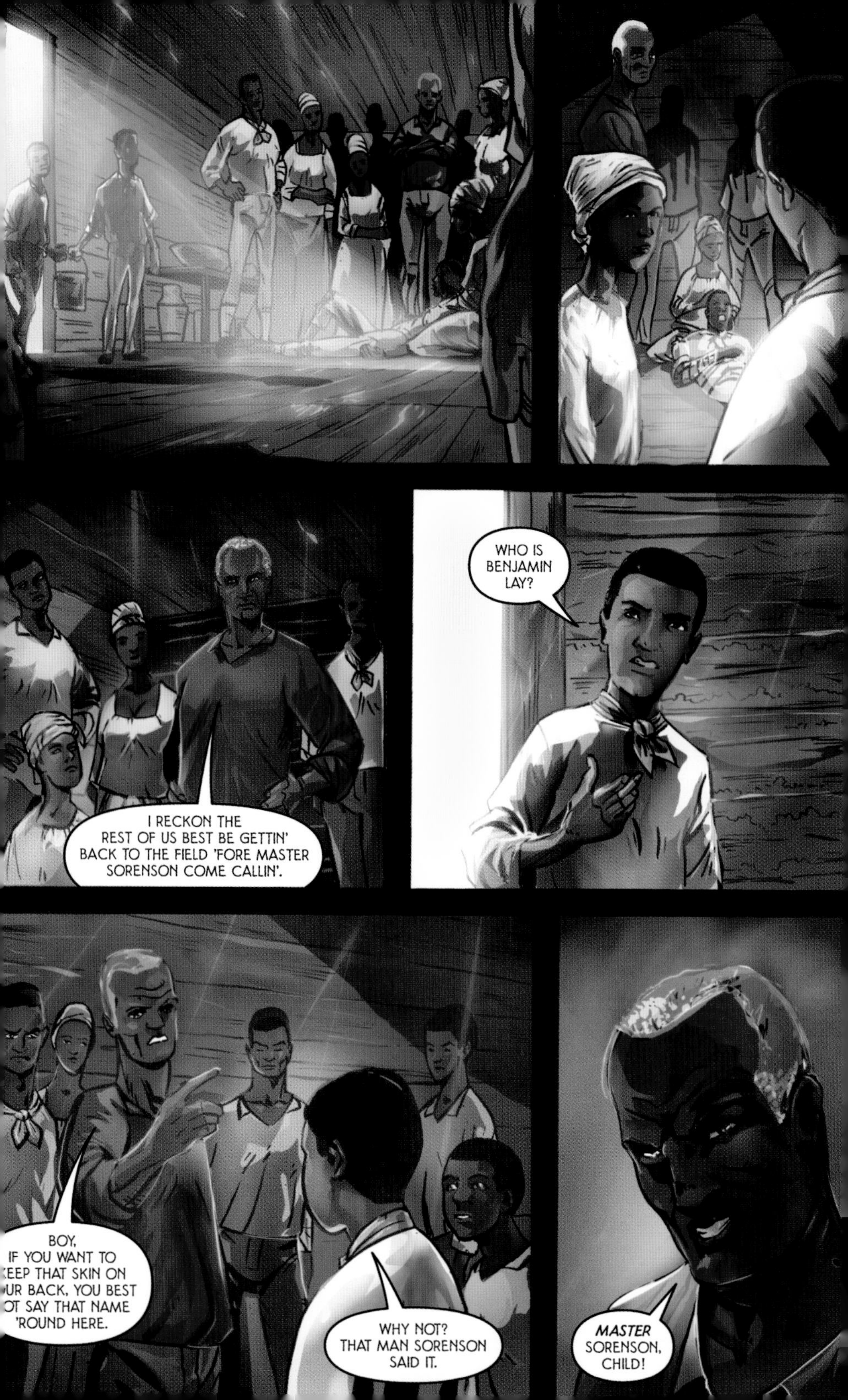
I RECKON THE REST OF US BEST BE GETTIN' BACK TO THE FIELD 'FORE MASTER SORENSON COME CALLIN'.
WHO IS BENJAMIN LAY?
BOY, IF YOU WANT TO KEEP THAT SKIN ON YOUR BACK, YOU BEST NOT SAY THAT NAME 'ROUND HERE.
WHY NOT? THAT MAN SORENSON SAID IT.
MASTER SORENSON, CHILD!

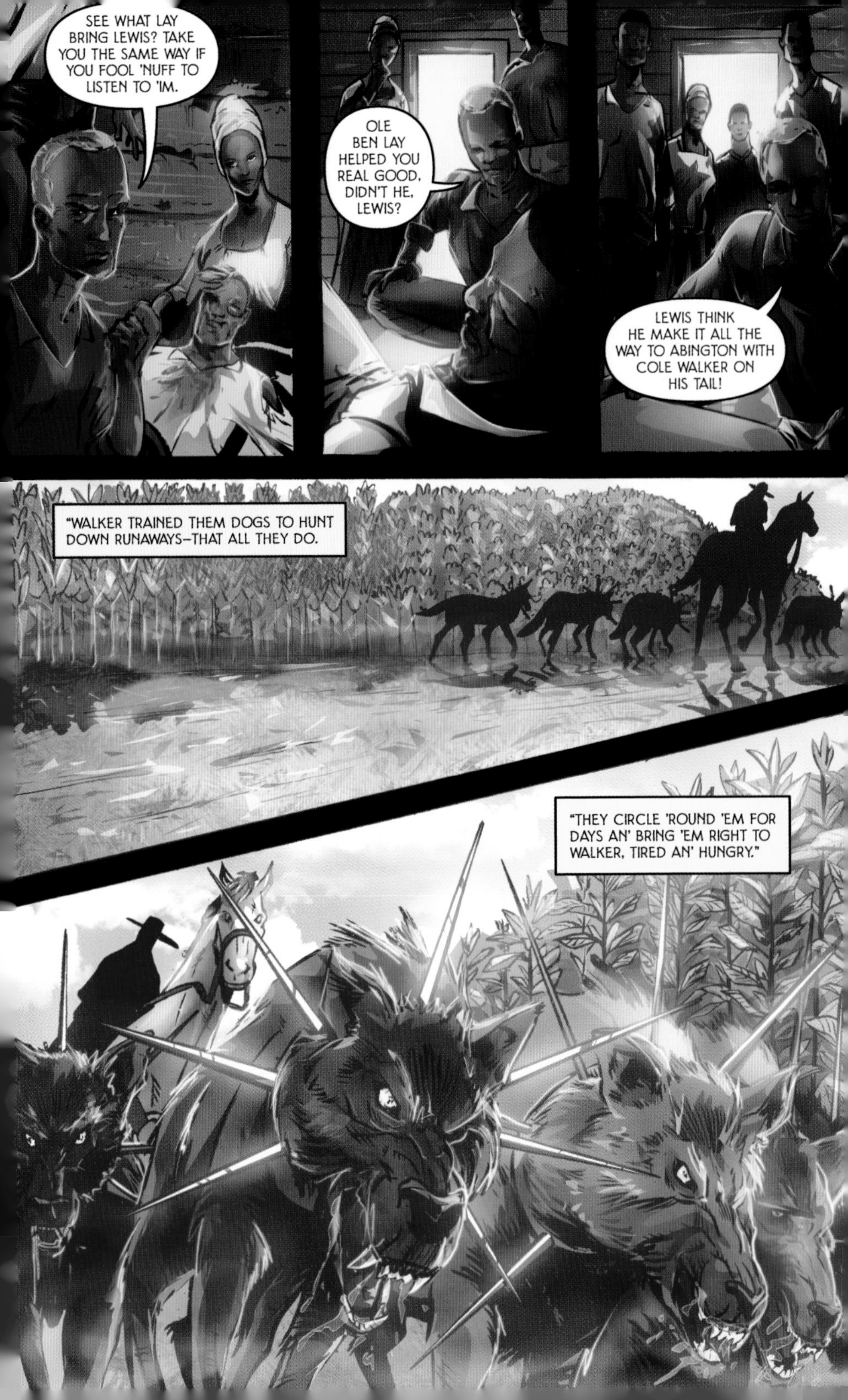
SEE WHAT LAY BRING LEWIS? TAKE YOU THE SAME WAY IF YOU FOOL 'NUFF TO LISTEN TO 'IM.
OLE BEN LAY HELPED YOU REAL GOOD, DIDN'T HE, LEWIS?
LEWIS THINK HE MAKE IT ALL THE WAY TO ABINGTON WITH COLE WALKER ON HIS TAIL!
"WALKER TRAINED THEM DOGS TO HUNT DOWN RUNAWAYS—THAT ALL THEY DO.
"THEY CIRCLE 'ROUND 'EM FOR DAYS AN' BRING 'EM RIGHT TO WALKER, TIRED AN' HUNGRY."

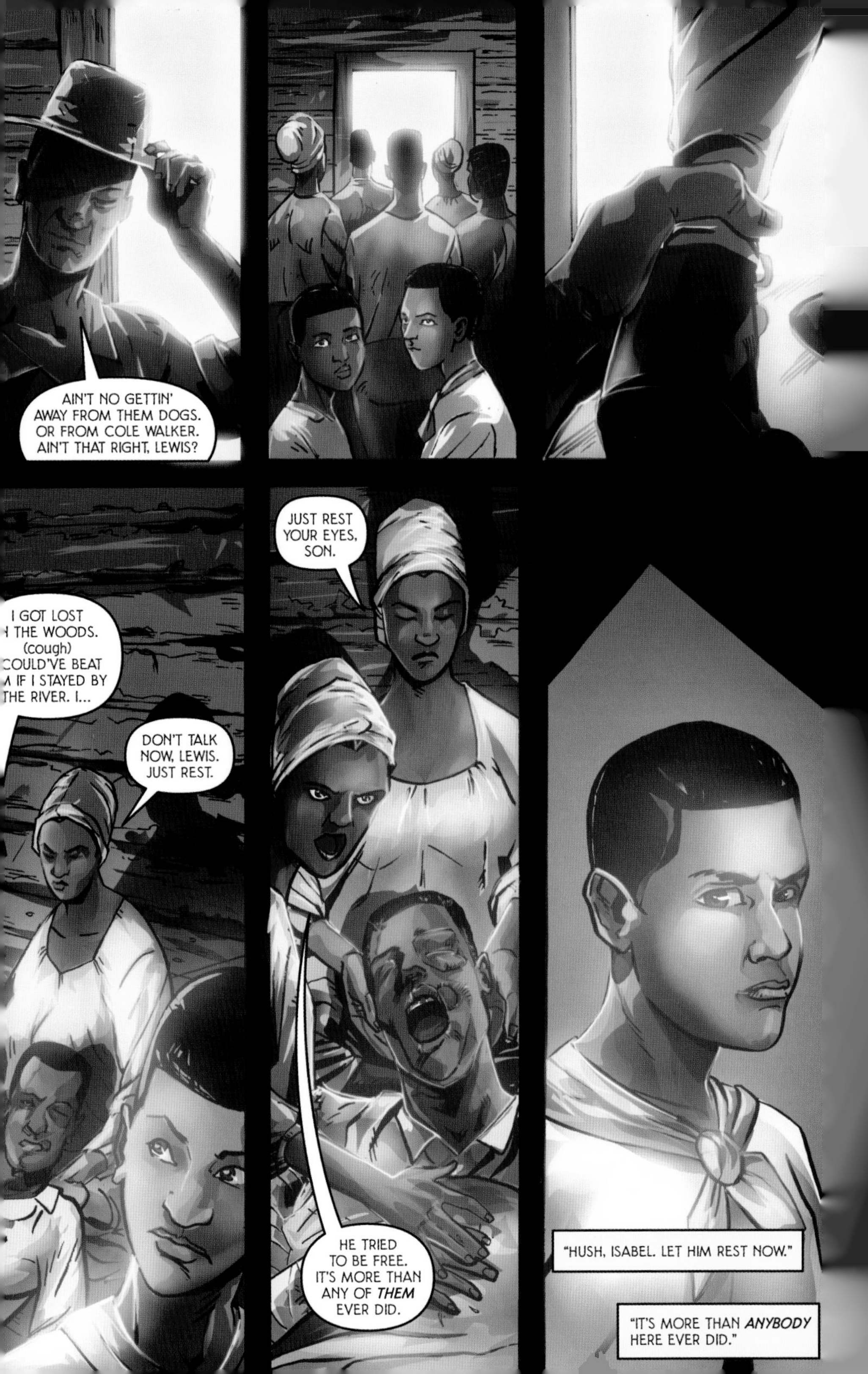
AIN'T NO GETTIN' AWAY FROM THEM DOGS. OR FROM COLE WALKER. AIN'T THAT RIGHT, LEWIS?
JUST REST YOUR EYES, SON.
I GOT LOST THE WOODS. (cough) COULD'VE BEAT IF I STAYED BY THE RIVER. I...
DON'T TALK NOW, LEWIS. JUST REST.
HE TRIED TO BE FREE. IT'S MORE THAN ANY OF *THEM* EVER DID.
"HUSH, ISABEL. LET HIM REST NOW."
"IT'S MORE THAN *ANYBODY* HERE EVER DID."

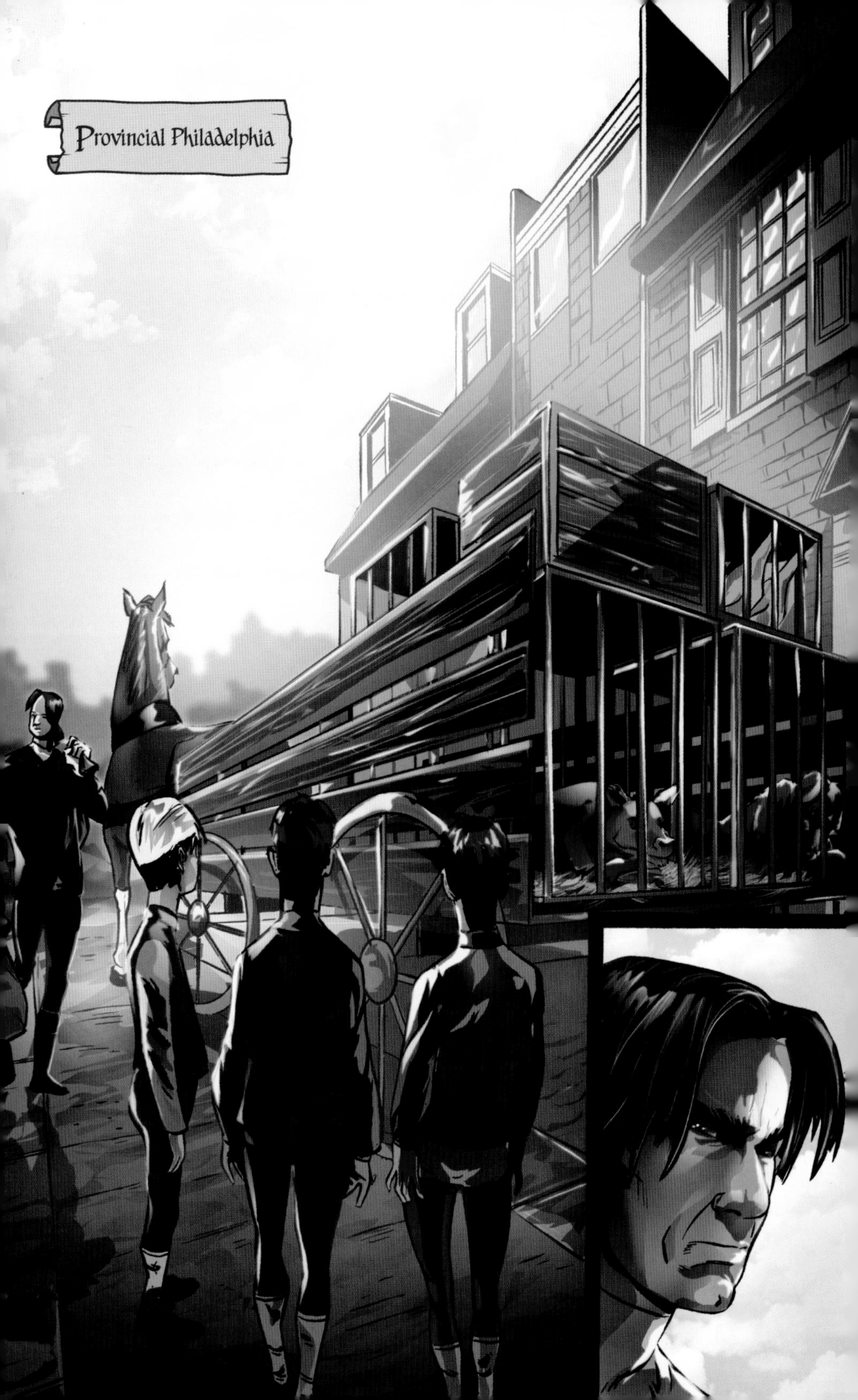
Provincial Philadelphia

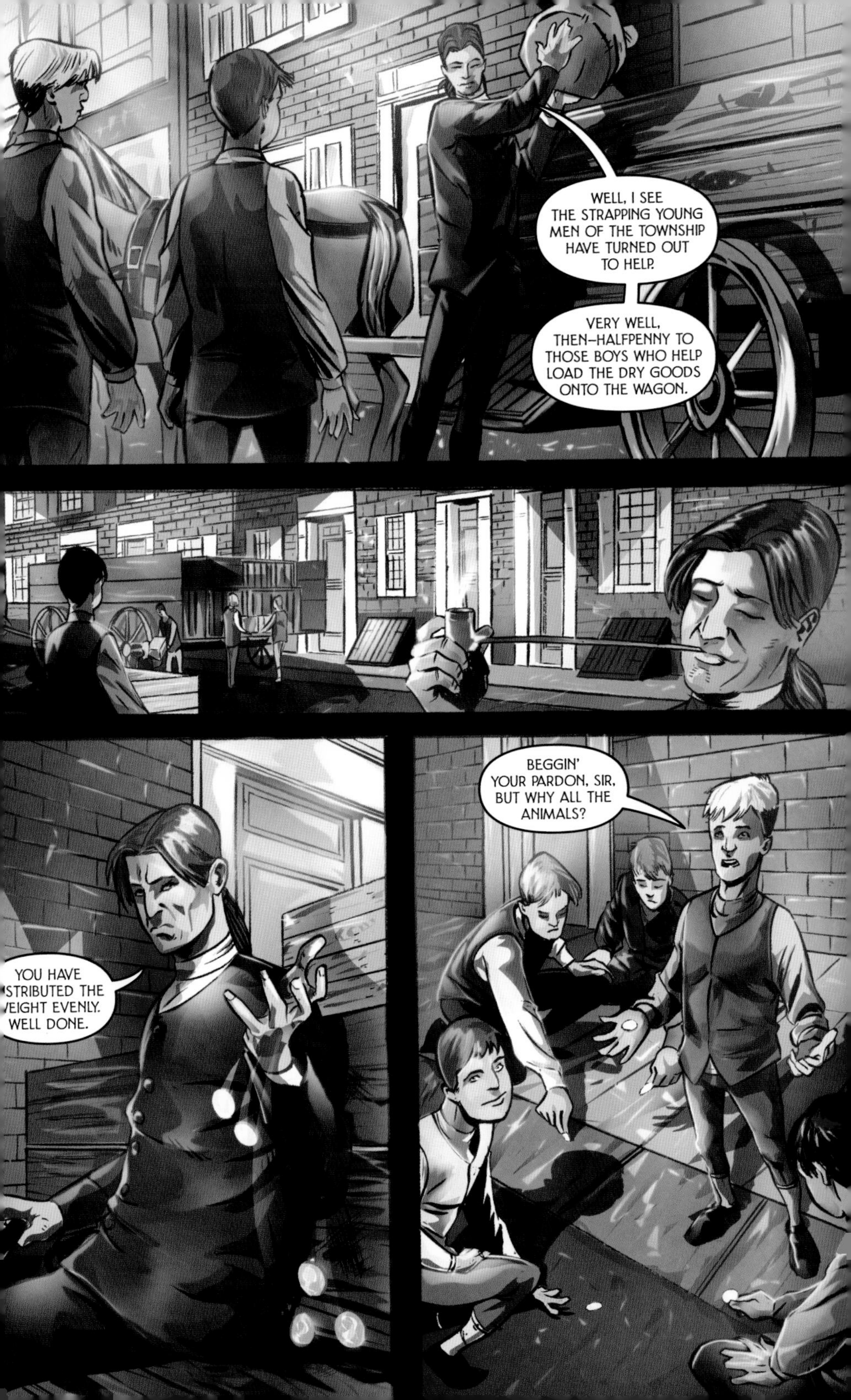
WELL, I SEE THE STRAPPING YOUNG MEN OF THE TOWNSHIP HAVE TURNED OUT TO HELP.
VERY WELL, THEN—HALFPENNY TO THOSE BOYS WHO HELP LOAD THE DRY GOODS ONTO THE WAGON.
YOU HAVE STRIBUTED THE VEIGHT EVENLY. WELL DONE.
BEGGIN' YOUR PARDON, SIR, BUT WHY ALL THE ANIMALS?

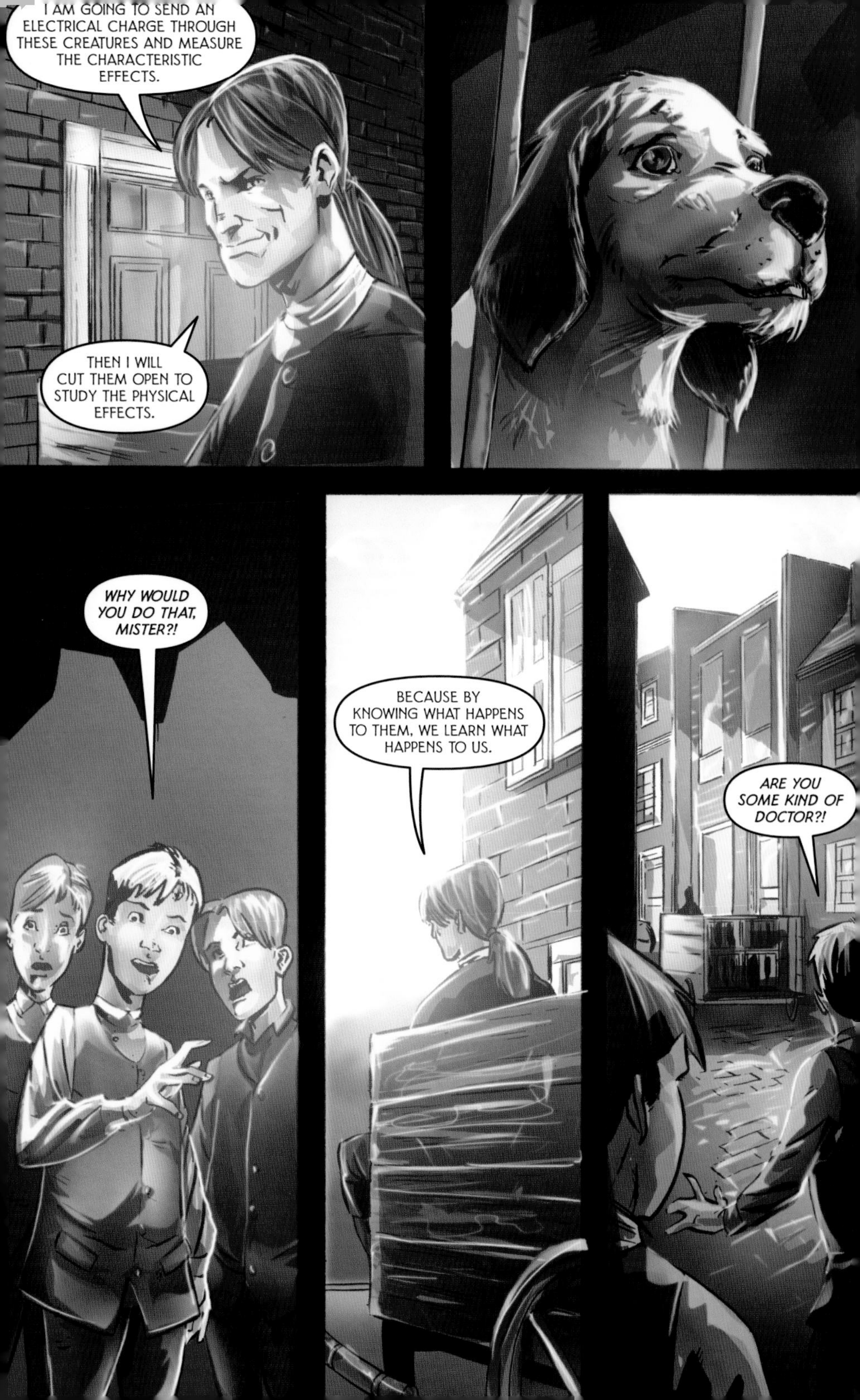
I AM GOING TO SEND AN ELECTRICAL CHARGE THROUGH THESE CREATURES AND MEASURE THE CHARACTERISTIC EFFECTS.
THEN I WILL CUT THEM OPEN TO STUDY THE PHYSICAL EFFECTS.
WHY WOULD YOU DO THAT, MISTER?!
BECAUSE BY KNOWING WHAT HAPPENS TO THEM, WE LEARN WHAT HAPPENS TO US.
ARE YOU SOME KIND OF DOCTOR?!

COME, MY LOVELIES, WON'T WE HAVE A TIME!

Lightning in the sky is the same as the ordinary static charge generated by friction, only millions of times more powerful.

This simple explanation to an age-old mystery has brought me recognition the world over....

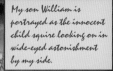

My son William is portrayed as the innocent child squire looking on in wide-eyed astonishment by my side.

...nce journals, as well as in art, ...ually depicted as a venerable ...aired wizard baiting the blue-white ...e fire from the heavens with a kite, ...read, and a brass key....

This artistic oversight (he is one and twenty years of age, after all) has perhaps caused William considerable strife....

As a result, the boy has now embraced my research with uncommon fervor, and I am both pleased and worried by it. Ambition and a desire to prove himself has filled him with a zeal that at times drives him forward at a reckless pace....

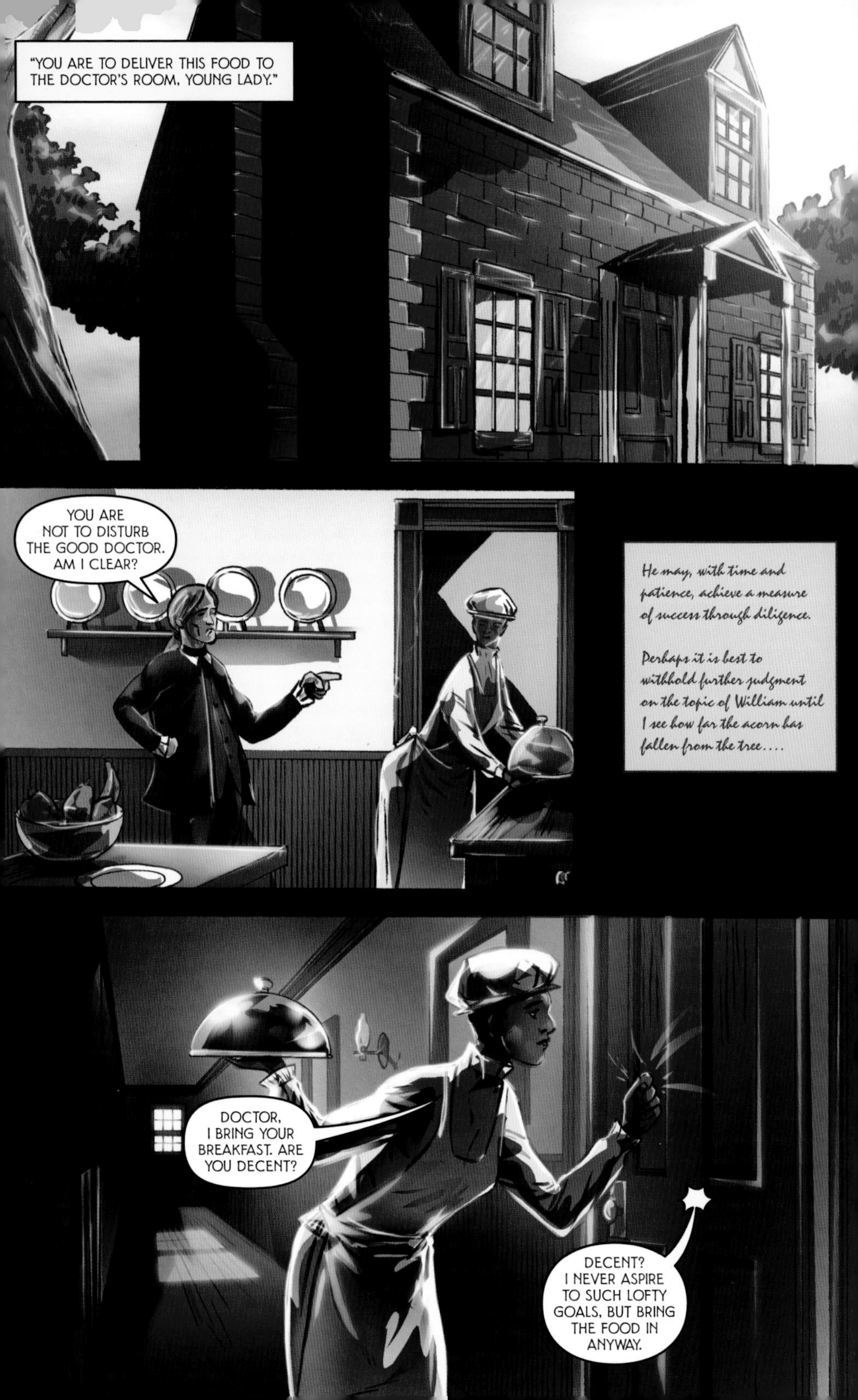
"YOU ARE TO DELIVER THIS FOOD TO THE DOCTOR'S ROOM, YOUNG LADY."
YOU ARE NOT TO DISTURB THE GOOD DOCTOR. AM I CLEAR?
He may, with time and patience, achieve a measure of success through diligence.
Perhaps it is best to withhold further judgment on the topic of William until I see how far the acorn has fallen from the tree....
DOCTOR, I BRING YOUR BREAKFAST. ARE YOU DECENT?
DECENT? I NEVER ASPIRE TO SUCH LOFTY GOALS, BUT BRING THE FOOD IN ANYWAY.

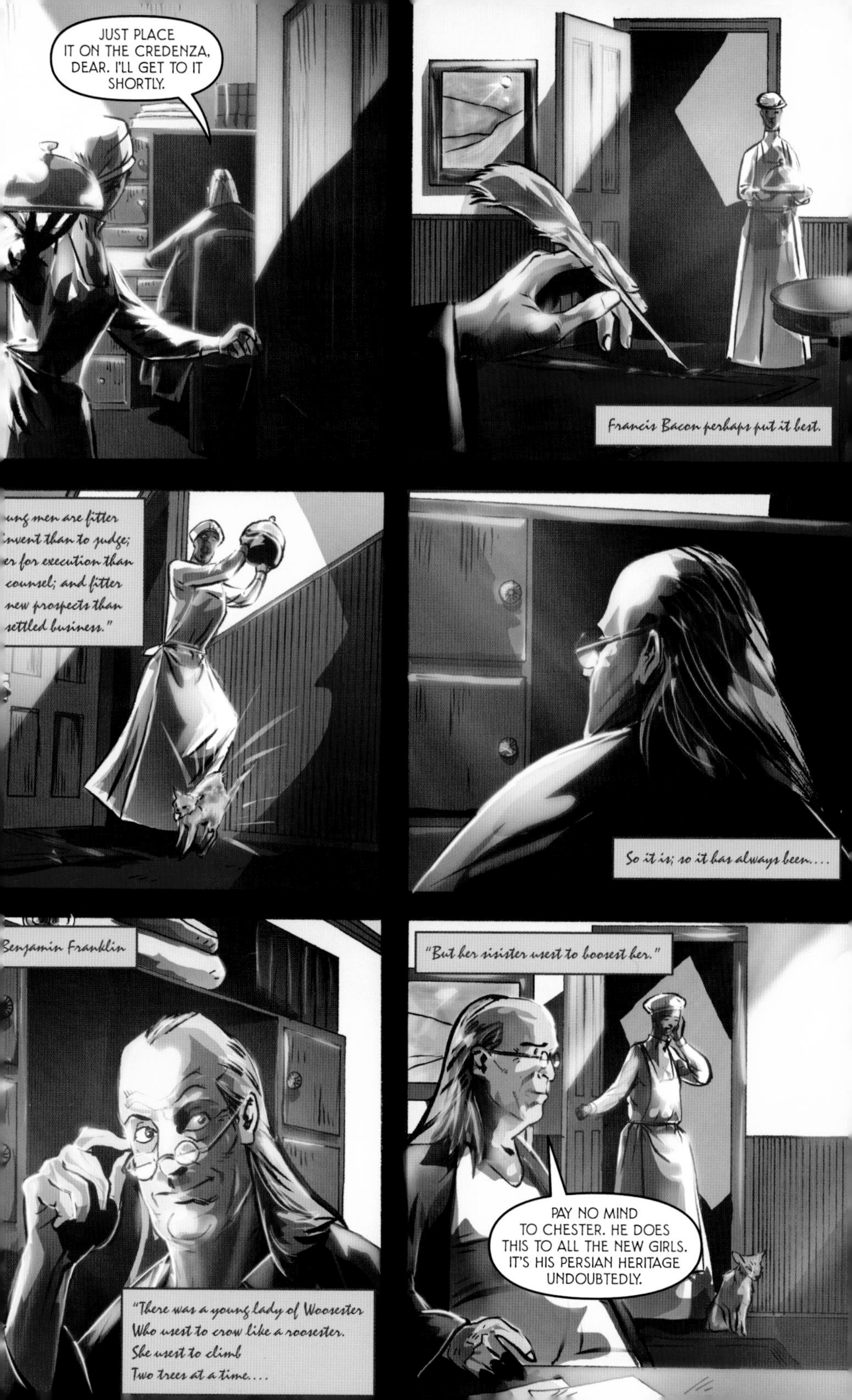
JUST PLACE IT ON THE CREDENZA, DEAR. I'LL GET TO IT SHORTLY.
Francis Bacon perhaps put it best.
ung men are fitter
nvent than to judge;
er for execution than
counsel; and fitter
new prospects than
settled business."
So it is; so it has always been....
Benjamin Franklin
"There was a young lady of Woosester
Who usest to crow like a roosester.
She usest to climb
Two trees at a time....
"But her sisister usest to boosest her."
PAY NO MIND TO CHESTER. HE DOES THIS TO ALL THE NEW GIRLS. IT'S HIS PERSIAN HERITAGE UNDOUBTEDLY.

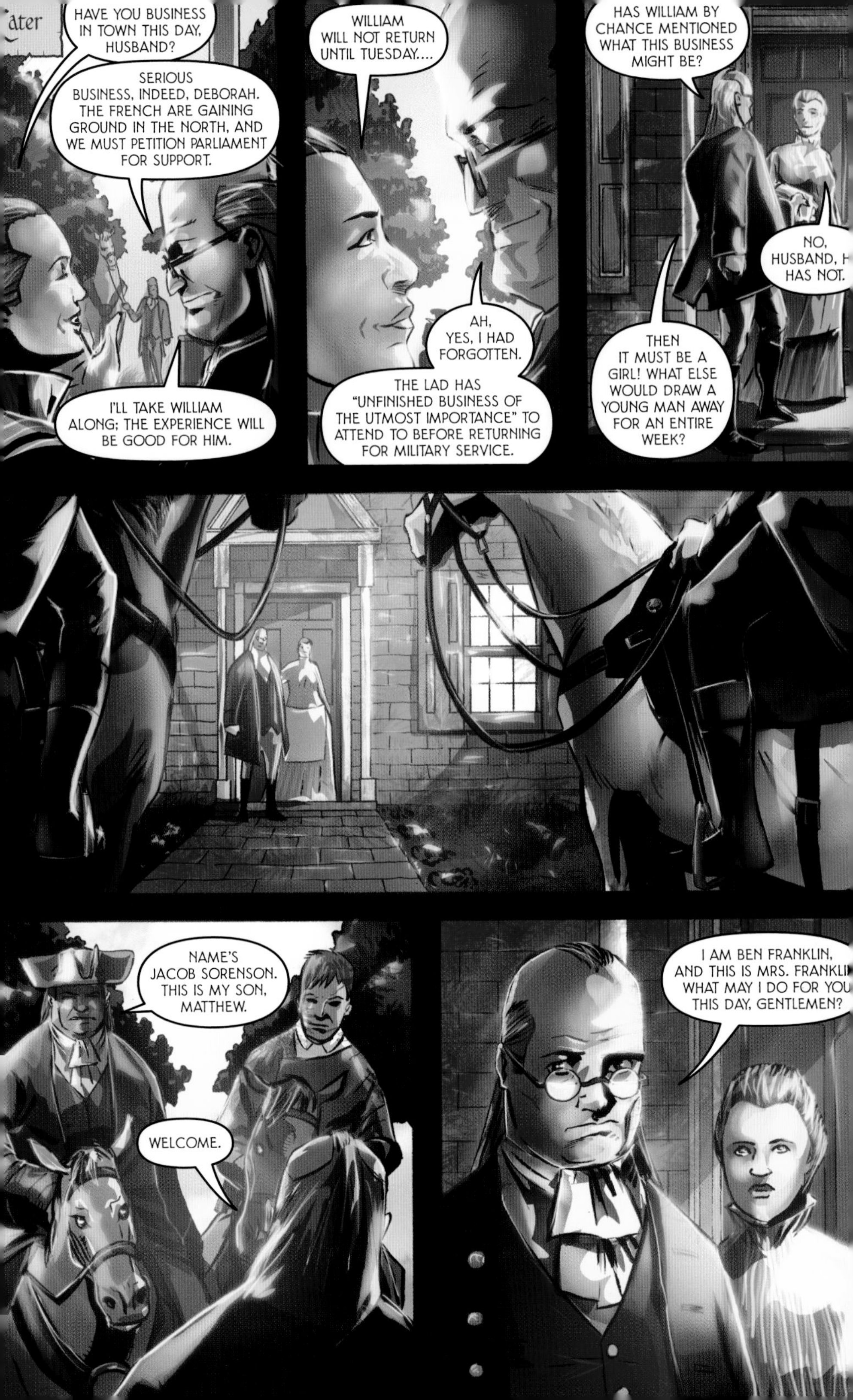
ater
HAVE YOU BUSINESS IN TOWN THIS DAY, HUSBAND?
SERIOUS BUSINESS, INDEED, DEBORAH. THE FRENCH ARE GAINING GROUND IN THE NORTH, AND WE MUST PETITION PARLIAMENT FOR SUPPORT.
I'LL TAKE WILLIAM ALONG; THE EXPERIENCE WILL BE GOOD FOR HIM.
WILLIAM WILL NOT RETURN UNTIL TUESDAY....
AH, YES, I HAD FORGOTTEN.
THE LAD HAS "UNFINISHED BUSINESS OF THE UTMOST IMPORTANCE" TO ATTEND TO BEFORE RETURNING FOR MILITARY SERVICE.
HAS WILLIAM BY CHANCE MENTIONED WHAT THIS BUSINESS MIGHT BE?
NO, HUSBAND, H HAS NOT.
THEN IT MUST BE A GIRL! WHAT ELSE WOULD DRAW A YOUNG MAN AWAY FOR AN ENTIRE WEEK?
NAME'S JACOB SORENSON. THIS IS MY SON, MATTHEW.
WELCOME.
I AM BEN FRANKLIN, AND THIS IS MRS. FRANKLI WHAT MAY I DO FOR YOU THIS DAY, GENTLEMEN?

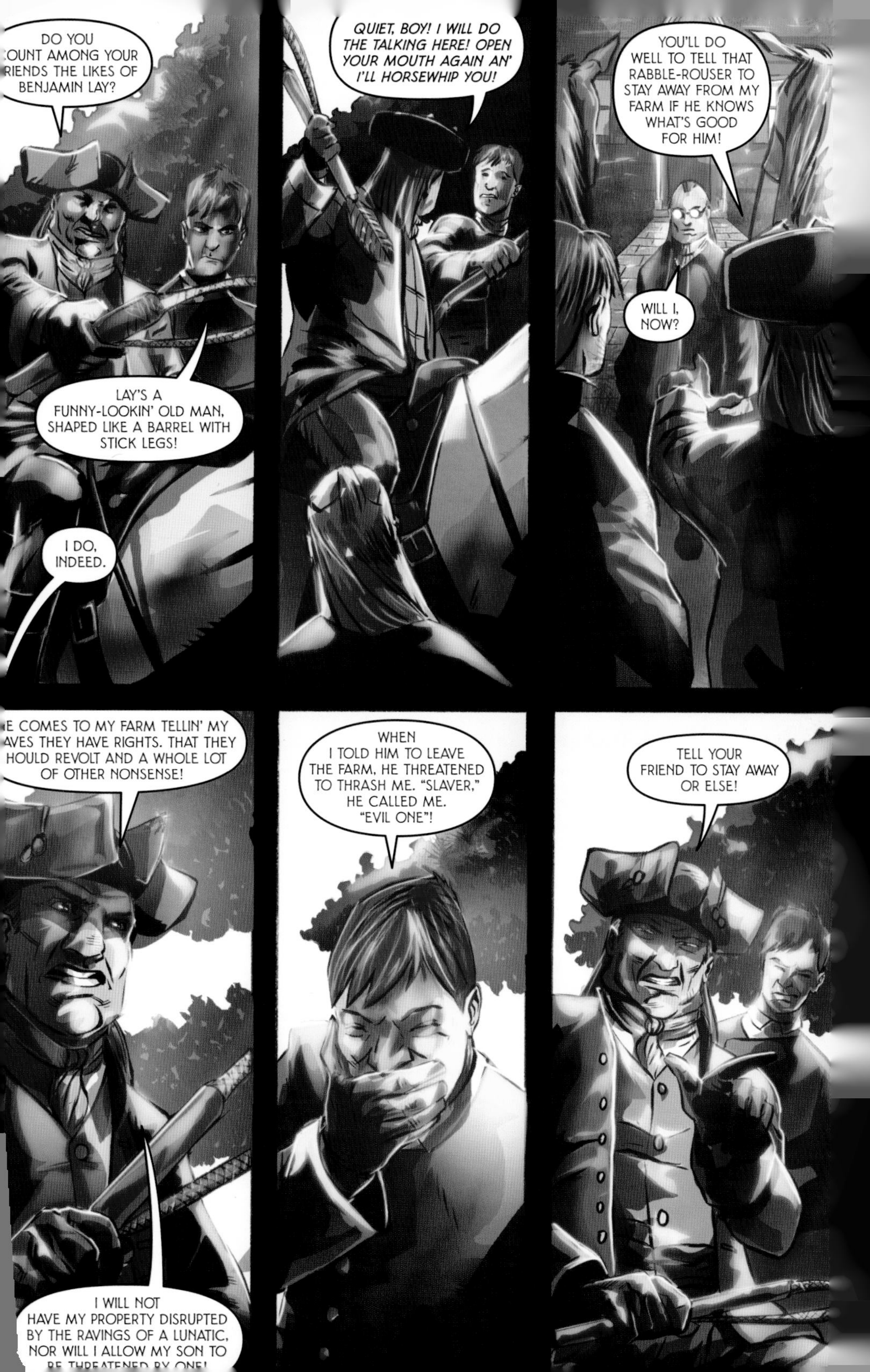
DO YOU
COUNT AMONG YOUR
FRIENDS THE LIKES OF
BENJAMIN LAY?
LAY'S A FUNNY-LOOKIN' OLD MAN, SHAPED LIKE A BARREL WITH STICK LEGS!
I DO, INDEED.
QUIET, BOY! I WILL DO THE TALKING HERE! OPEN YOUR MOUTH AGAIN AN' I'LL HORSEWHIP YOU!
YOU'LL DO WELL TO TELL THAT RABBLE-ROUSER TO STAY AWAY FROM MY FARM IF HE KNOWS WHAT'S GOOD FOR HIM!
WILL I, NOW?
HE COMES TO MY FARM TELLIN' MY SLAVES THEY HAVE RIGHTS. THAT THEY SHOULD REVOLT AND A WHOLE LOT OF OTHER NONSENSE!
I WILL NOT HAVE MY PROPERTY DISRUPTED BY THE RAVINGS OF A LUNATIC, NOR WILL I ALLOW MY SON TO BE THREATENED BY ONE!
WHEN I TOLD HIM TO LEAVE THE FARM, HE THREATENED TO THRASH ME. "SLAVER," HE CALLED ME. "EVIL ONE"!
TELL YOUR FRIEND TO STAY AWAY OR ELSE!

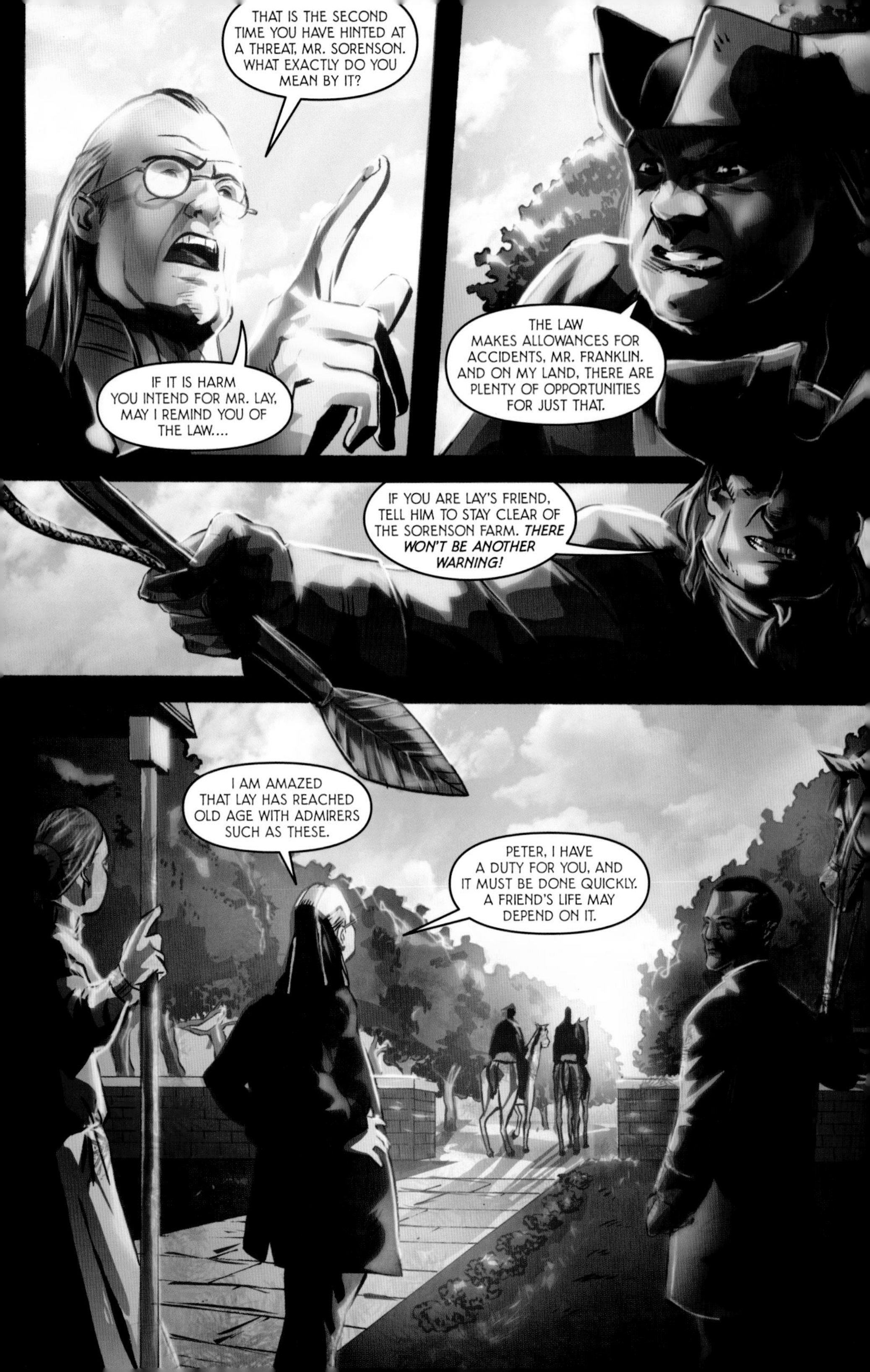
THAT IS THE SECOND TIME YOU HAVE HINTED AT A THREAT, MR. SORENSON. WHAT EXACTLY DO YOU MEAN BY IT?
IF IT IS HARM YOU INTEND FOR MR. LAY, MAY I REMIND YOU OF THE LAW....
THE LAW MAKES ALLOWANCES FOR ACCIDENTS, MR. FRANKLIN. AND ON MY LAND, THERE ARE PLENTY OF OPPORTUNITIES FOR JUST THAT.
IF YOU ARE LAY'S FRIEND, TELL HIM TO STAY CLEAR OF THE SORENSON FARM. *THERE WON'T BE ANOTHER WARNING!*
I AM AMAZED THAT LAY HAS REACHED OLD AGE WITH ADMIRERS SUCH AS THESE.
PETER, I HAVE A DUTY FOR YOU, AND IT MUST BE DONE QUICKLY. A FRIEND'S LIFE MAY DEPEND ON IT.

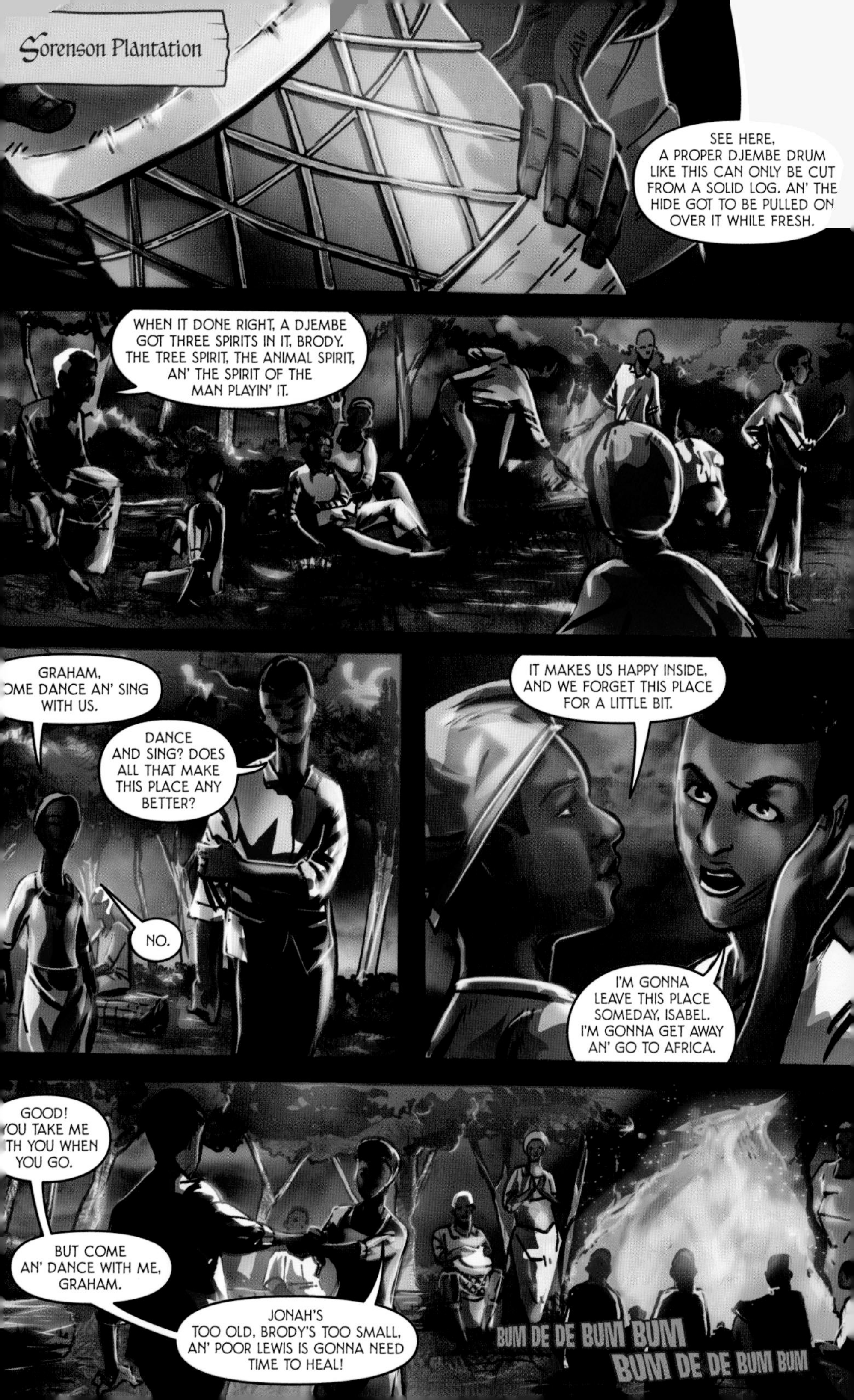
Sorenson Plantation
SEE HERE, A PROPER DJEMBE DRUM LIKE THIS CAN ONLY BE CUT FROM A SOLID LOG. AN' THE HIDE GOT TO BE PULLED ON OVER IT WHILE FRESH.
WHEN IT DONE RIGHT, A DJEMBE GOT THREE SPIRITS IN IT, BRODY. THE TREE SPIRIT, THE ANIMAL SPIRIT, AN' THE SPIRIT OF THE MAN PLAYIN' IT.
GRAHAM, OME DANCE AN' SING WITH US.
DANCE AND SING? DOES ALL THAT MAKE THIS PLACE ANY BETTER?
NO.
IT MAKES US HAPPY INSIDE, AND WE FORGET THIS PLACE FOR A LITTLE BIT.
I'M GONNA LEAVE THIS PLACE SOMEDAY, ISABEL. I'M GONNA GET AWAY AN' GO TO AFRICA.
GOOD! OU TAKE ME TH YOU WHEN YOU GO.
BUT COME AN' DANCE WITH ME, GRAHAM.
JONAH'S TOO OLD, BRODY'S TOO SMALL, AN' POOR LEWIS IS GONNA NEED TIME TO HEAL!
BUM DE DE BUM BUM
BUM DE DE BUM BUM

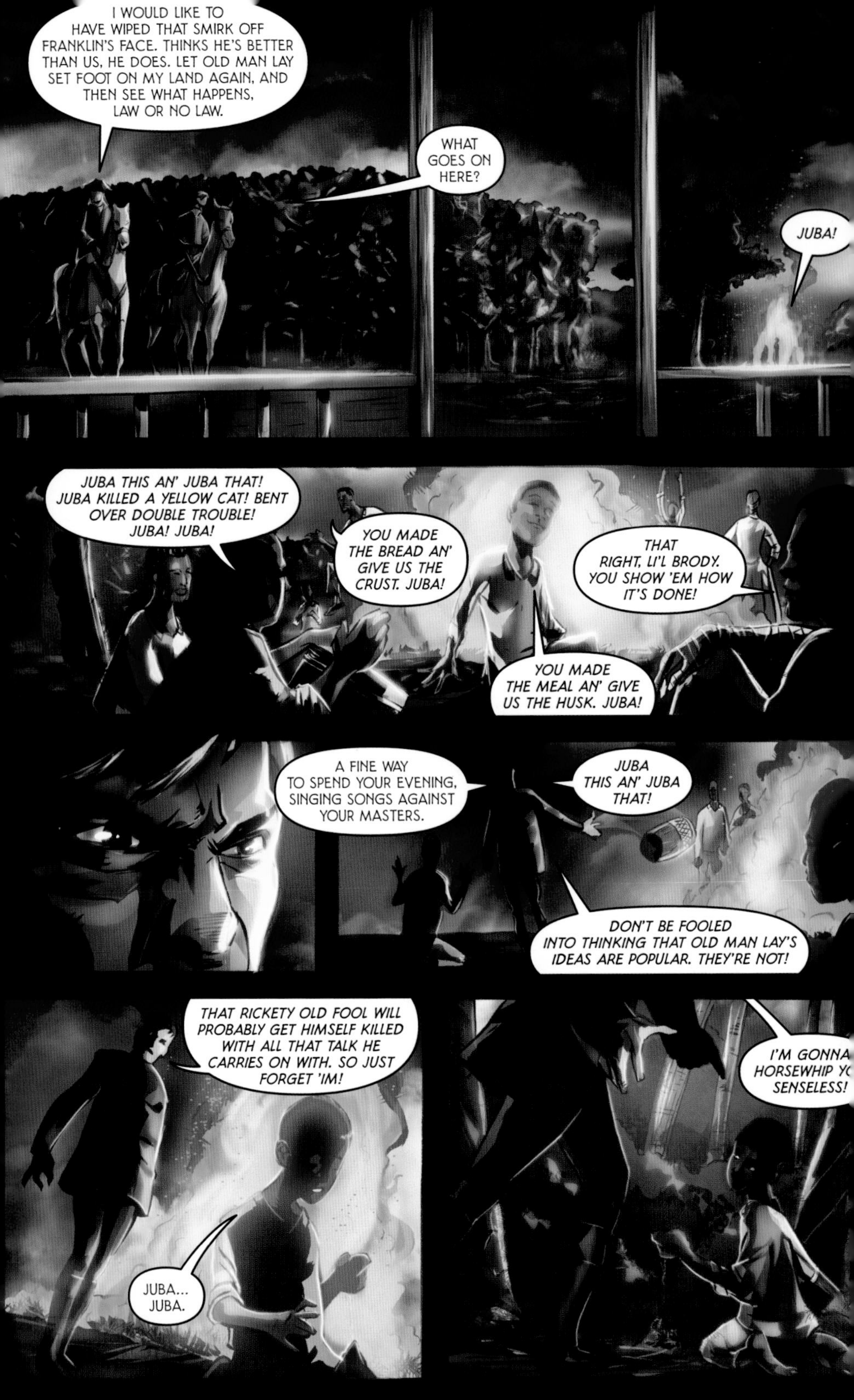
I WOULD LIKE TO HAVE WIPED THAT SMIRK OFF FRANKLIN'S FACE. THINKS HE'S BETTER THAN US, HE DOES. LET OLD MAN LAY SET FOOT ON MY LAND AGAIN, AND THEN SEE WHAT HAPPENS, LAW OR NO LAW.
WHAT GOES ON HERE?
JUBA!
JUBA THIS AN' JUBA THAT! JUBA KILLED A YELLOW CAT! BENT OVER DOUBLE TROUBLE! JUBA! JUBA!
YOU MADE THE BREAD AN' GIVE US THE CRUST. JUBA!
THAT RIGHT, LI'L BRODY. YOU SHOW 'EM HOW IT'S DONE!
YOU MADE THE MEAL AN' GIVE US THE HUSK. JUBA!
A FINE WAY TO SPEND YOUR EVENING, SINGING SONGS AGAINST YOUR MASTERS.
JUBA THIS AN' JUBA THAT!
DON'T BE FOOLED INTO THINKING THAT OLD MAN LAY'S IDEAS ARE POPULAR. THEY'RE NOT!
THAT RICKETY OLD FOOL WILL PROBABLY GET HIMSELF KILLED WITH ALL THAT TALK HE CARRIES ON WITH. SO JUST FORGET 'IM!
JUBA... JUBA.
I'M GONNA HORSEWHIP YO SENSELESS!

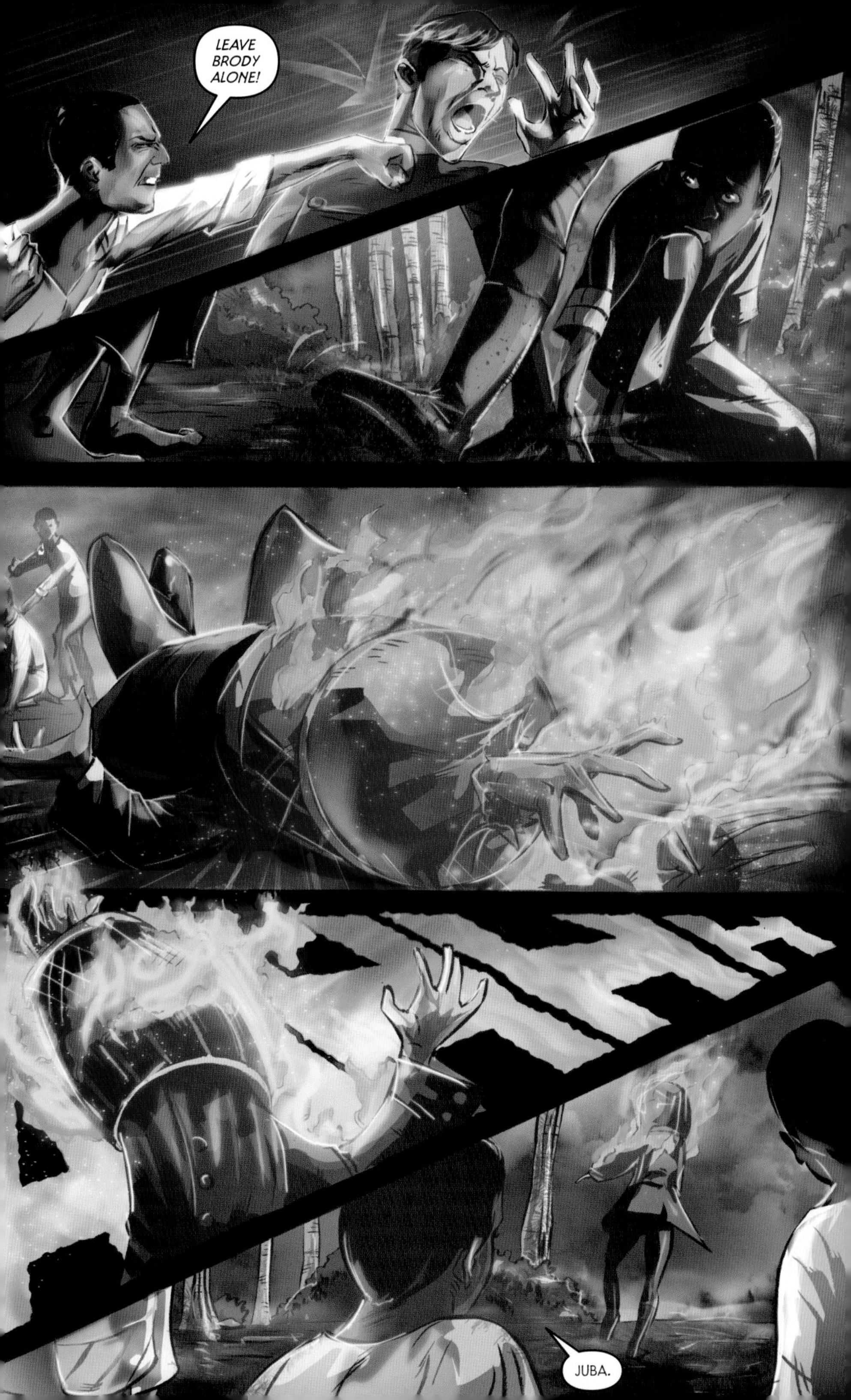
LEAVE BRODY ALONE!
JUBA.

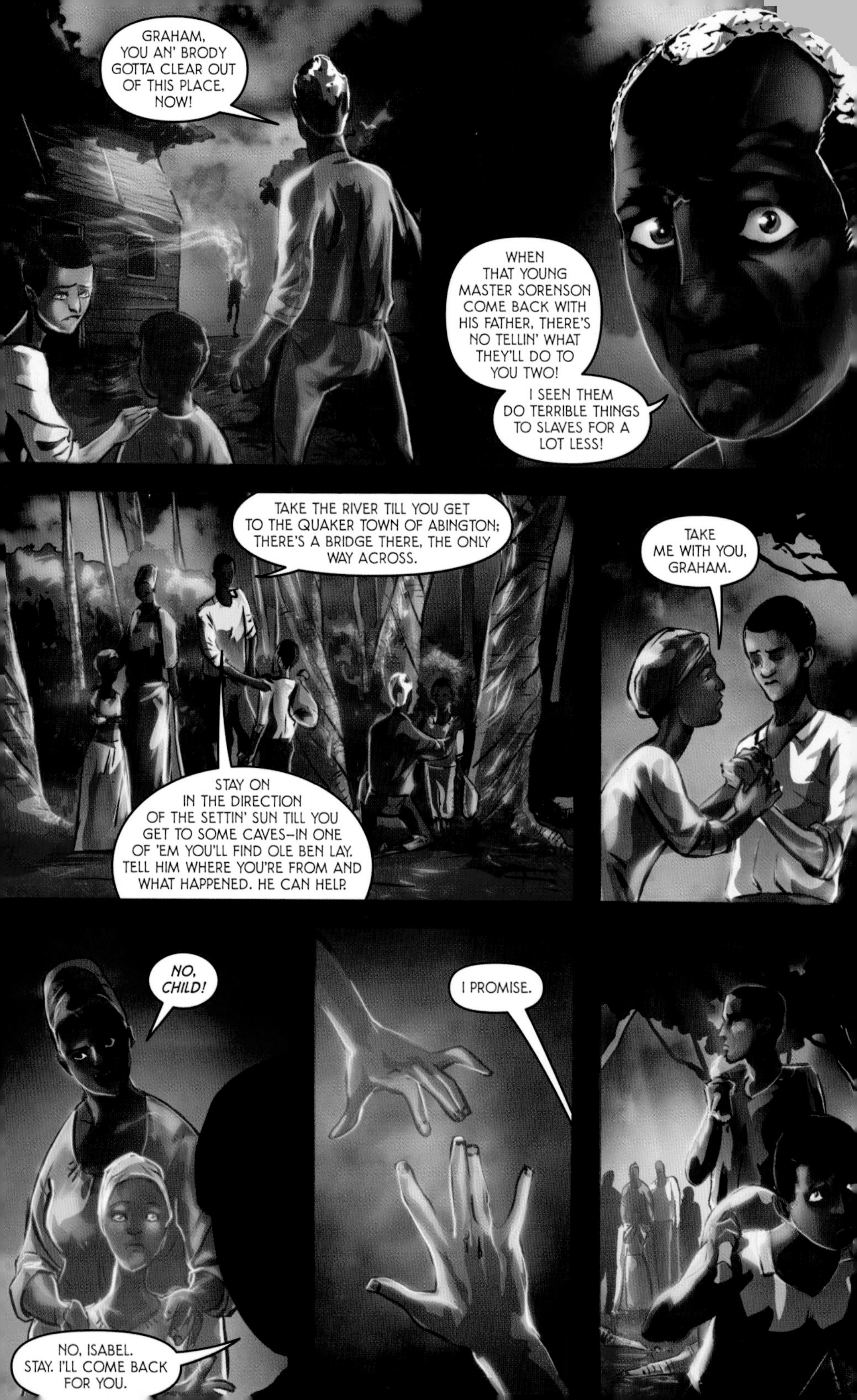
GRAHAM, YOU AN' BRODY GOTTA CLEAR OUT OF THIS PLACE, NOW!
WHEN THAT YOUNG MASTER SORENSON COME BACK WITH HIS FATHER, THERE'S NO TELLIN' WHAT THEY'LL DO TO YOU TWO!
I SEEN THEM DO TERRIBLE THINGS TO SLAVES FOR A LOT LESS!
TAKE THE RIVER TILL YOU GET TO THE QUAKER TOWN OF ABINGTON; THERE'S A BRIDGE THERE, THE ONLY WAY ACROSS.
STAY ON IN THE DIRECTION OF THE SETTIN' SUN TILL YOU GET TO SOME CAVES—IN ONE OF 'EM YOU'LL FIND OLE BEN LAY. TELL HIM WHERE YOU'RE FROM AND WHAT HAPPENED. HE CAN HELP.
TAKE ME WITH YOU, GRAHAM.
NO, CHILD!
NO, ISABEL. STAY. I'LL COME BACK FOR YOU.
I PROMISE.

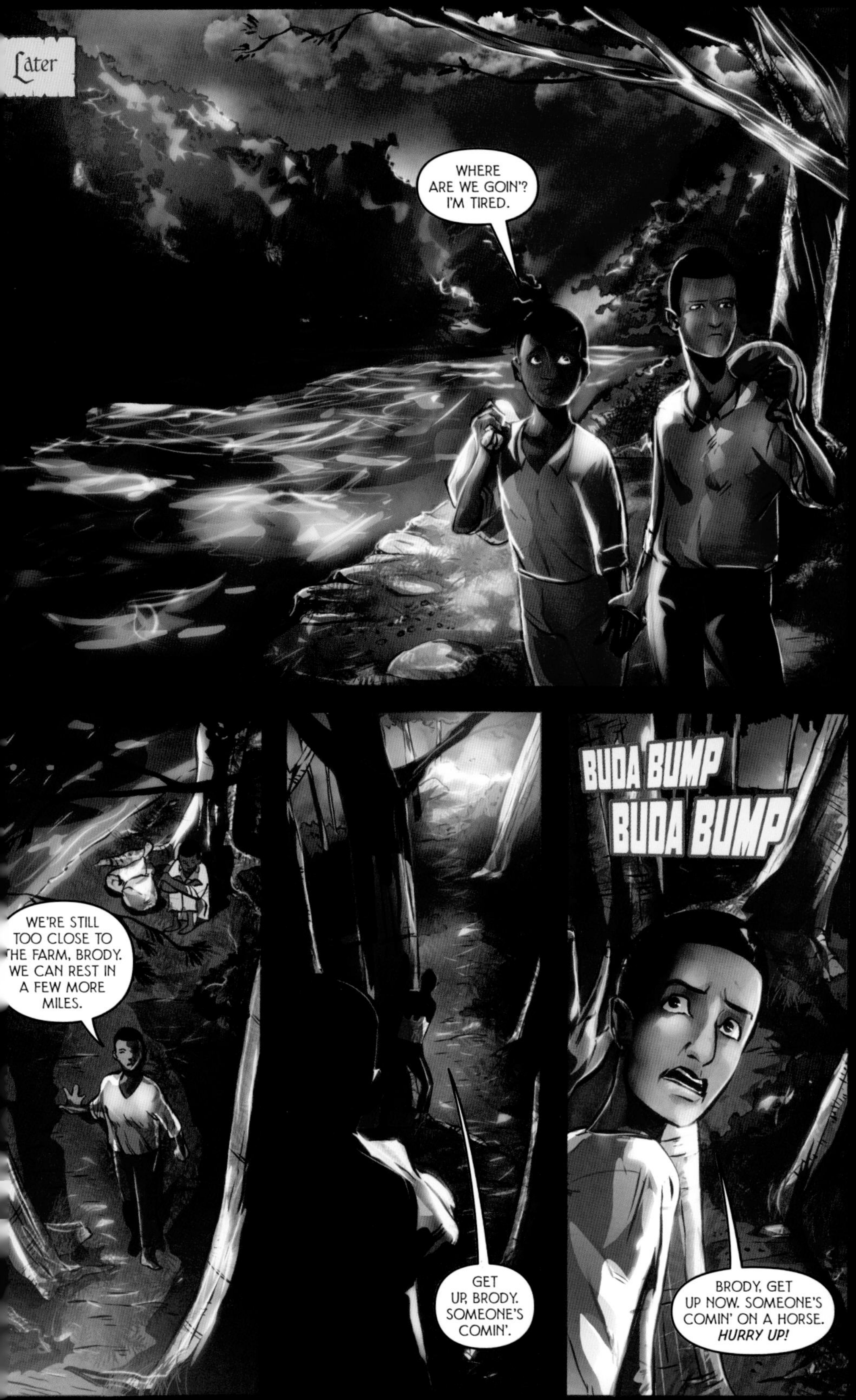
Later
WHERE ARE WE GOIN'? I'M TIRED.
WE'RE STILL TOO CLOSE TO THE FARM, BRODY. WE CAN REST IN A FEW MORE MILES.
GET UP, BRODY. SOMEONE'S COMIN'.
BUDA BUMP
BUDA BUMP
BRODY, GET UP NOW. SOMEONE'S COMIN' ON A HORSE. *HURRY UP!*

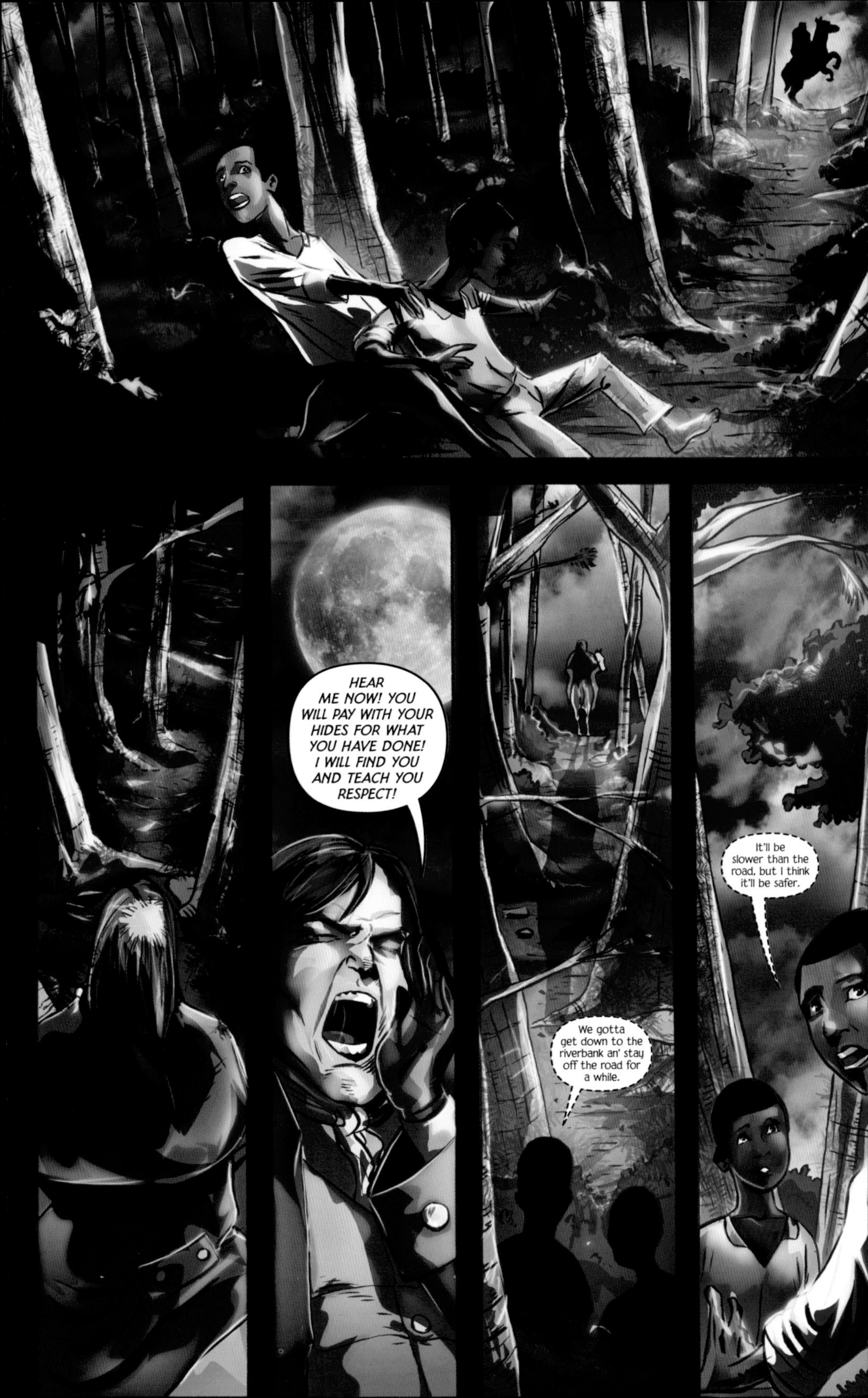
HEAR ME NOW! YOU WILL PAY WITH YOUR HIDES FOR WHAT YOU HAVE DONE! I WILL FIND YOU AND TEACH YOU RESPECT!
We gotta get down to the riverbank an' stay off the road for a while.
It'll be slower than the road, but I think it'll be safer.

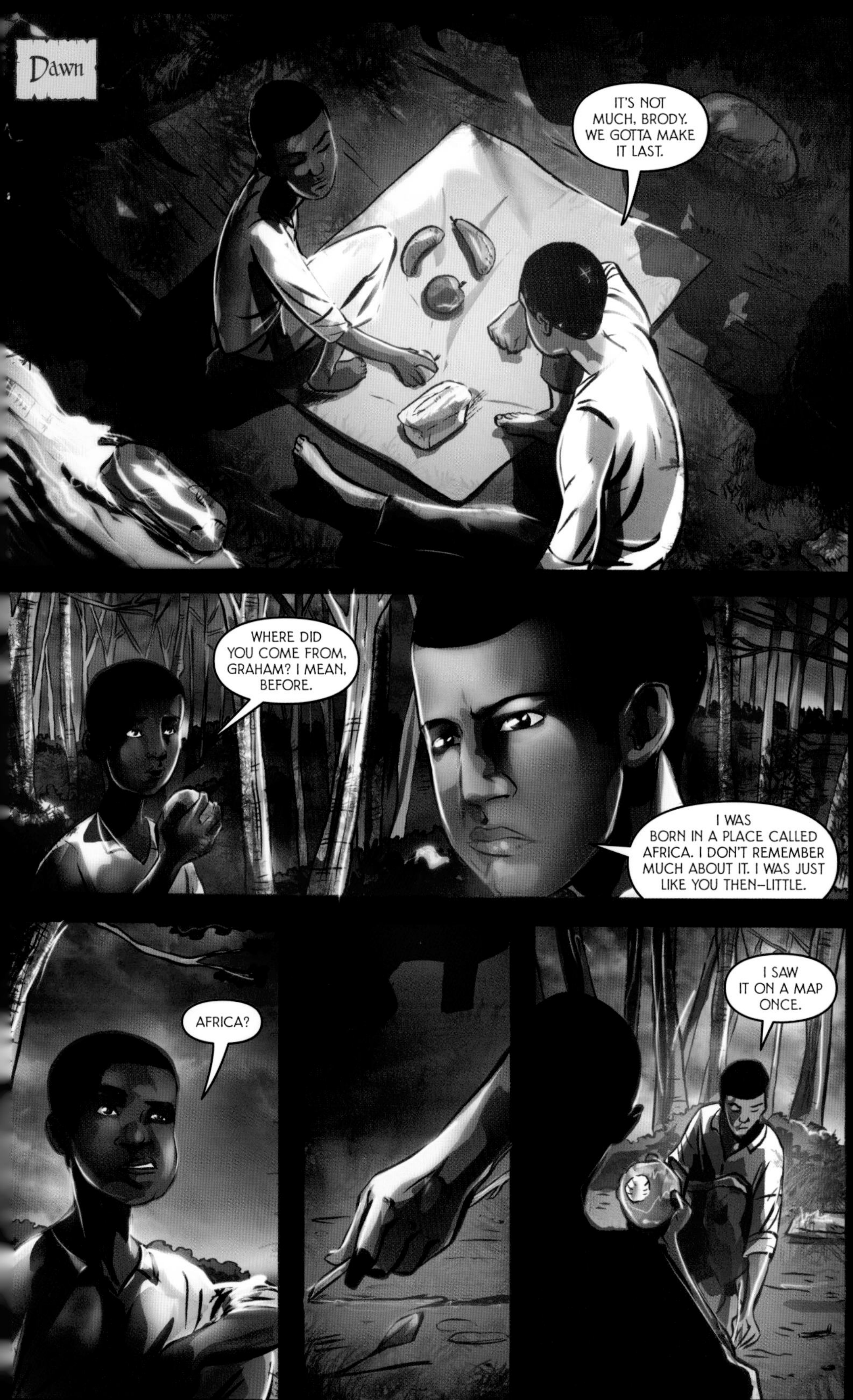
Dawn
IT'S NOT MUCH, BRODY. WE GOTTA MAKE IT LAST.
WHERE DID YOU COME FROM, GRAHAM? I MEAN, BEFORE.
I WAS BORN IN A PLACE CALLED AFRICA. I DON'T REMEMBER MUCH ABOUT IT. I WAS JUST LIKE YOU THEN—LITTLE.
AFRICA?
I SAW IT ON A MAP ONCE.

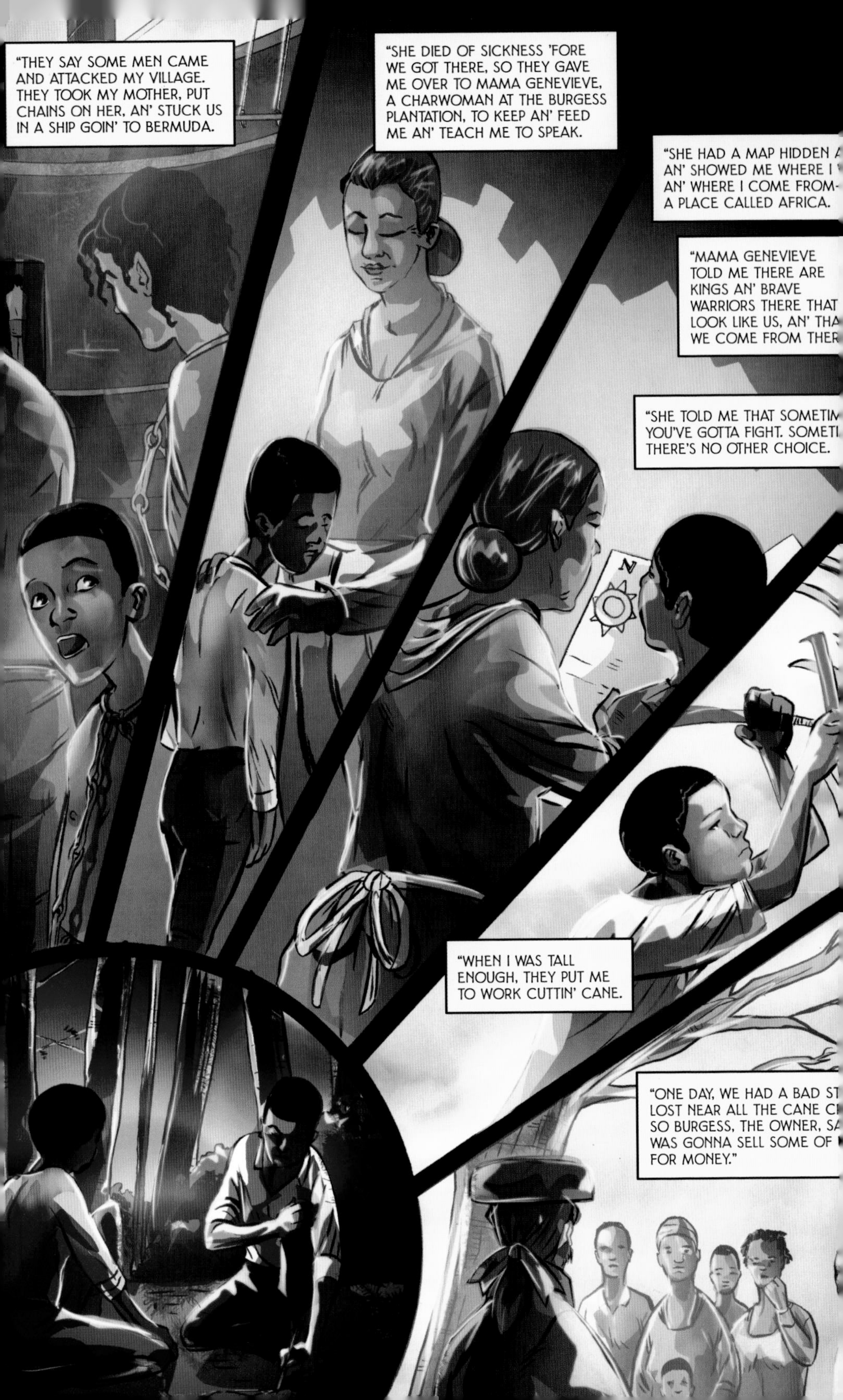
"THEY SAY SOME MEN CAME AND ATTACKED MY VILLAGE. THEY TOOK MY MOTHER, PUT CHAINS ON HER, AN' STUCK US IN A SHIP GOIN' TO BERMUDA.
"SHE DIED OF SICKNESS 'FORE WE GOT THERE, SO THEY GAVE ME OVER TO MAMA GENEVIEVE, A CHARWOMAN AT THE BURGESS PLANTATION, TO KEEP AN' FEED ME AN' TEACH ME TO SPEAK.
"SHE HAD A MAP HIDDEN A AN' SHOWED ME WHERE I AN' WHERE I COME FROM- A PLACE CALLED AFRICA.
"MAMA GENEVIEVE TOLD ME THERE ARE KINGS AN' BRAVE WARRIORS THERE THAT LOOK LIKE US, AN' THA WE COME FROM THER
"SHE TOLD ME THAT SOMETIM YOU'VE GOTTA FIGHT. SOMETI THERE'S NO OTHER CHOICE.
N
"WHEN I WAS TALL ENOUGH, THEY PUT ME TO WORK CUTTIN' CANE.
"ONE DAY, WE HAD A BAD ST LOST NEAR ALL THE CANE C SO BURGESS, THE OWNER, SA WAS GONNA SELL SOME OF FOR MONEY."

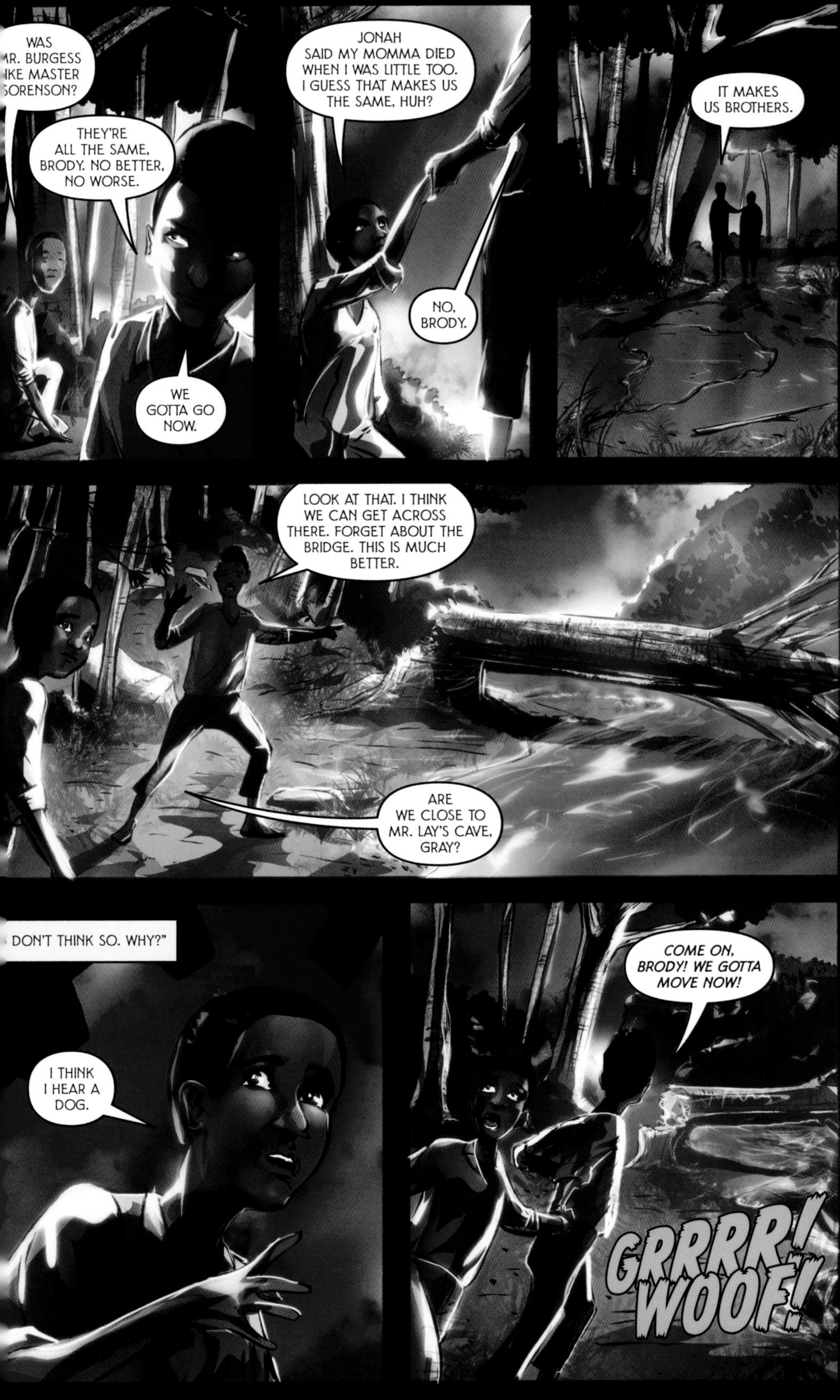
WAS
MR. BURGESS
IKE MASTER
SORENSON?
THEY'RE ALL THE SAME, BRODY. NO BETTER, NO WORSE.
WE GOTTA GO NOW.
JONAH SAID MY MOMMA DIED WHEN I WAS LITTLE TOO. I GUESS THAT MAKES US THE SAME, HUH?
NO, BRODY.
IT MAKES US BROTHERS.
LOOK AT THAT. I THINK WE CAN GET ACROSS THERE. FORGET ABOUT THE BRIDGE. THIS IS MUCH BETTER.
ARE WE CLOSE TO MR. LAY'S CAVE, GRAY?
DON'T THINK SO. WHY?"
I THINK I HEAR A DOG.
COME ON, BRODY! WE GOTTA MOVE NOW!
GRRRR! WOOF!

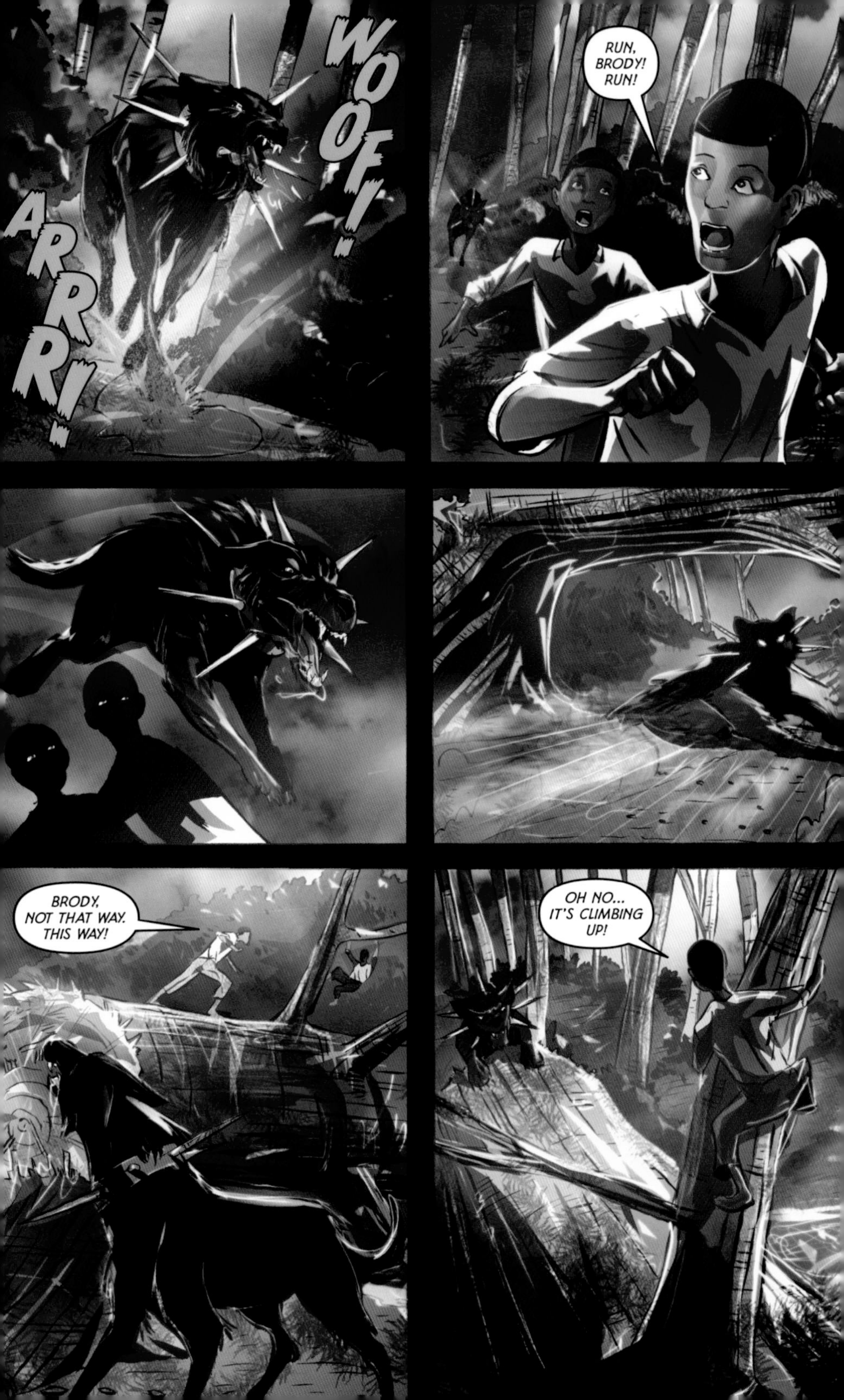
WOOF!!
ARRR!
RUN, BRODY! RUN!
BRODY, NOT THAT WAY. THIS WAY!
OH NO... IT'S CLIMBING UP!

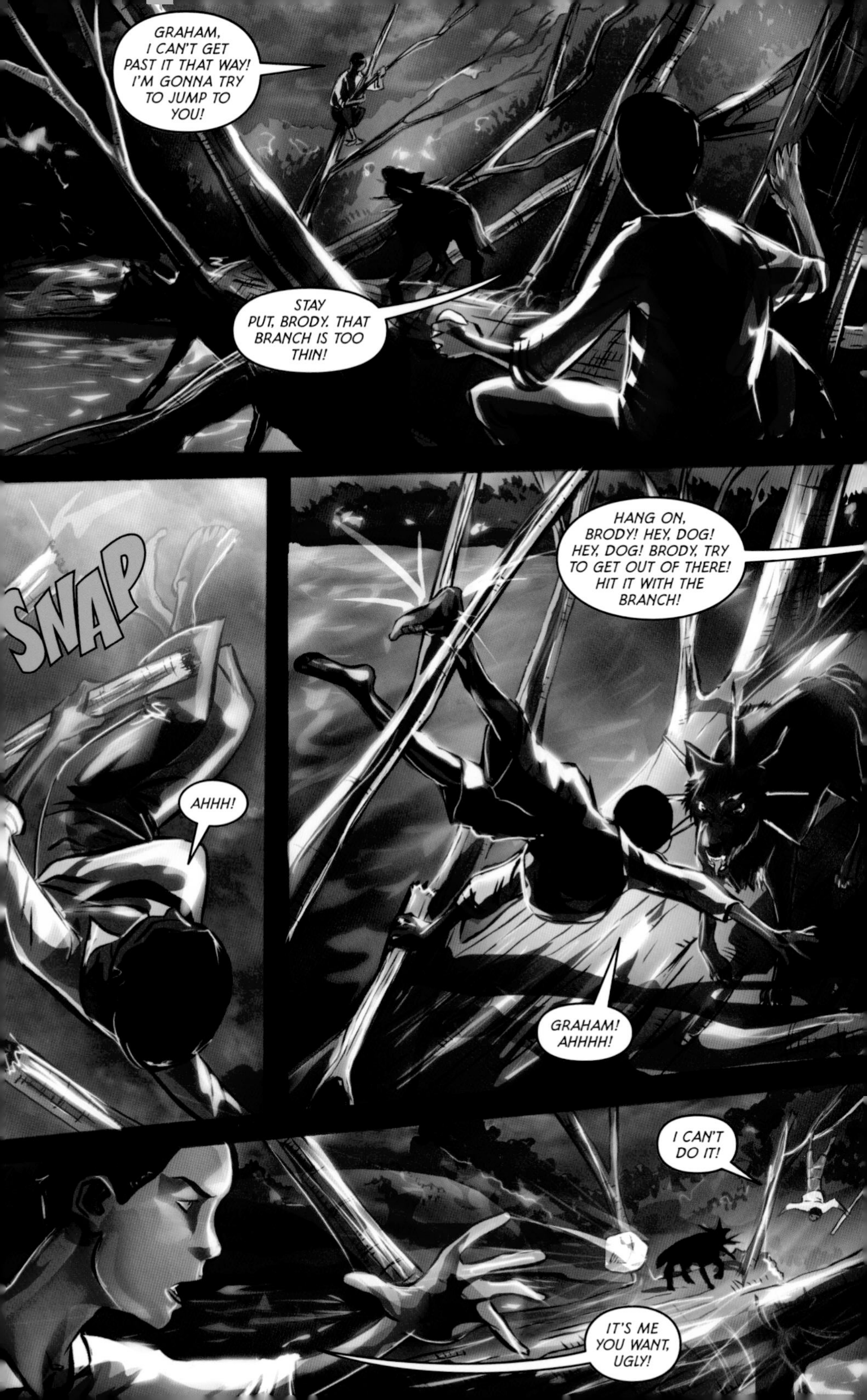
GRAHAM, I CAN'T GET PAST IT THAT WAY! I'M GONNA TRY TO JUMP TO YOU!
STAY PUT, BRODY. THAT BRANCH IS TOO THIN!
SNAP
AHHH!
HANG ON, BRODY! HEY, DOG! HEY, DOG! BRODY, TRY TO GET OUT OF THERE! HIT IT WITH THE BRANCH!
GRAHAM! AHHHH!
I CAN'T DO IT!
IT'S ME YOU WANT, UGLY!

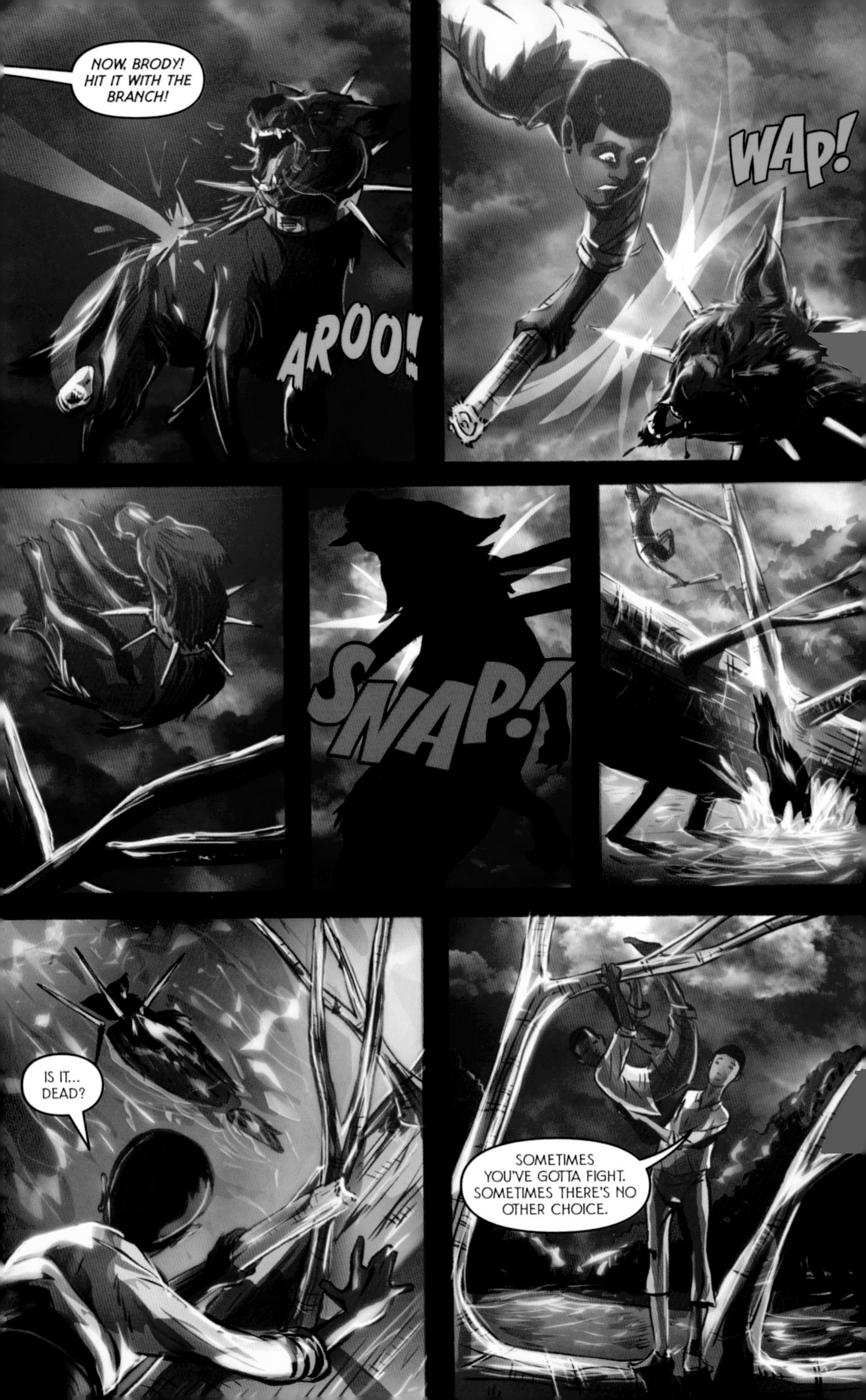
NOW, BRODY! HIT IT WITH THE BRANCH!
AROO!
WAP!
SNAP!
IS IT... DEAD?
SOMETIMES YOU'VE GOTTA FIGHT. SOMETIMES THERE'S NO OTHER CHOICE.

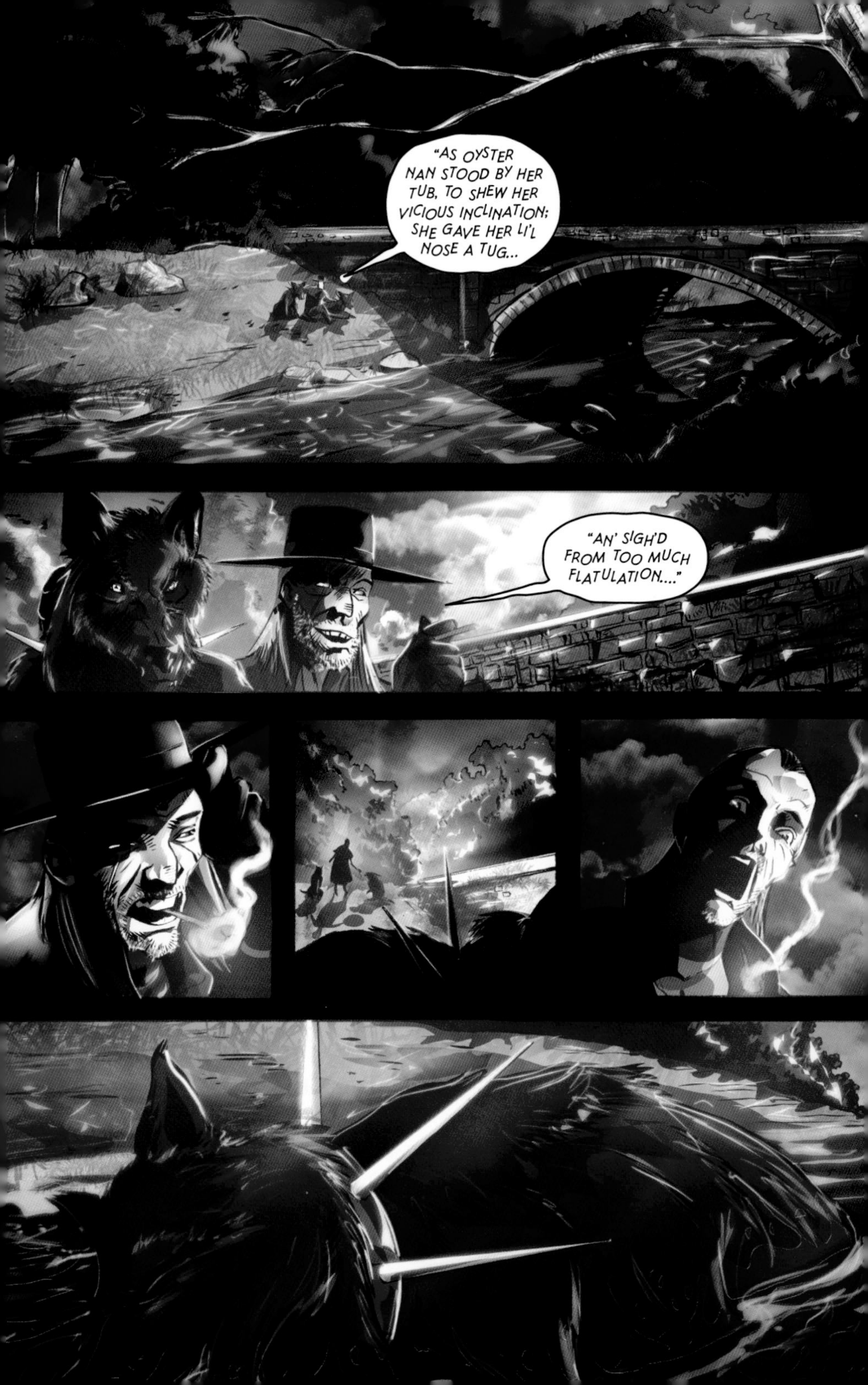
"AS OYSTER NAN STOOD BY HER TUB, TO SHEW HER VICIOUS INCLINATION; SHE GAVE HER LI'L NOSE A TUG...
"AN' SIGH'D FROM TOO MUCH FLATULATION..."

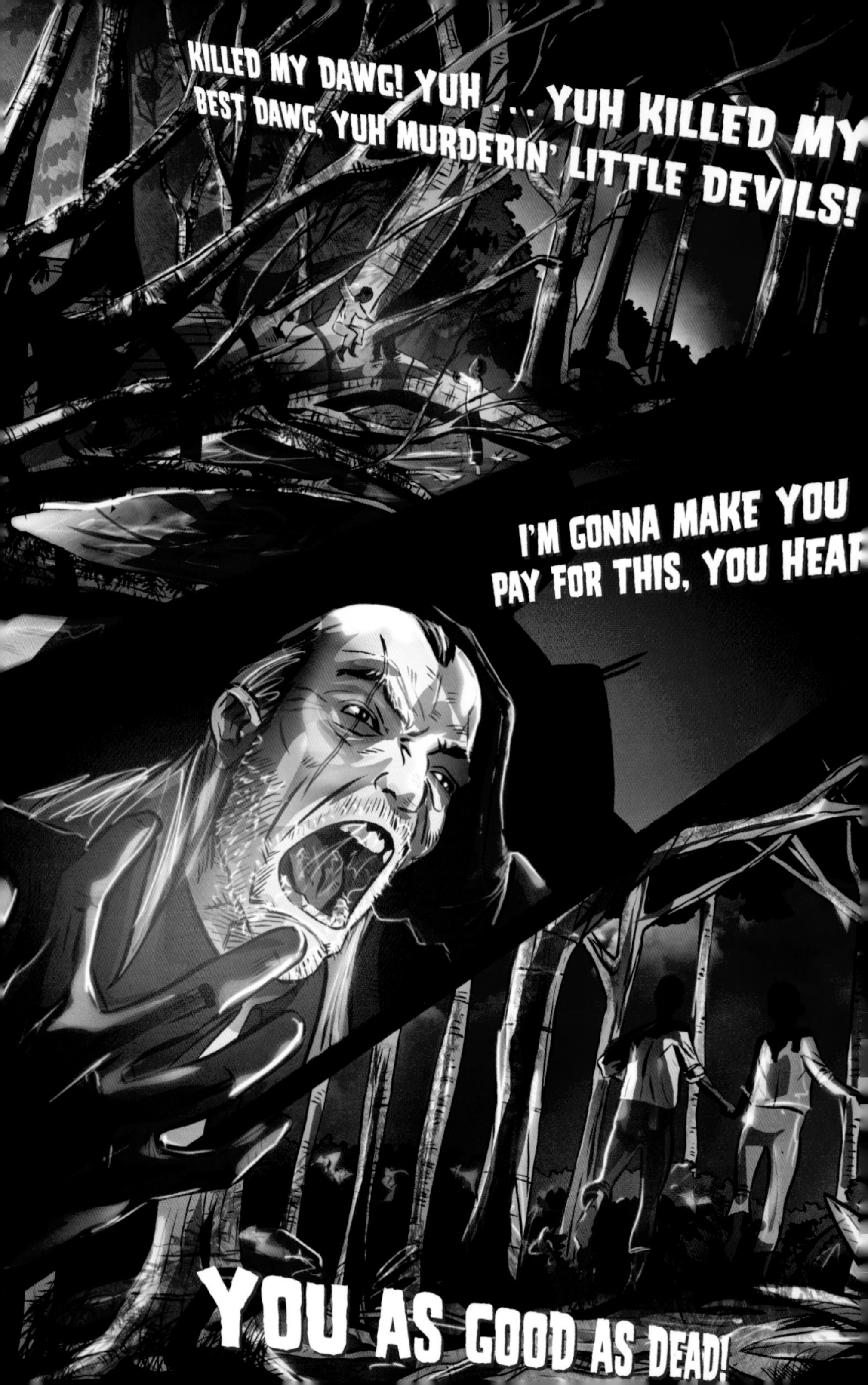
KILLED MY DAWG! YUH . . . YUH KILLED MY BEST DAWG, YUH MURDERIN' LITTLE DEVILS!
I'M GONNA MAKE YOU PAY FOR THIS, YOU HEAR
YOU AS GOOD AS DEAD!

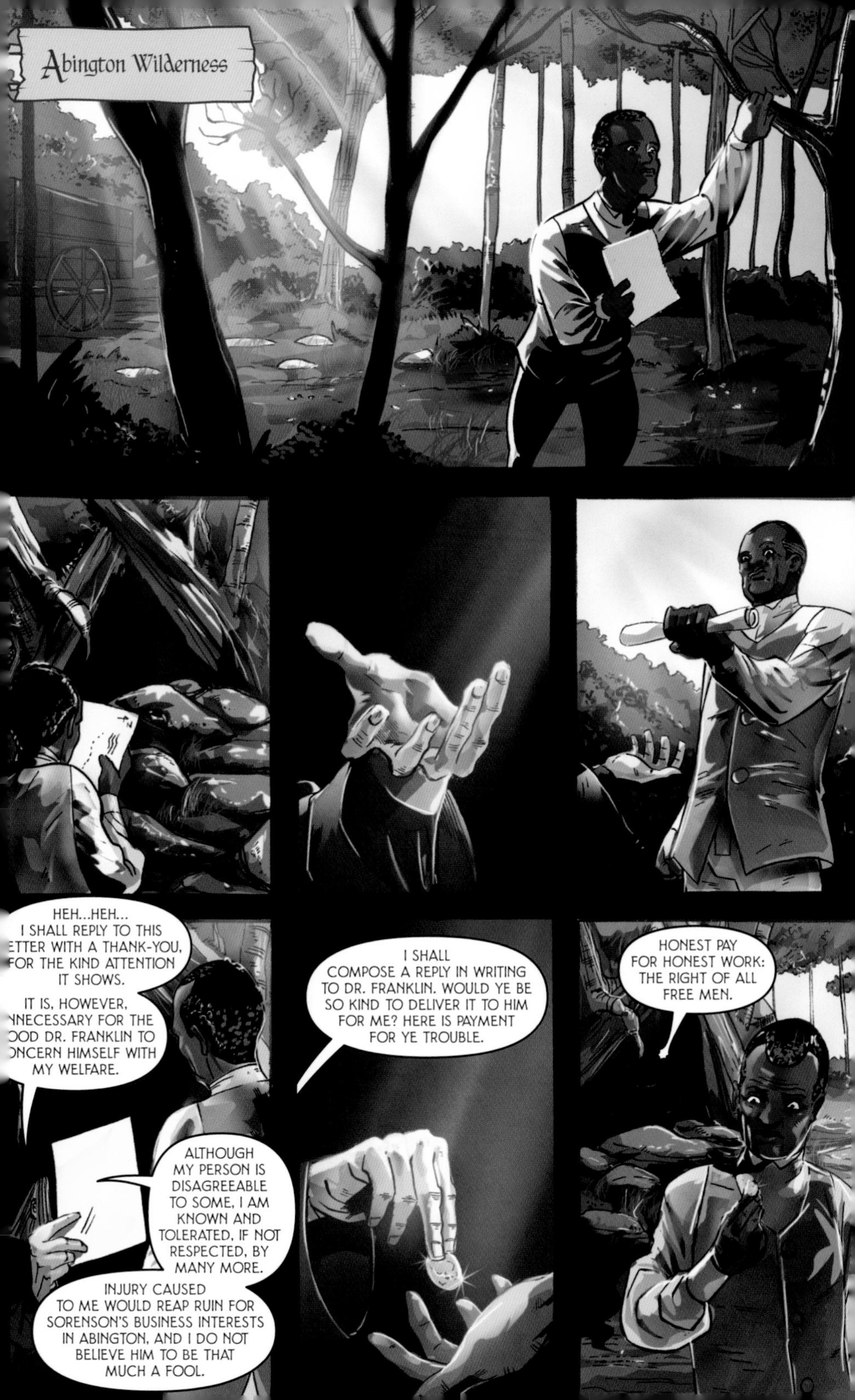
Abington Wilderness
HEH...HEH... I SHALL REPLY TO THIS ETTER WITH A THANK-YOU, FOR THE KIND ATTENTION IT SHOWS.
IT IS, HOWEVER, NNECESSARY FOR THE OOD DR. FRANKLIN TO ONCERN HIMSELF WITH MY WELFARE.
ALTHOUGH MY PERSON IS DISAGREEABLE TO SOME, I AM KNOWN AND TOLERATED, IF NOT RESPECTED, BY MANY MORE.
INJURY CAUSED TO ME WOULD REAP RUIN FOR SORENSON'S BUSINESS INTERESTS IN ABINGTON, AND I DO NOT BELIEVE HIM TO BE THAT MUCH A FOOL.
I SHALL COMPOSE A REPLY IN WRITING TO DR. FRANKLIN. WOULD YE BE SO KIND TO DELIVER IT TO HIM FOR ME? HERE IS PAYMENT FOR YE TROUBLE.
HONEST PAY FOR HONEST WORK: THE RIGHT OF ALL FREE MEN.

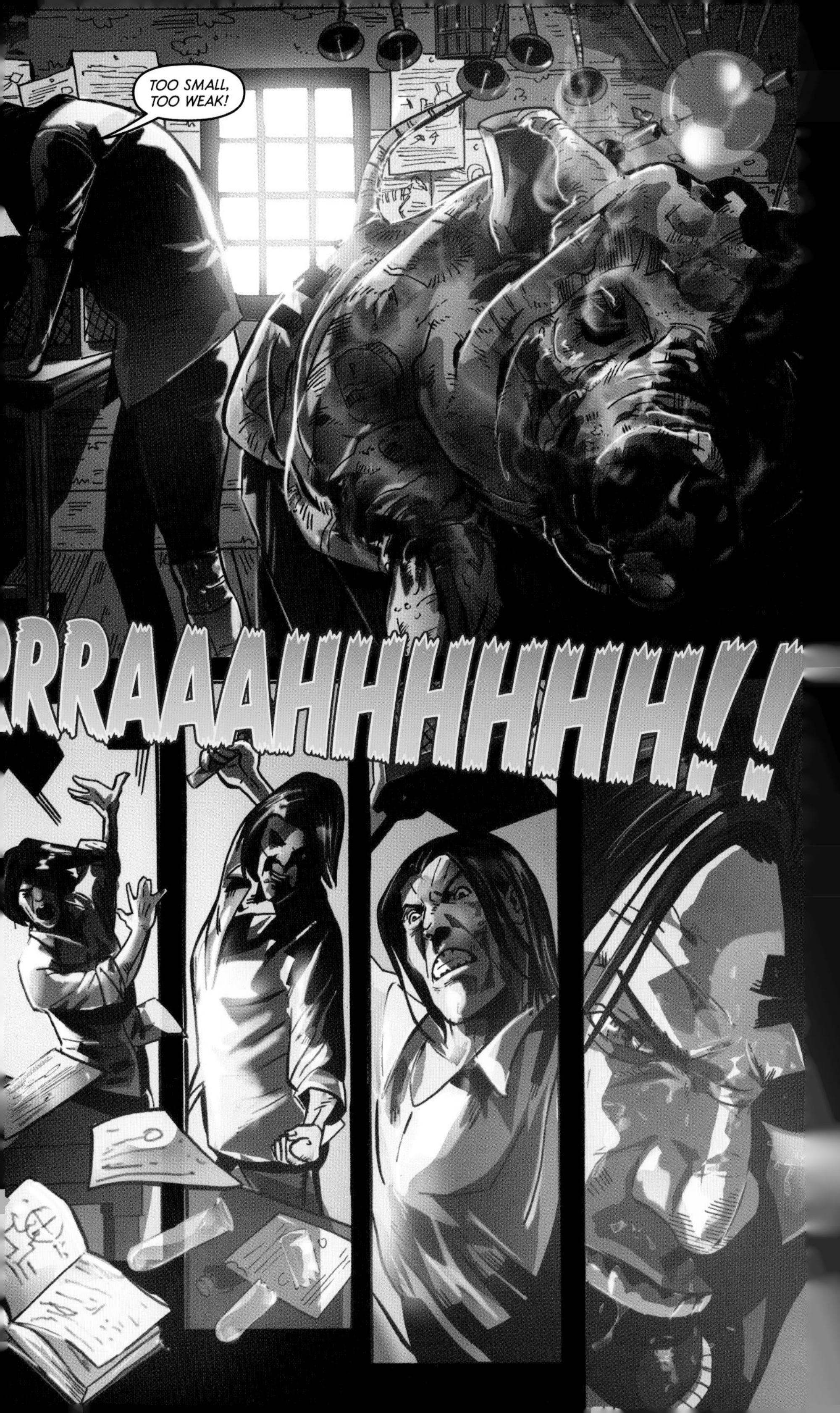
TOO SMALL, TOO WEAK!
RRAAAHHHHHHH!!

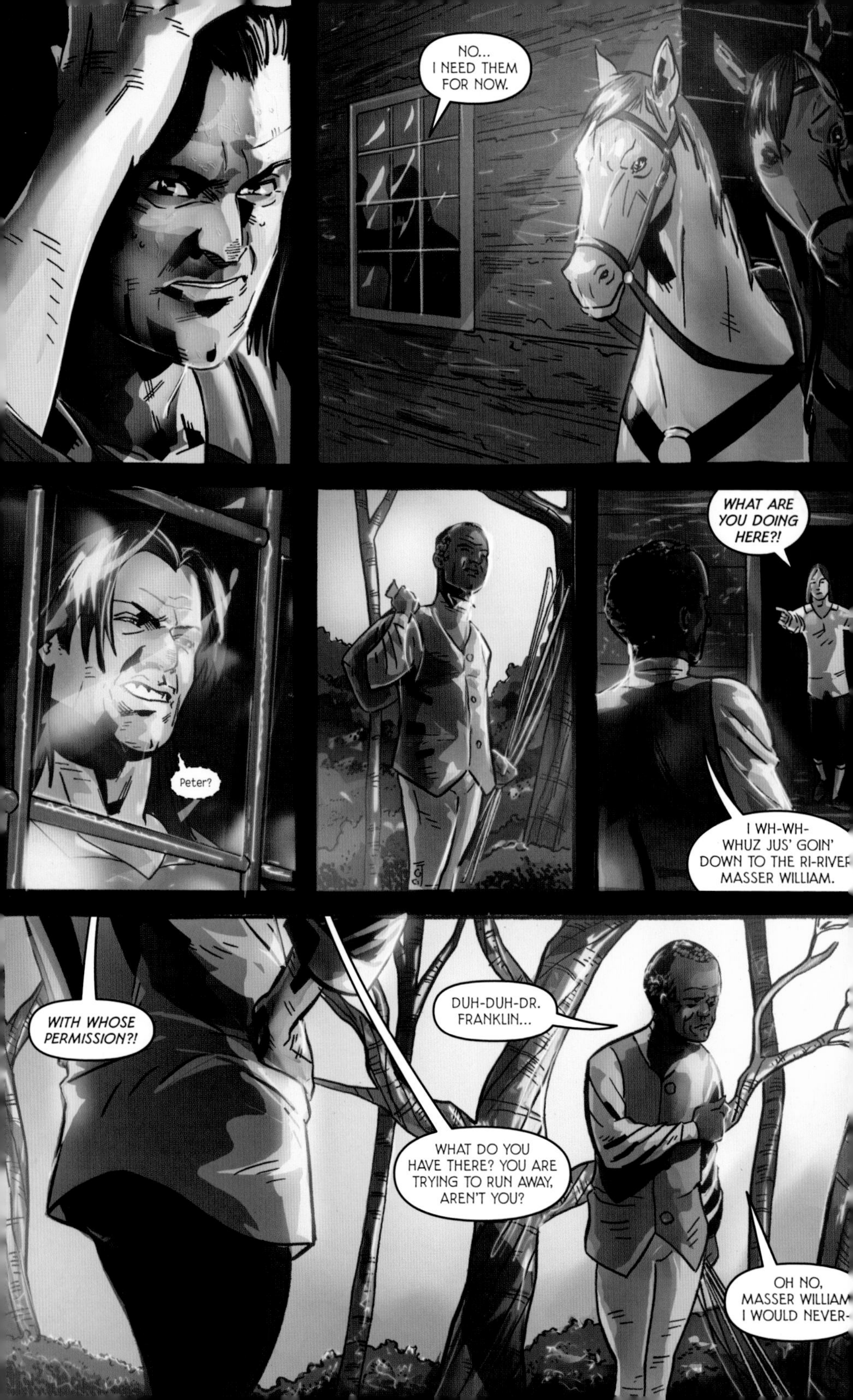
NO...
I NEED THEM
FOR NOW.
Peter?
WHAT ARE
YOU DOING
HERE?!
I WH-WH-
WHUZ JUS' GOIN'
DOWN TO THE RI-RIVER
MASSER WILLIAM.
WITH WHOSE
PERMISSION?!
DUH-DUH-DR.
FRANKLIN...
WHAT DO YOU
HAVE THERE? YOU ARE
TRYING TO RUN AWAY,
AREN'T YOU?
OH NO,
MASSER WILLIAM
I WOULD NEVER-

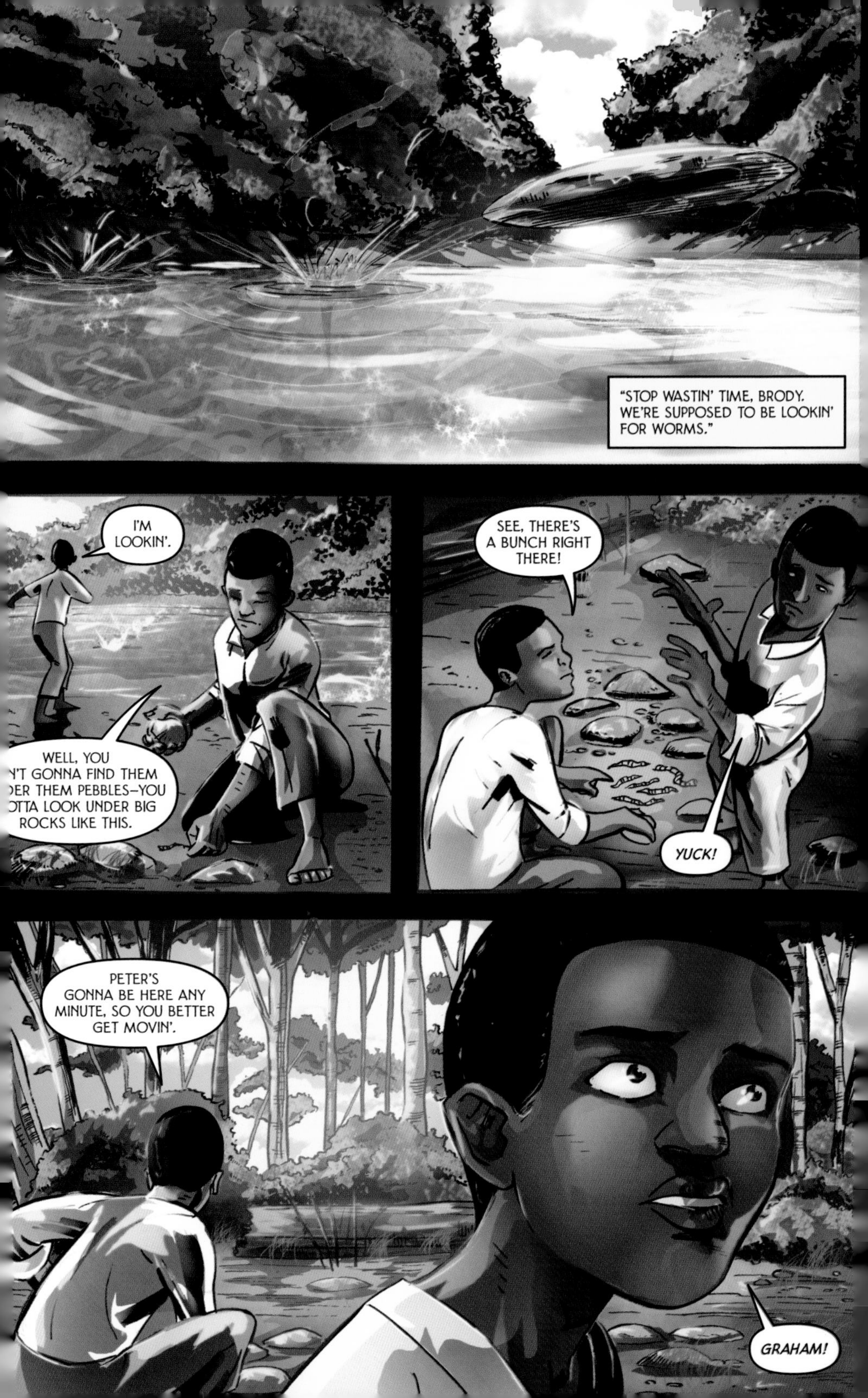
"STOP WASTIN' TIME, BRODY. WE'RE SUPPOSED TO BE LOOKIN' FOR WORMS."
I'M LOOKIN'.
WELL, YOU N'T GONNA FIND THEM DER THEM PEBBLES—YOU OTTA LOOK UNDER BIG ROCKS LIKE THIS.
SEE, THERE'S A BUNCH RIGHT THERE!
YUCK!
PETER'S GONNA BE HERE ANY MINUTE, SO YOU BETTER GET MOVIN'.
GRAHAM!

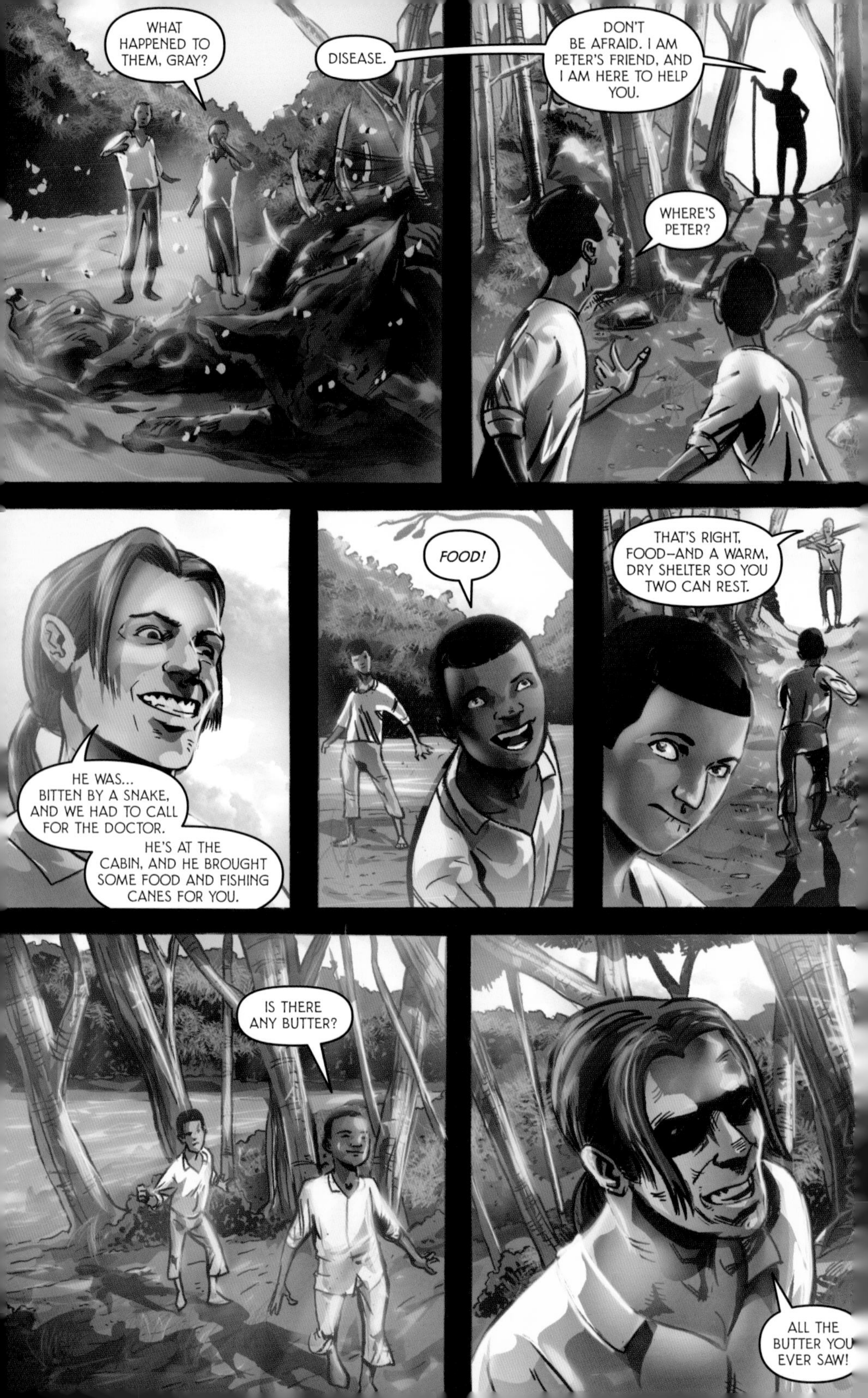
WHAT HAPPENED TO THEM, GRAY?
DISEASE.
DON'T BE AFRAID. I AM PETER'S FRIEND, AND I AM HERE TO HELP YOU.
WHERE'S PETER?
HE WAS... BITTEN BY A SNAKE, AND WE HAD TO CALL FOR THE DOCTOR.
HE'S AT THE CABIN, AND HE BROUGHT SOME FOOD AND FISHING CANES FOR YOU.
FOOD!
THAT'S RIGHT, FOOD—AND A WARM, DRY SHELTER SO YOU TWO CAN REST.
IS THERE ANY BUTTER?
ALL THE BUTTER YOU EVER SAW!

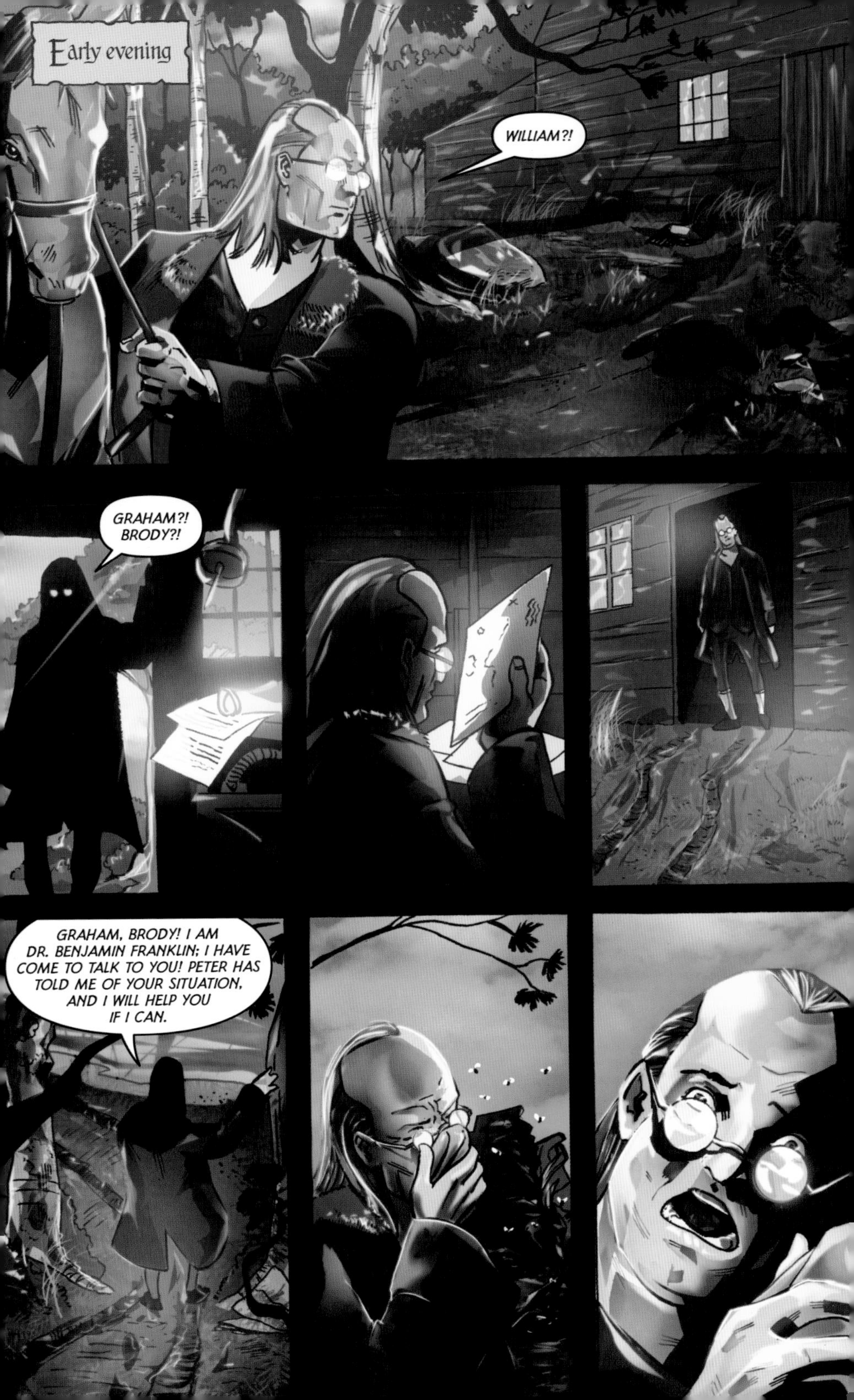
Early evening
WILLIAM?!
GRAHAM?! BRODY?!
GRAHAM, BRODY! I AM DR. BENJAMIN FRANKLIN; I HAVE COME TO TALK TO YOU! PETER HAS TOLD ME OF YOUR SITUATION, AND I WILL HELP YOU IF I CAN.

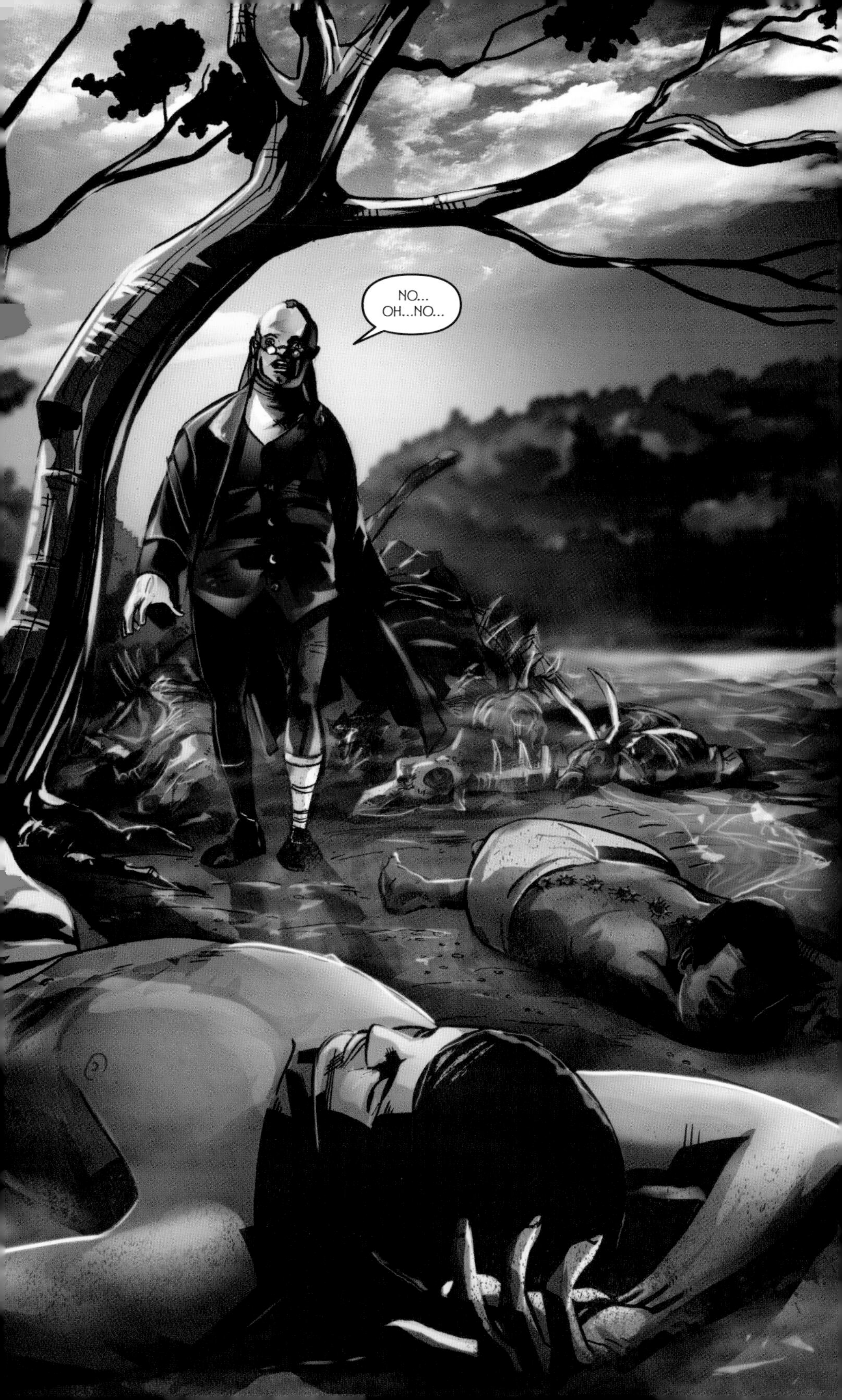
NO...
OH...NO...

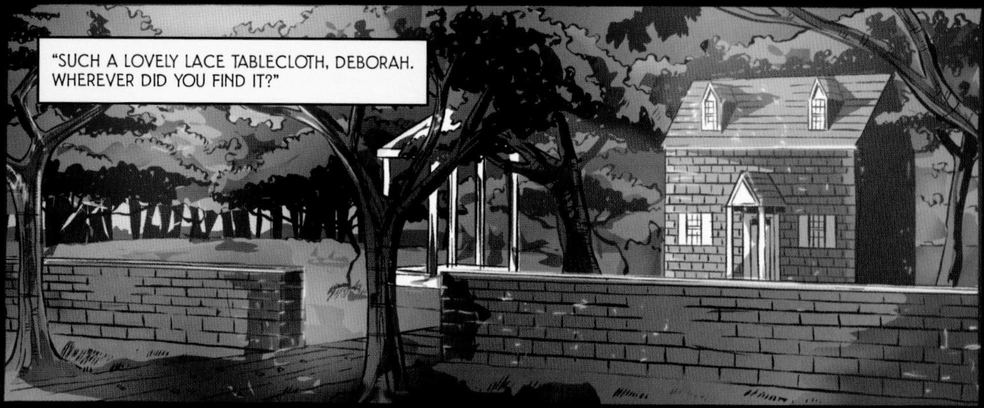
"SUCH A LOVELY LACE TABLECLOTH, DEBORAH. WHEREVER DID YOU FIND IT?"

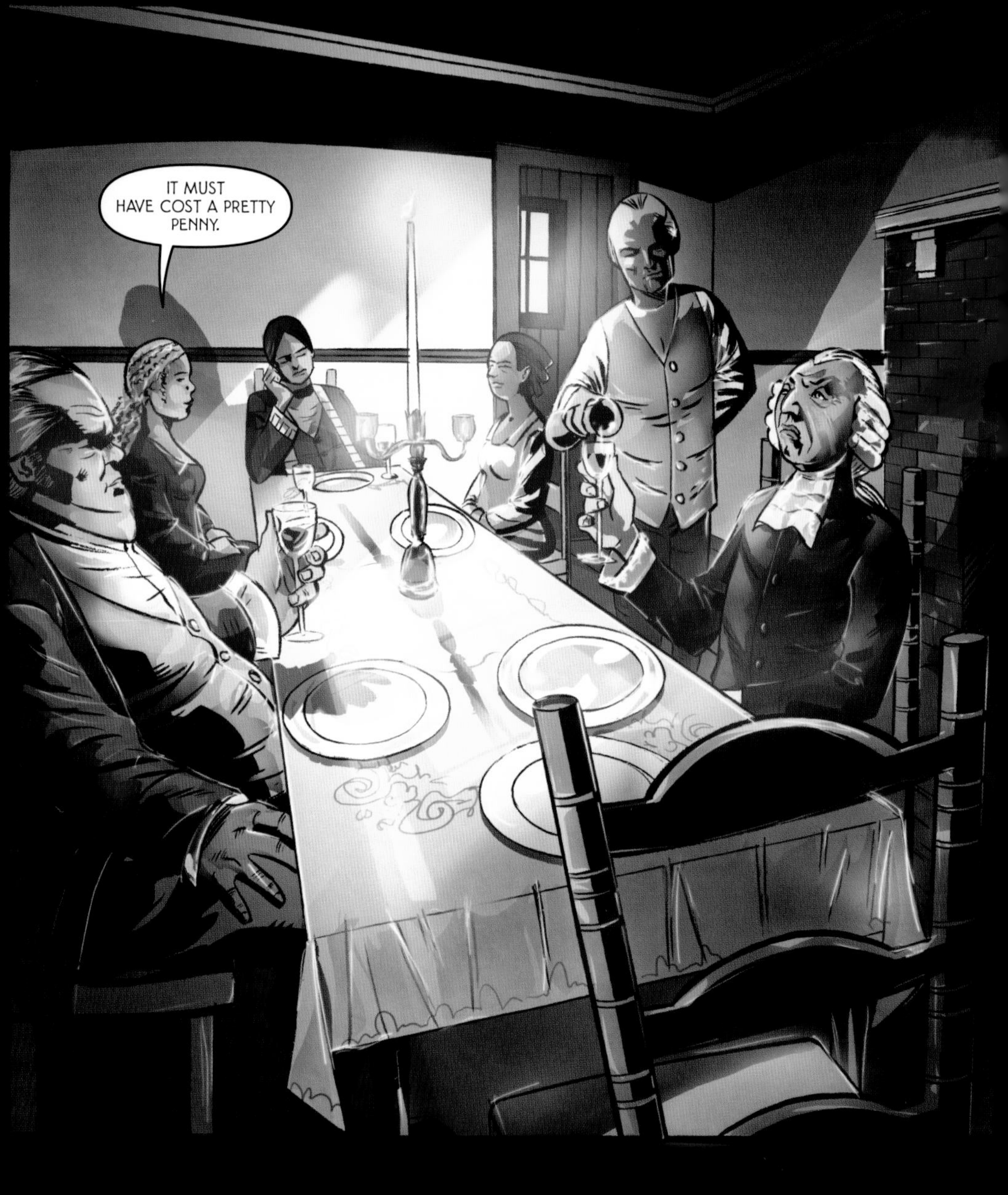
IT MUST HAVE COST A PRETTY PENNY.

IT IS POSSIBLE BEN HAS SIMPLY OVERLOOKED THE TIME; THOSE JUNTO MEETINGS ARE QUITE ABSORBING, I UNDERSTAND.

OH, A JUNTO MEETING, IS IT? WELL, I BEEN TO ONE OR TWO OF THOSE MYSELF, AND YOU ARE RIGHT— THEY ARE ABSORBING.

ESPECIALLY THE ENDLESS TOASTING. *HA, HA, HA, SUWEEE, SUWEEE!*

PERHAPS YOU COULD DISCU[ ] YOUR BUSINESS WIT[ ] ME?

IT'S BEEN MY BLESSIN' TO KNOW THE FRANKLIN CLAN FOR THIRTY OR MORE YEARS. I WATCHED LITTLE BILLY HERE GROW UP FROM A WEE LAD. YES, I DID.

FEW MEN HAVE DONE GREATER SERVICE FOR THE BRITISH EMPIRE AND FOR HIS FRIENDS THA[ ] BENJAMIN FRANKLIN, AND I SALUTE HIM HERE IN THE PRESENCE OF HIS FRIENDS AND FAMILY.

HEAR, HEAR!

I'M SORRY, LAD. I KNOW YE MEAN WELL, AN' I DUNNA MEAN TO LAUGH AT YE, BUT THIS SORT OF BUSINESS NEEDS YER FATHER'S EXPERIENCE BEHIND IT. YE UNDERSTAND THAT, DON'T YE?

ARE YOU FORGETTING SOMETHING?

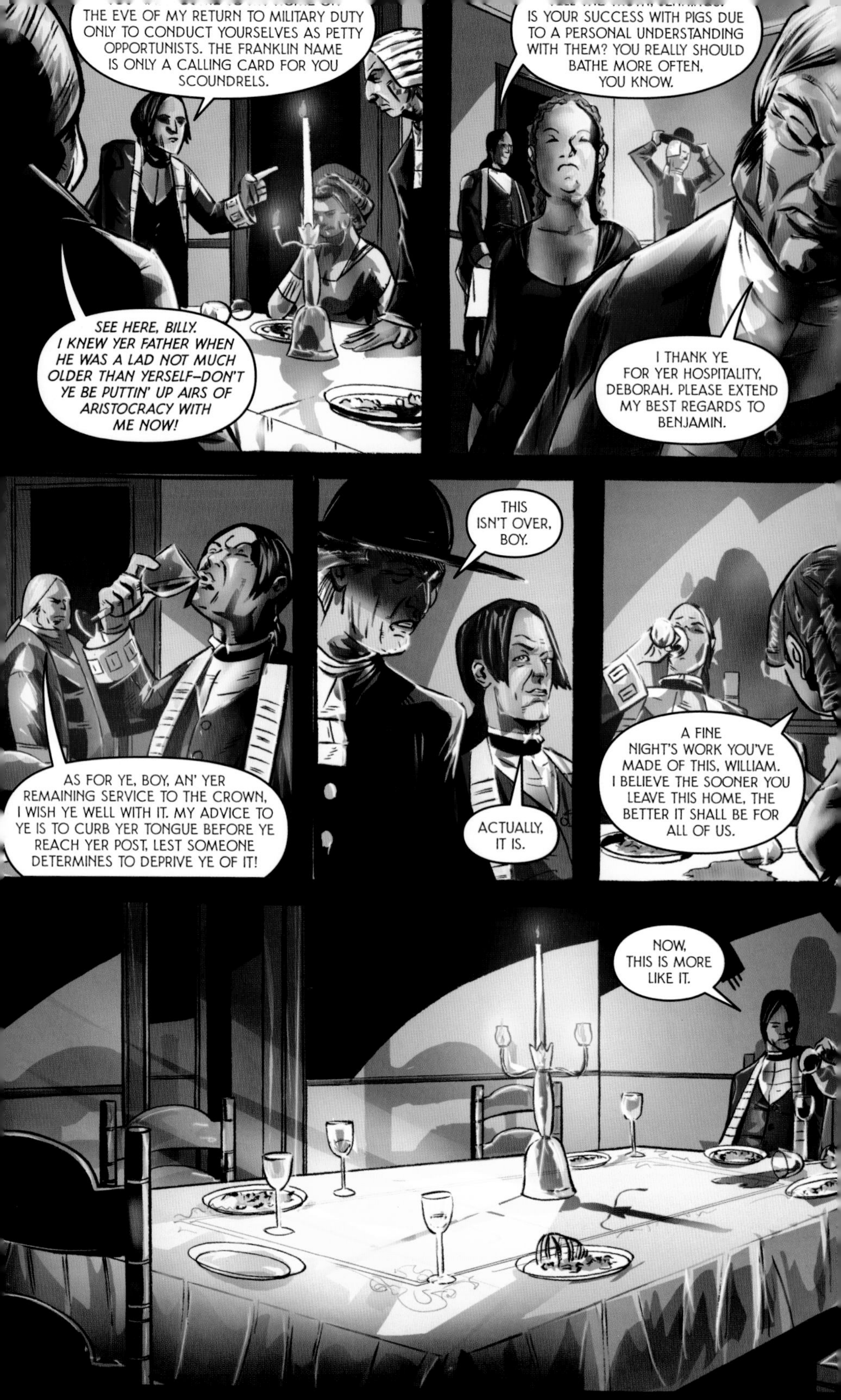
THE EVE OF MY RETURN TO MILITARY DUTY ONLY TO CONDUCT YOURSELVES AS PETTY OPPORTUNISTS. THE FRANKLIN NAME IS ONLY A CALLING CARD FOR YOU SCOUNDRELS.
SEE HERE, BILLY. I KNEW YER FATHER WHEN HE WAS A LAD NOT MUCH OLDER THAN YERSELF—DON'T YE BE PUTTIN' UP AIRS OF ARISTOCRACY WITH ME NOW!
IS YOUR SUCCESS WITH PIGS DUE TO A PERSONAL UNDERSTANDING WITH THEM? YOU REALLY SHOULD BATHE MORE OFTEN, YOU KNOW.
I THANK YE FOR YER HOSPITALITY, DEBORAH. PLEASE EXTEND MY BEST REGARDS TO BENJAMIN.
AS FOR YE, BOY, AN' YER REMAINING SERVICE TO THE CROWN, I WISH YE WELL WITH IT. MY ADVICE TO YE IS TO CURB YER TONGUE BEFORE YE REACH YER POST, LEST SOMEONE DETERMINES TO DEPRIVE YE OF IT!
THIS ISN'T OVER, BOY.
ACTUALLY, IT IS.
A FINE NIGHT'S WORK YOU'VE MADE OF THIS, WILLIAM. I BELIEVE THE SOONER YOU LEAVE THIS HOME, THE BETTER IT SHALL BE FOR ALL OF US.
NOW, THIS IS MORE LIKE IT.

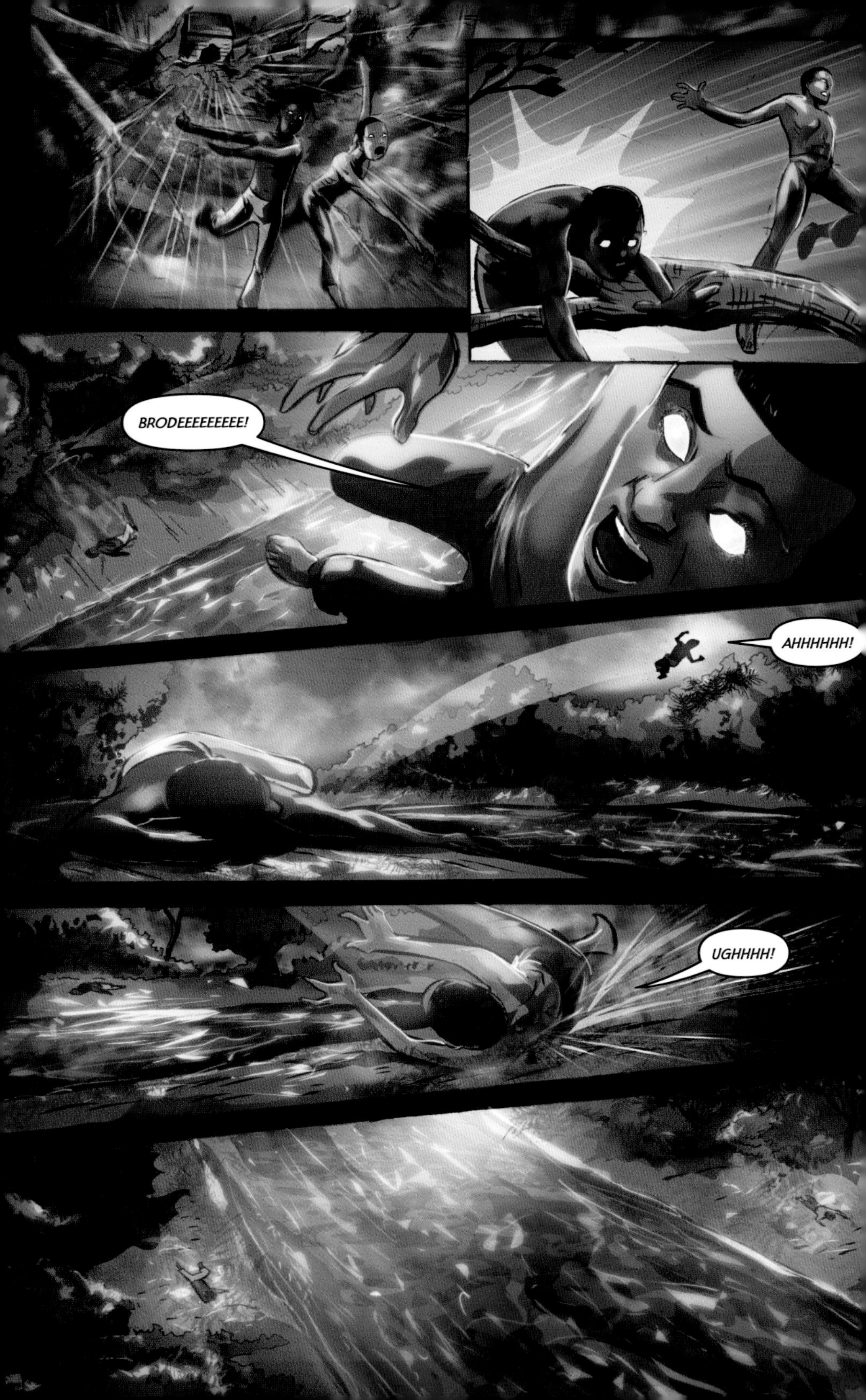
BRODEEEEEEEEE!
AHHHHHH!
UGHHHH!

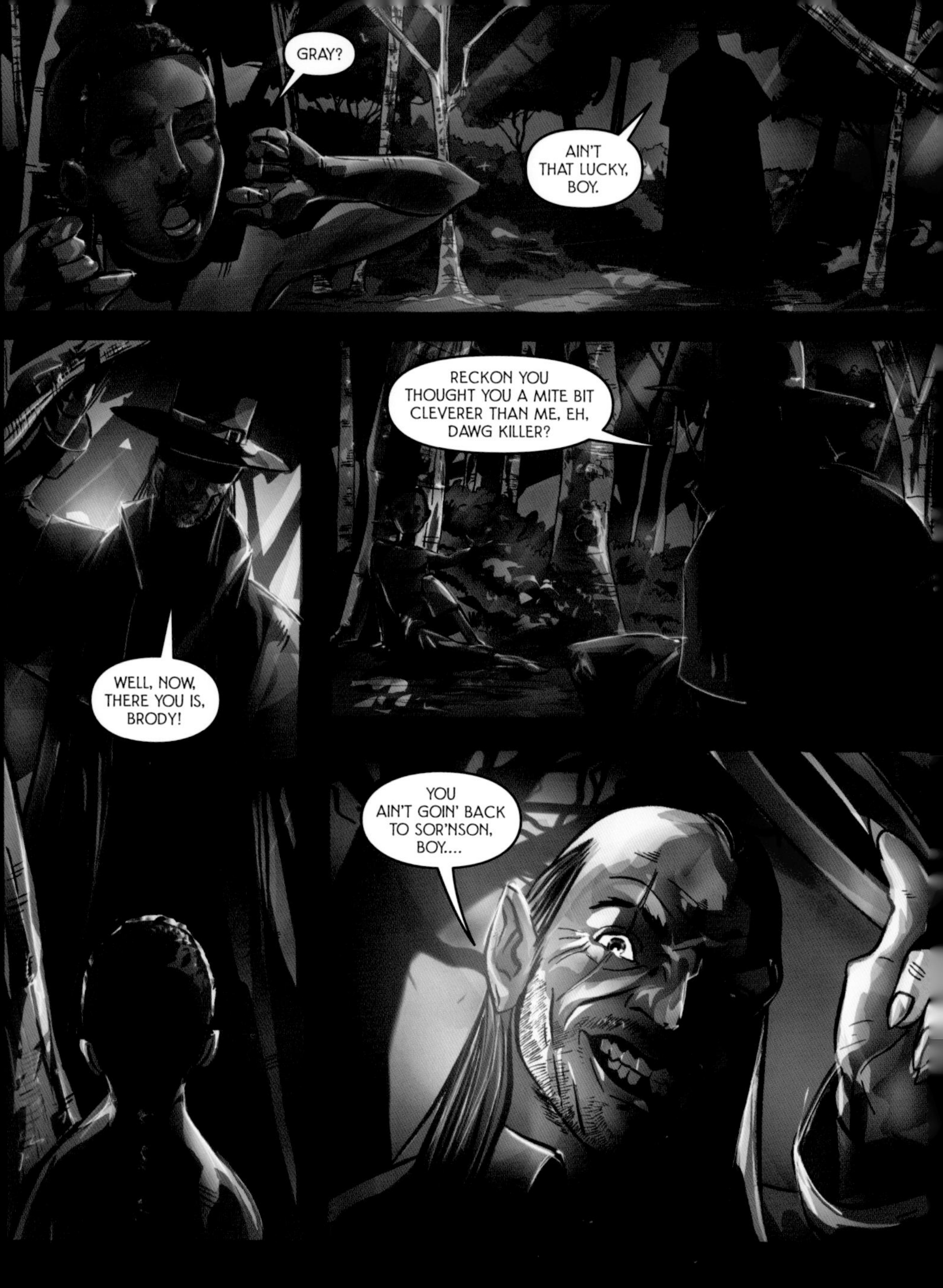
GRAY?
AIN'T THAT LUCKY, BOY.
RECKON YOU THOUGHT YOU A MITE BIT CLEVERER THAN ME, EH, DAWG KILLER?
WELL, NOW, THERE YOU IS, BRODY!
YOU AIN'T GOIN' BACK TO SOR'NSON, BOY....

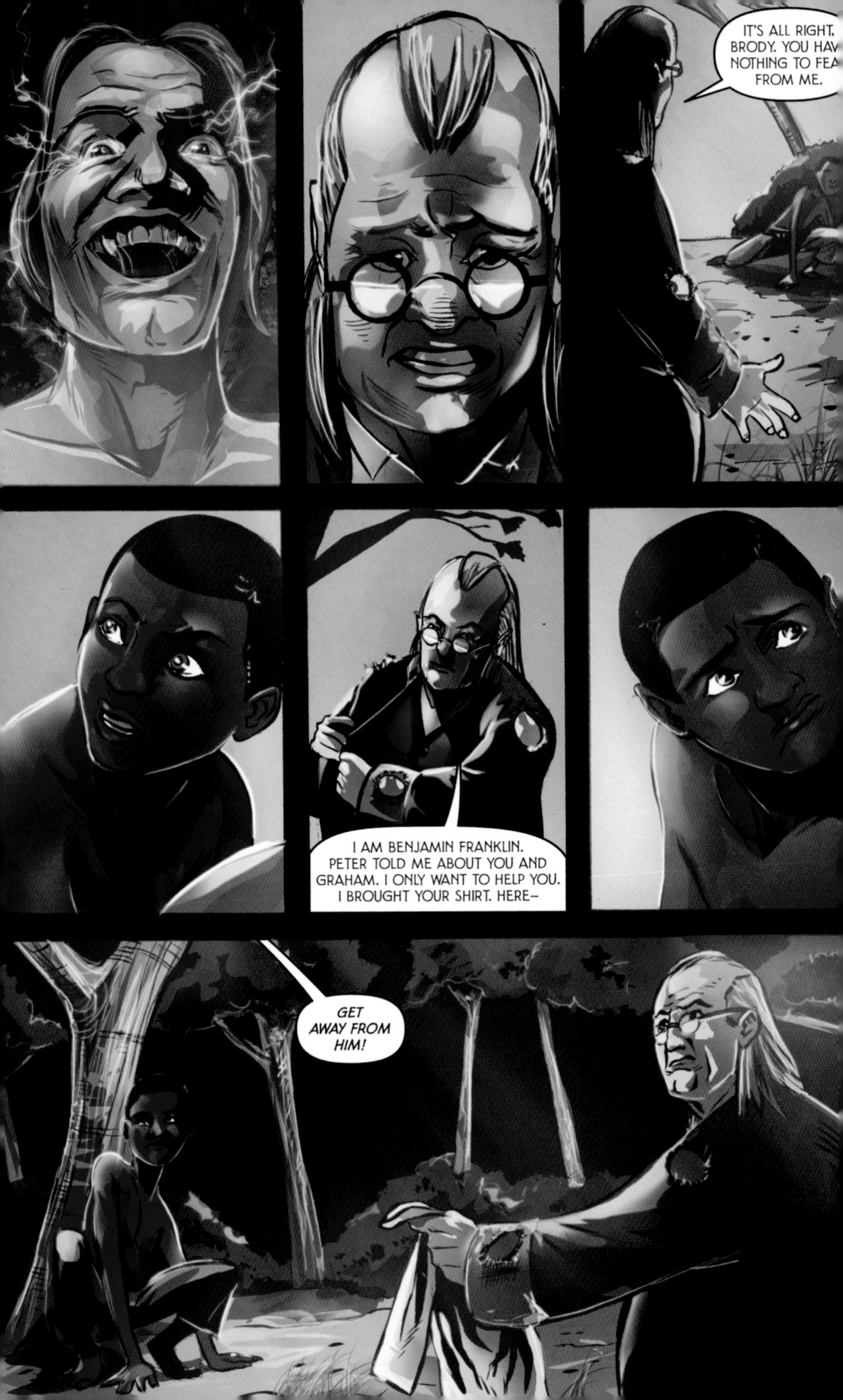
IT'S ALL RIGHT, BRODY. YOU HAV NOTHING TO FEA FROM ME.
I AM BENJAMIN FRANKLIN. PETER TOLD ME ABOUT YOU AND GRAHAM. I ONLY WANT TO HELP YOU. I BROUGHT YOUR SHIRT. HERE–
GET AWAY FROM HIM!

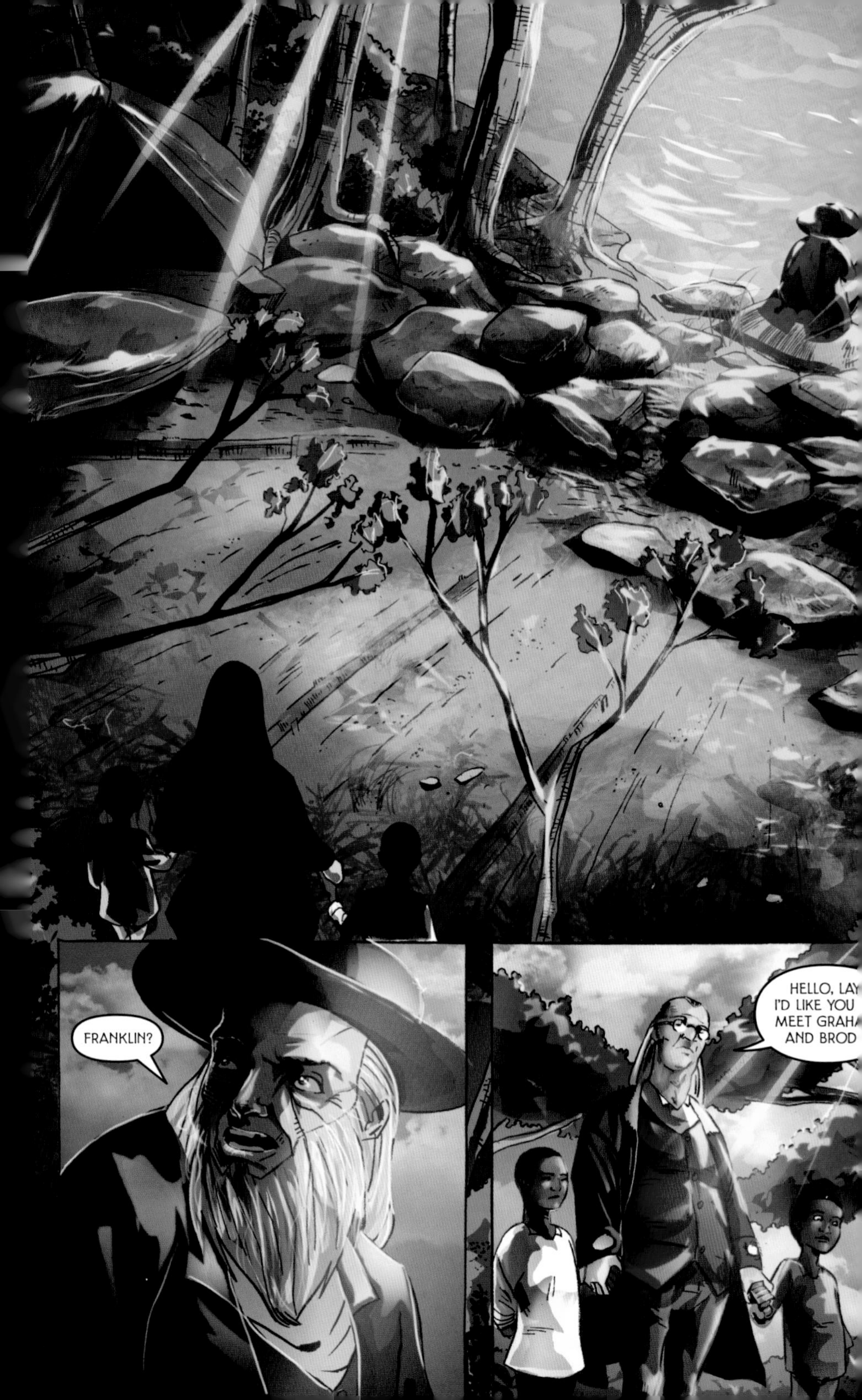
FRANKLIN?
HELLO, LAY
I'D LIKE YOU
MEET GRAH
AND BROD

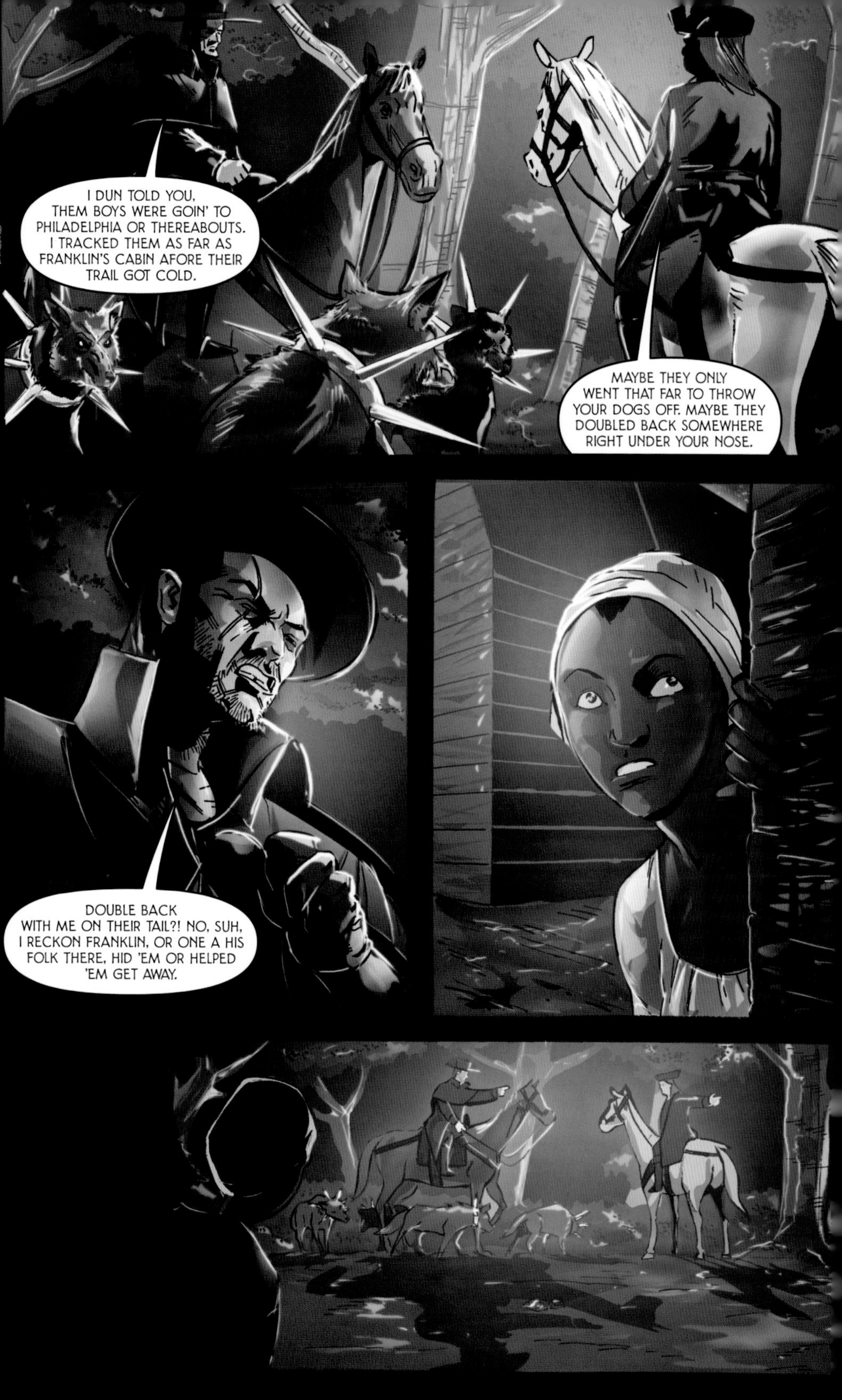
I DUN TOLD YOU, THEM BOYS WERE GOIN' TO PHILADELPHIA OR THEREABOUTS. I TRACKED THEM AS FAR AS FRANKLIN'S CABIN AFORE THEIR TRAIL GOT COLD.
MAYBE THEY ONLY WENT THAT FAR TO THROW YOUR DOGS OFF. MAYBE THEY DOUBLED BACK SOMEWHERE RIGHT UNDER YOUR NOSE.
DOUBLE BACK WITH ME ON THEIR TAIL?! NO, SUH, I RECKON FRANKLIN, OR ONE A HIS FOLK THERE, HID 'EM OR HELPED 'EM GET AWAY.

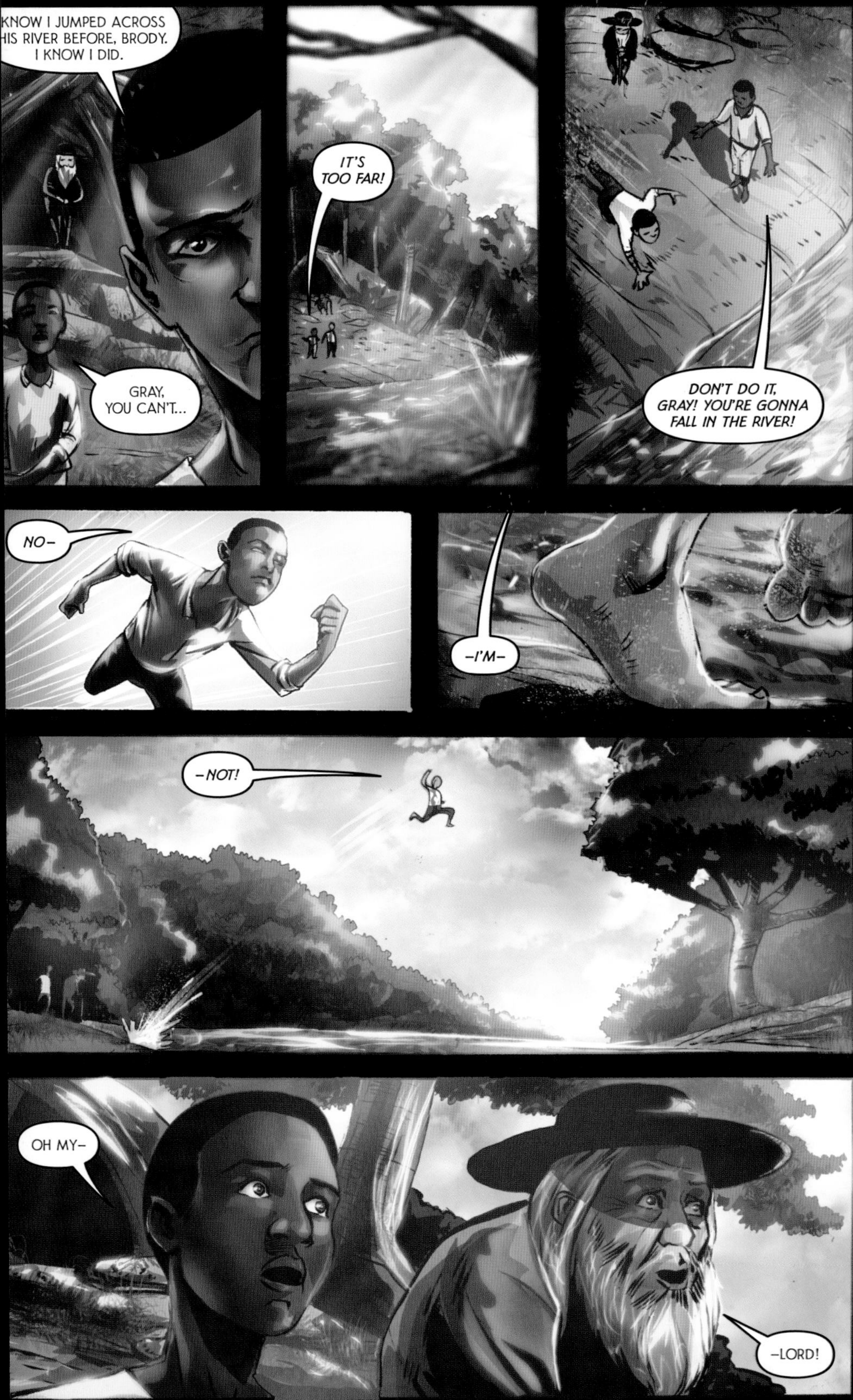
KNOW I JUMPED ACROSS
HIS RIVER BEFORE, BRODY.
I KNOW I DID.
GRAY,
YOU CAN'T...
IT'S
TOO FAR!
DON'T DO IT,
GRAY! YOU'RE GONNA
FALL IN THE RIVER!
NO–
–I'M–
–NOT!
OH MY–
–LORD!

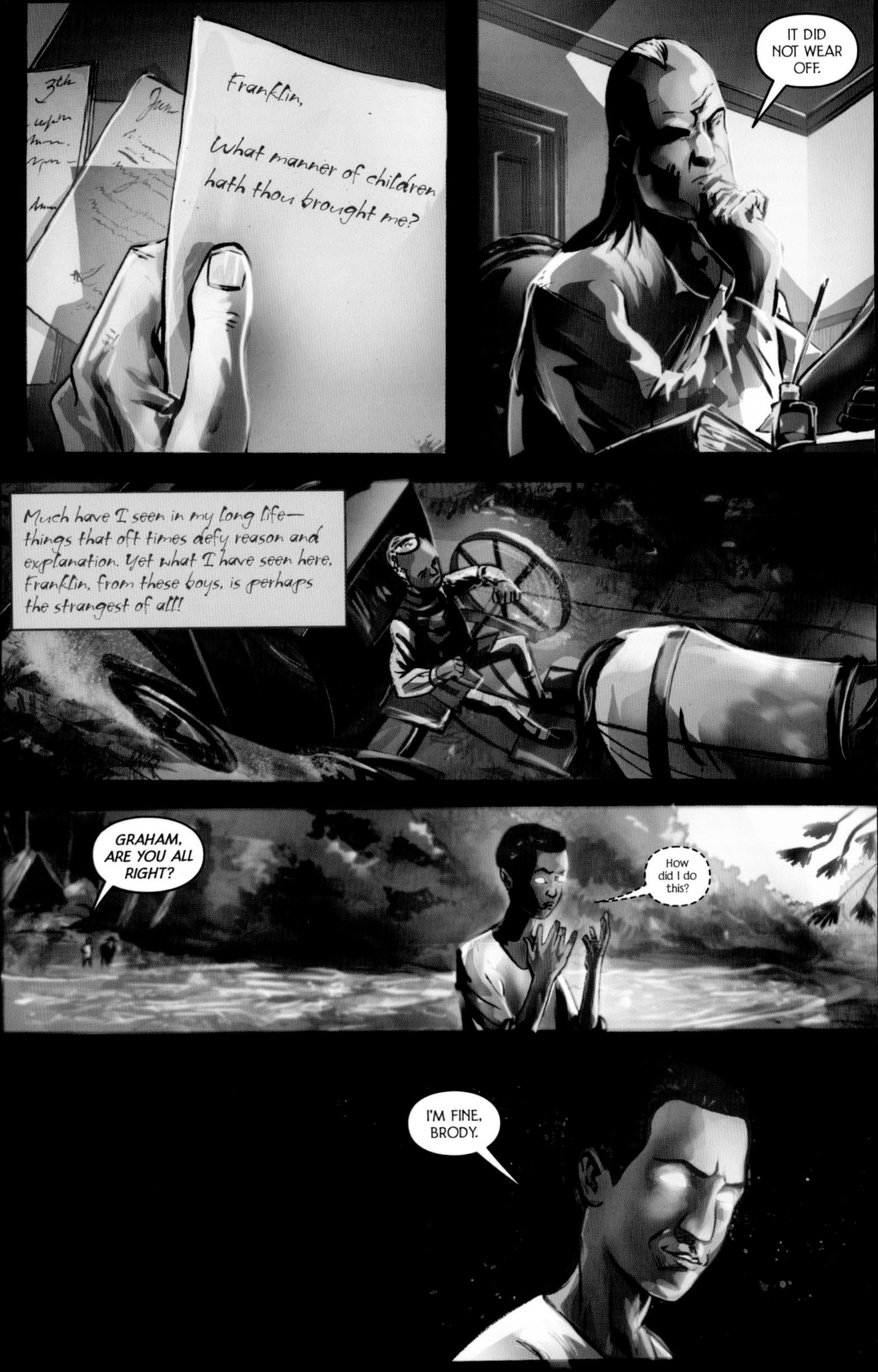
Franklin,
What manner of children hath thou brought me?
IT DID NOT WEAR OFF.
Much have I seen in my long life—things that oft times defy reason and explanation. Yet what I have seen here, Franklin, from these boys, is perhaps the strangest of all!
GRAHAM, ARE YOU ALL RIGHT?
How did I do this?
I'M FINE, BRODY.

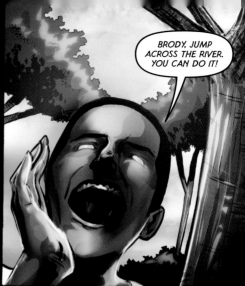

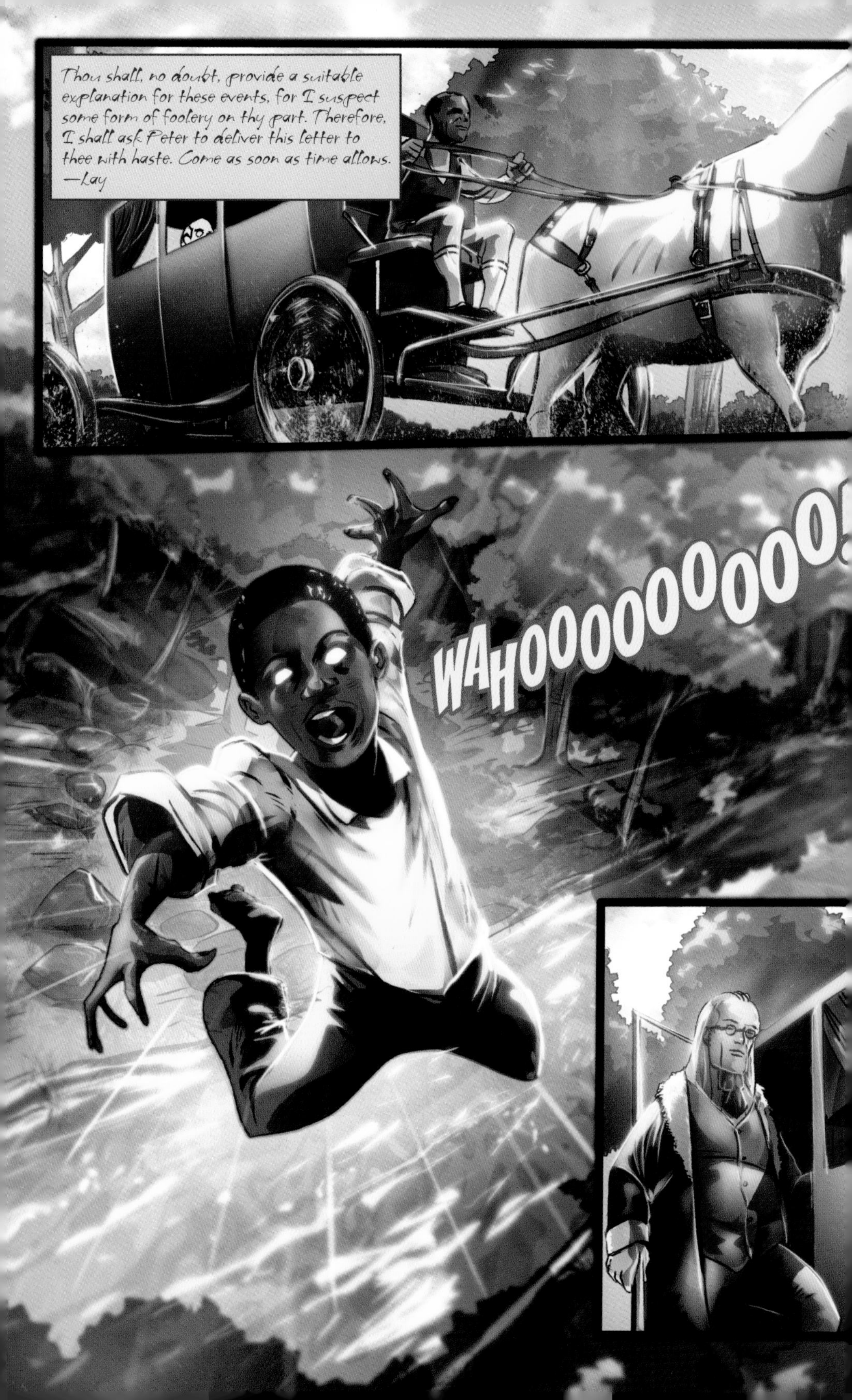
Thou shall, no doubt, provide a suitable explanation for these events, for I suspect some form of foolery on thy part. Therefore, I shall ask Peter to deliver this letter to thee with haste. Come as soon as time allows.
—Lay
WAHOOOOOOOOO!

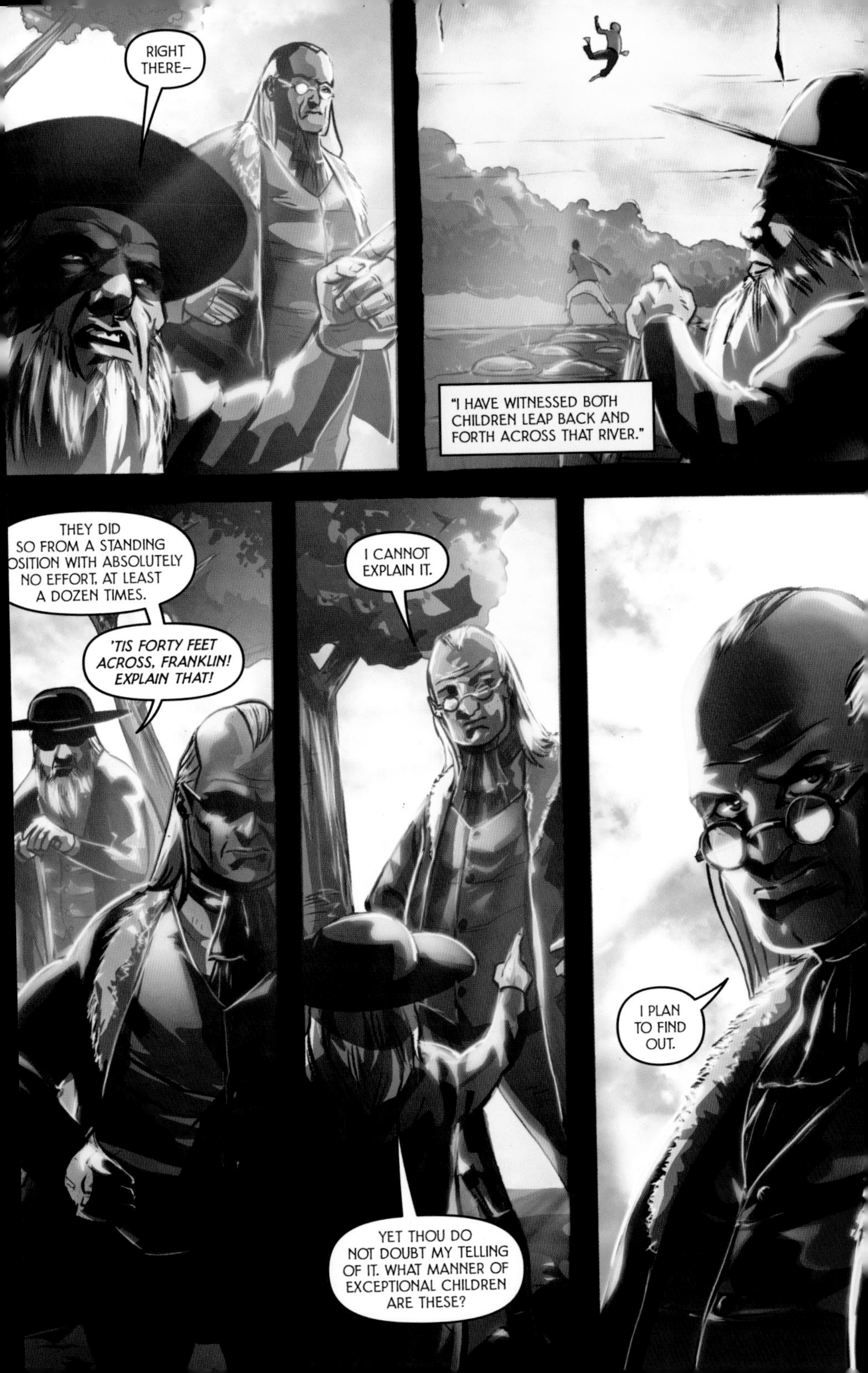
RIGHT THERE–
"I HAVE WITNESSED BOTH CHILDREN LEAP BACK AND FORTH ACROSS THAT RIVER."
THEY DID SO FROM A STANDING OSITION WITH ABSOLUTELY NO EFFORT, AT LEAST A DOZEN TIMES.
'TIS FORTY FEET ACROSS, FRANKLIN! EXPLAIN THAT!
I CANNOT EXPLAIN IT.
YET THOU DO NOT DOUBT MY TELLING OF IT. WHAT MANNER OF EXCEPTIONAL CHILDREN ARE THESE?
I PLAN TO FIND OUT.

THE FROG NEEDS THE HARNESS FOR THE CHARGE, BUT BRODY AND I CAN MAKE IT HAPPEN. WE CAN FEEL THE CHARGE AND MAKE IT HAPPEN, DR. FRANKLIN.

A SEA RAY WAS BORN THAT WAY—BRODY AND I WEREN'T. SOMETHING CHANGED INSIDE OF US, DIDN'T IT, DR. FRANKLIN? WHY CAN'T WE REMEMBER WHAT HAPPENED TO US? I MEAN, I REMEMBER SORENSON, AND PETER, BUT THEN NOTHING ELSE. WHY?

SO, TOO, THE SEA RAY. IT GENERATES A CHARGE THAT IT USES IN DEFENSE AND FOR HUNTING, AT WILL. THE GREEKS AND ROMANS USED SUCH CREATURES TO CURE HEADACHES, BY PLACING THEM ON THE FOREHEAD.

I REMEMBER DREAMING ABOUT A BLUE FACE, GETTING CLOSE TO ME AND LAUGHING, AND...PAIN... LIKE I WAS BURNING ALL OVER.

YOU DIDN'T COME OUT TODAY JUST TO SHOW US THE FROG, DID YOU, DR. FRANKLIN?

GRAHAM, BRODY, I WANT YOU TO KNOW I WILL DO ALL I CAN FOR YOU. THAT I PROMISE.

LAY IS RIGHT—YOU ARE VERY PERCEPTIVE, GRAHAM.

I HAVE A PROPOSITION THAT I SHALL PUT TO YOU NOW. THEN, DEPENDING ON YOUR REPLY, I WILL DELIVER THE SAME MESSAGE TO BENJAMIN LAY MYSELF. AGREED?

VERY WELL, HELP ME WITH THE EQUIPMENT, AND I WILL TELL YOU THE OTHER REASON FOR MY COMING THIS DAY.

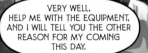

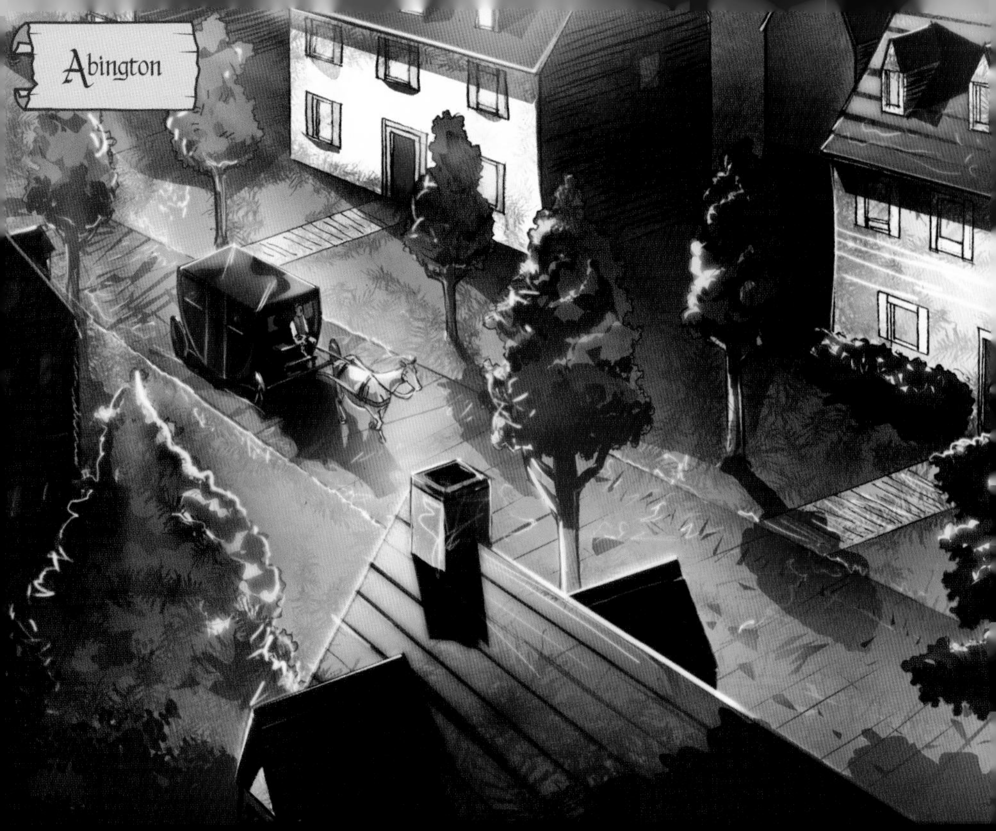
Abington

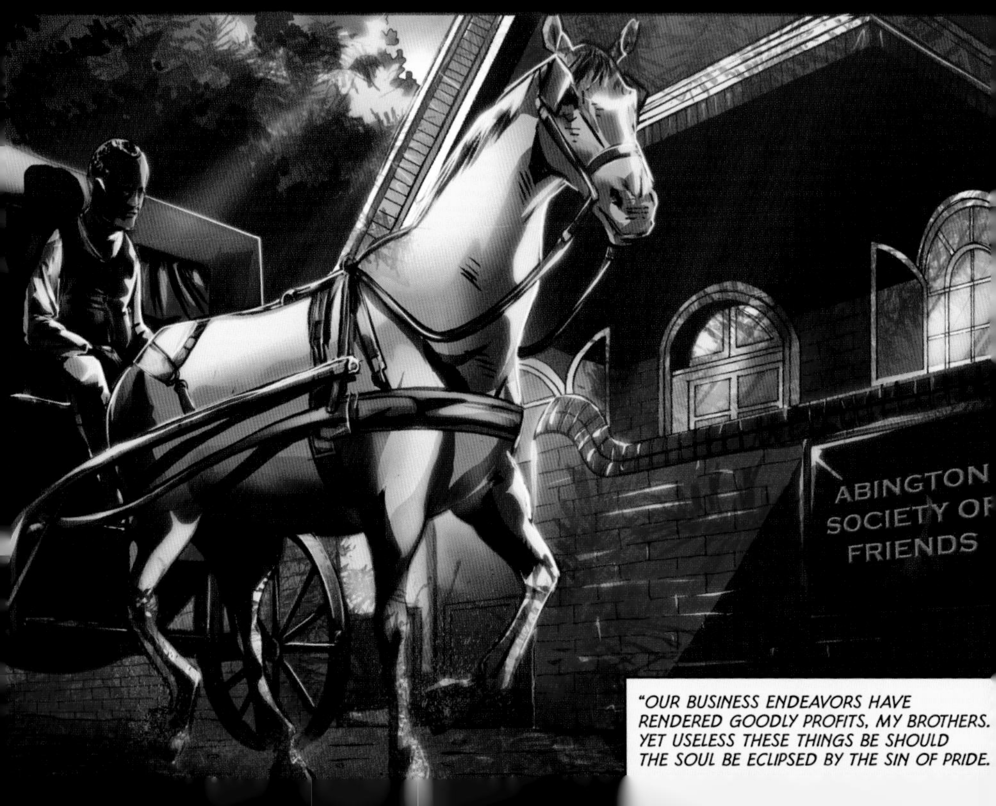
ABINGTON
SOCIETY O
FRIENDS
"OUR BUSINESS ENDEAVORS HAVE RENDERED GOODLY PROFITS, MY BROTHERS. YET USELESS THESE THINGS BE SHOULD THE SOUL BE ECLIPSED BY THE SIN OF PRIDE.

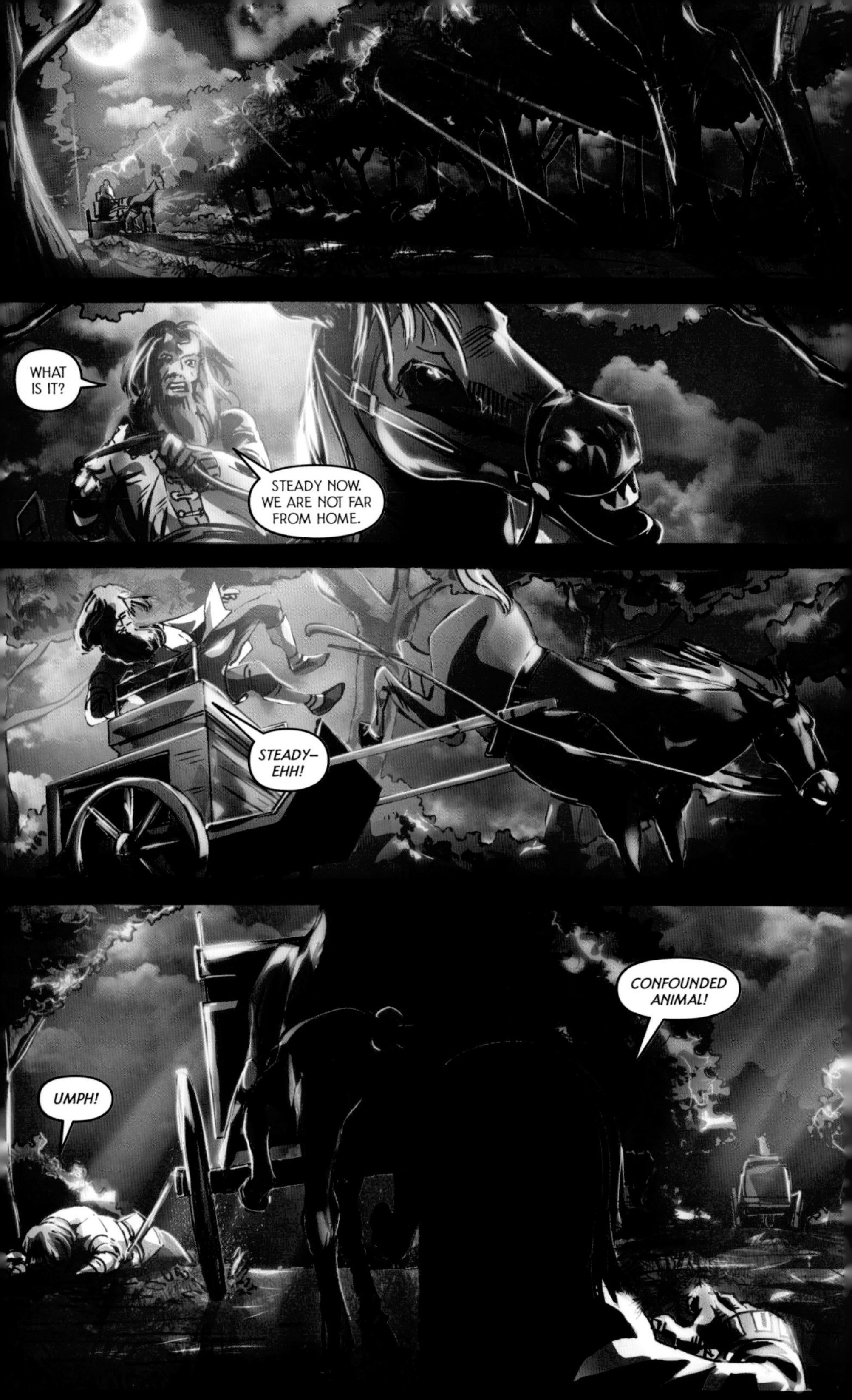
WHAT IS IT?
STEADY NOW. WE ARE NOT FAR FROM HOME.
STEADY—EHH!
CONFOUNDED ANIMAL!
UMPH!

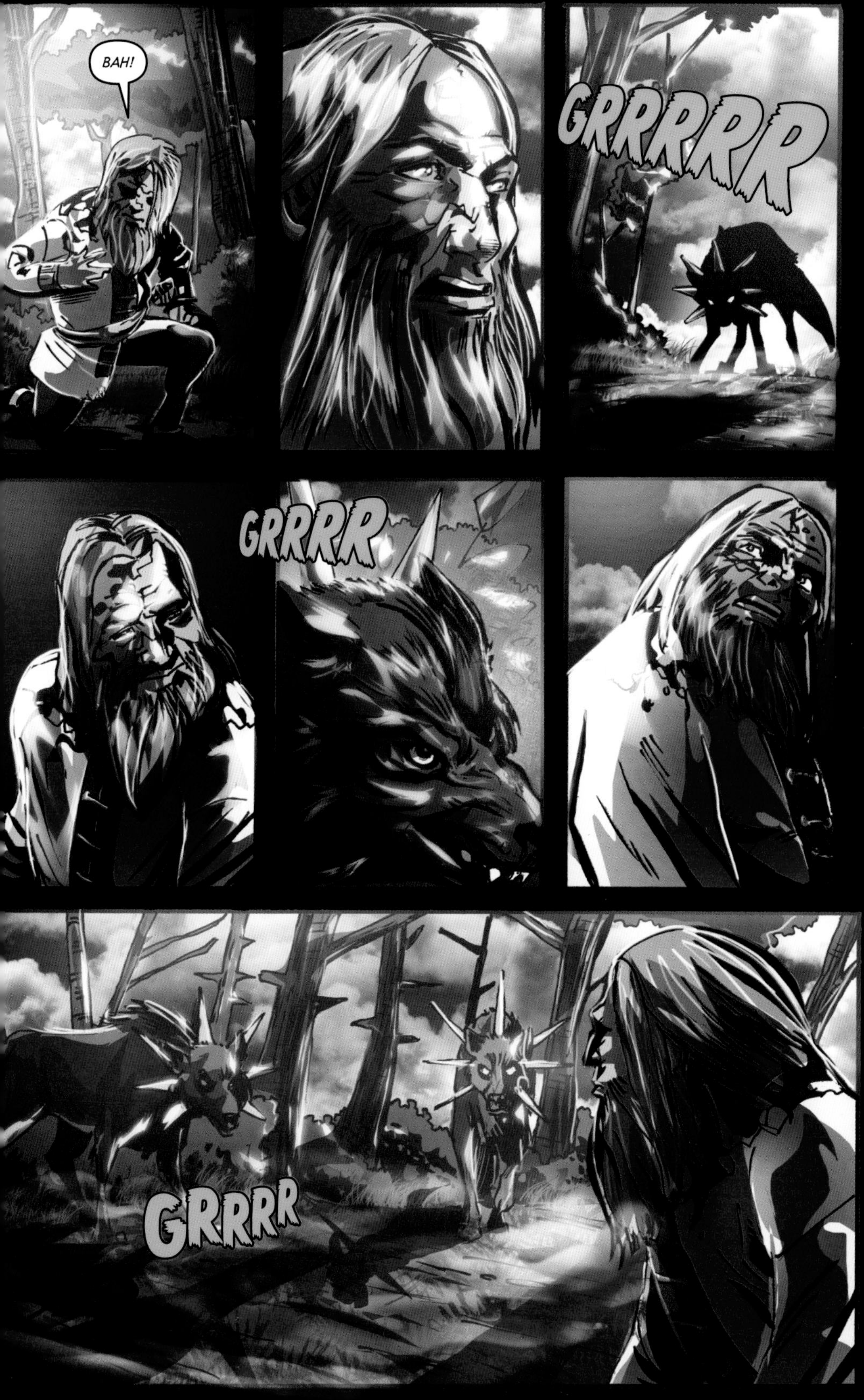
BAH!
GRRRRRR
GRRRR
GRRRR

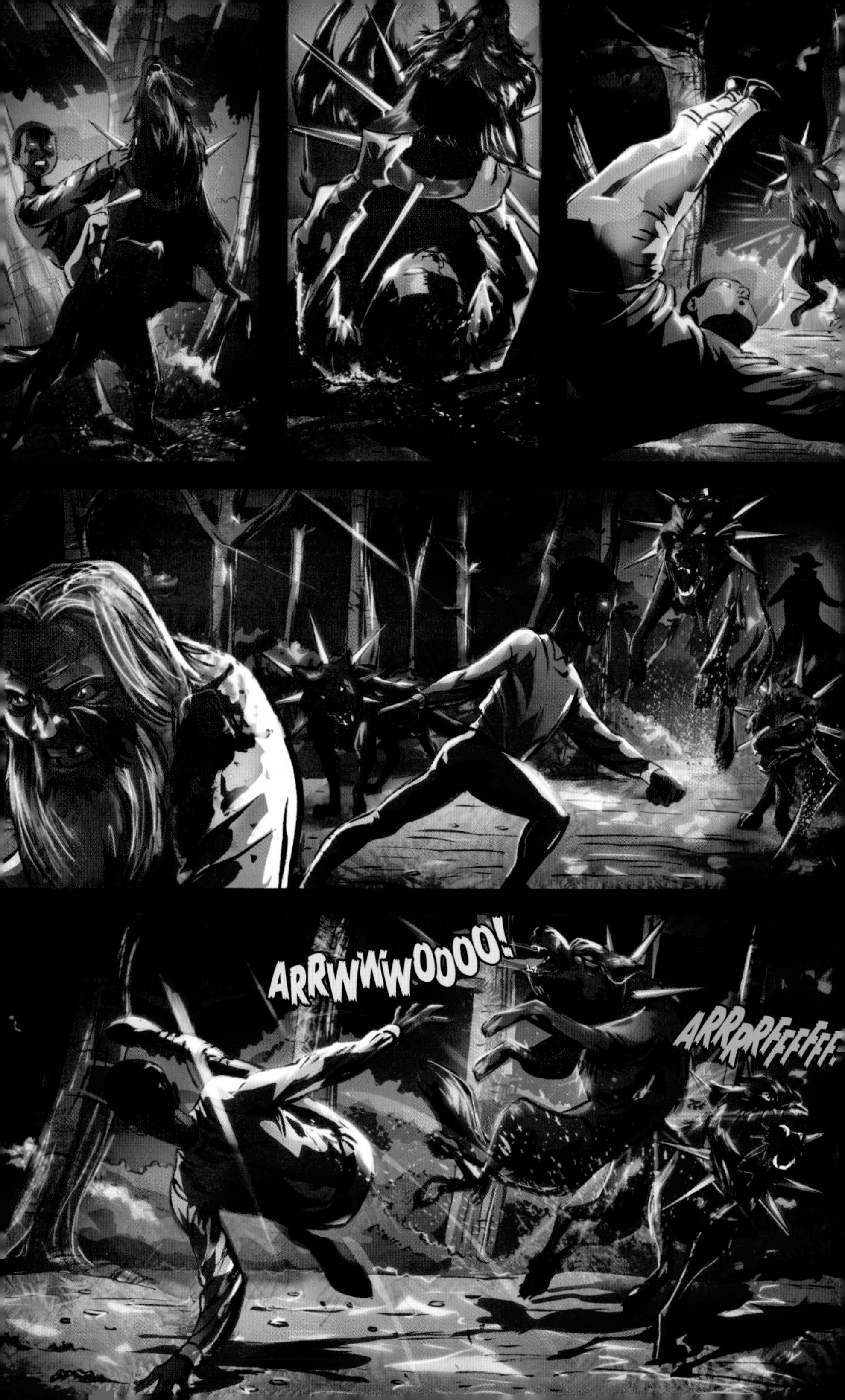
ARRWWWOOOO!
ARRRRFFFFFF.

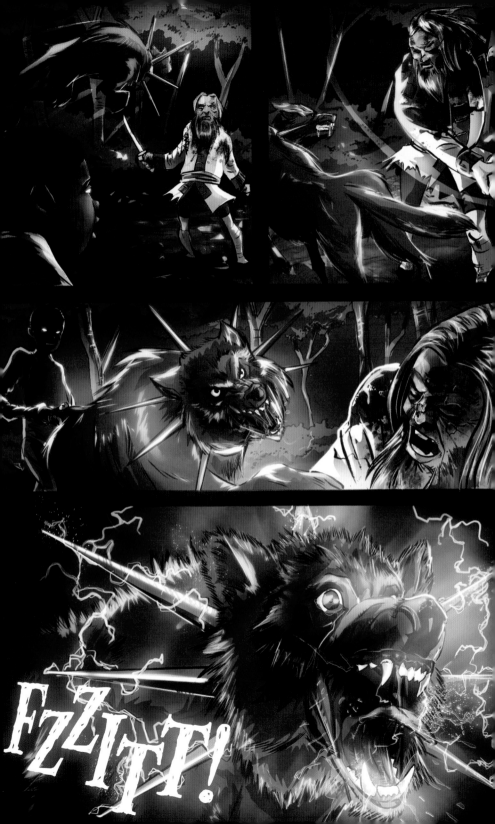

FZZITT!

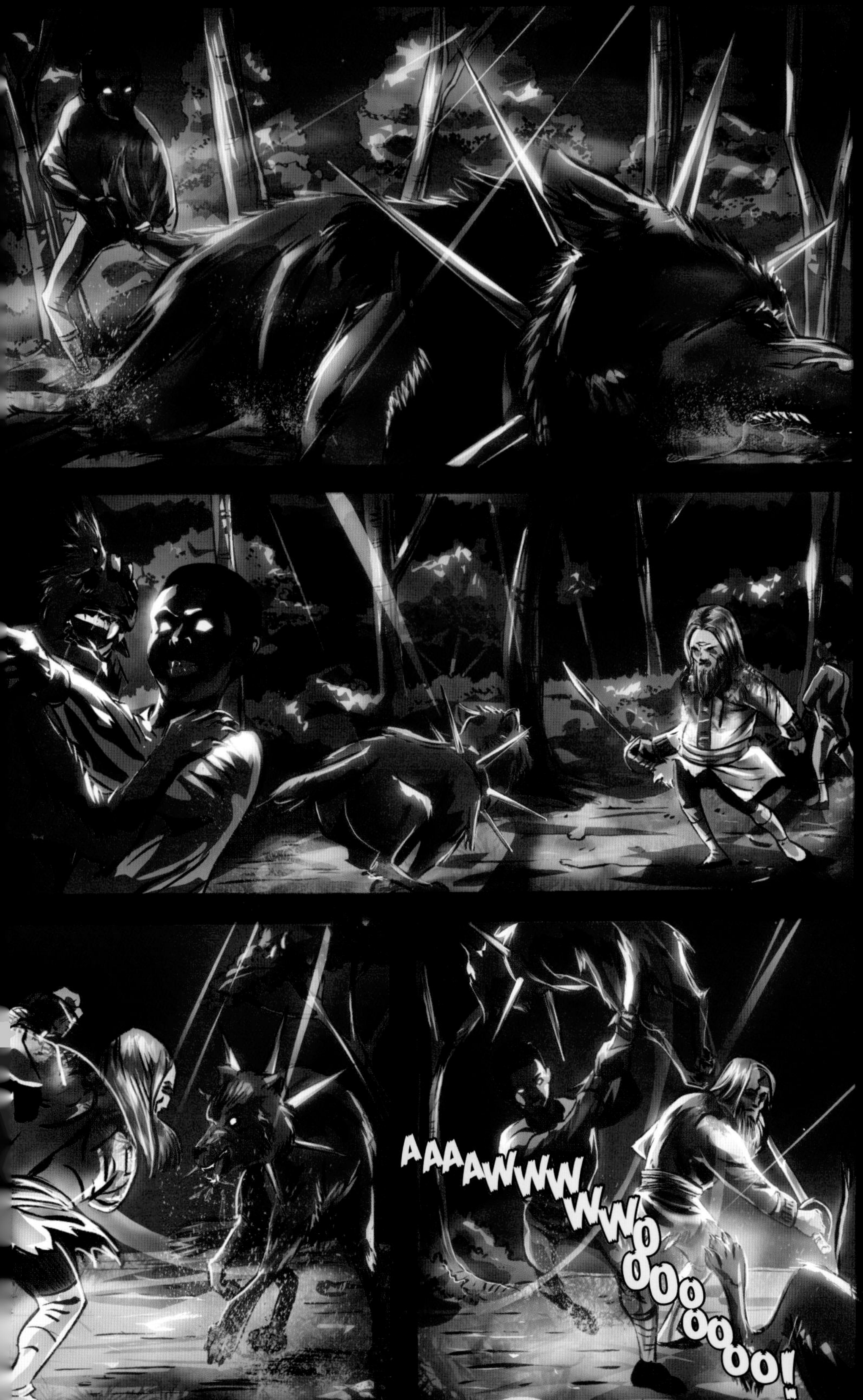
AAAAWWWWWWOOOOOOOO!

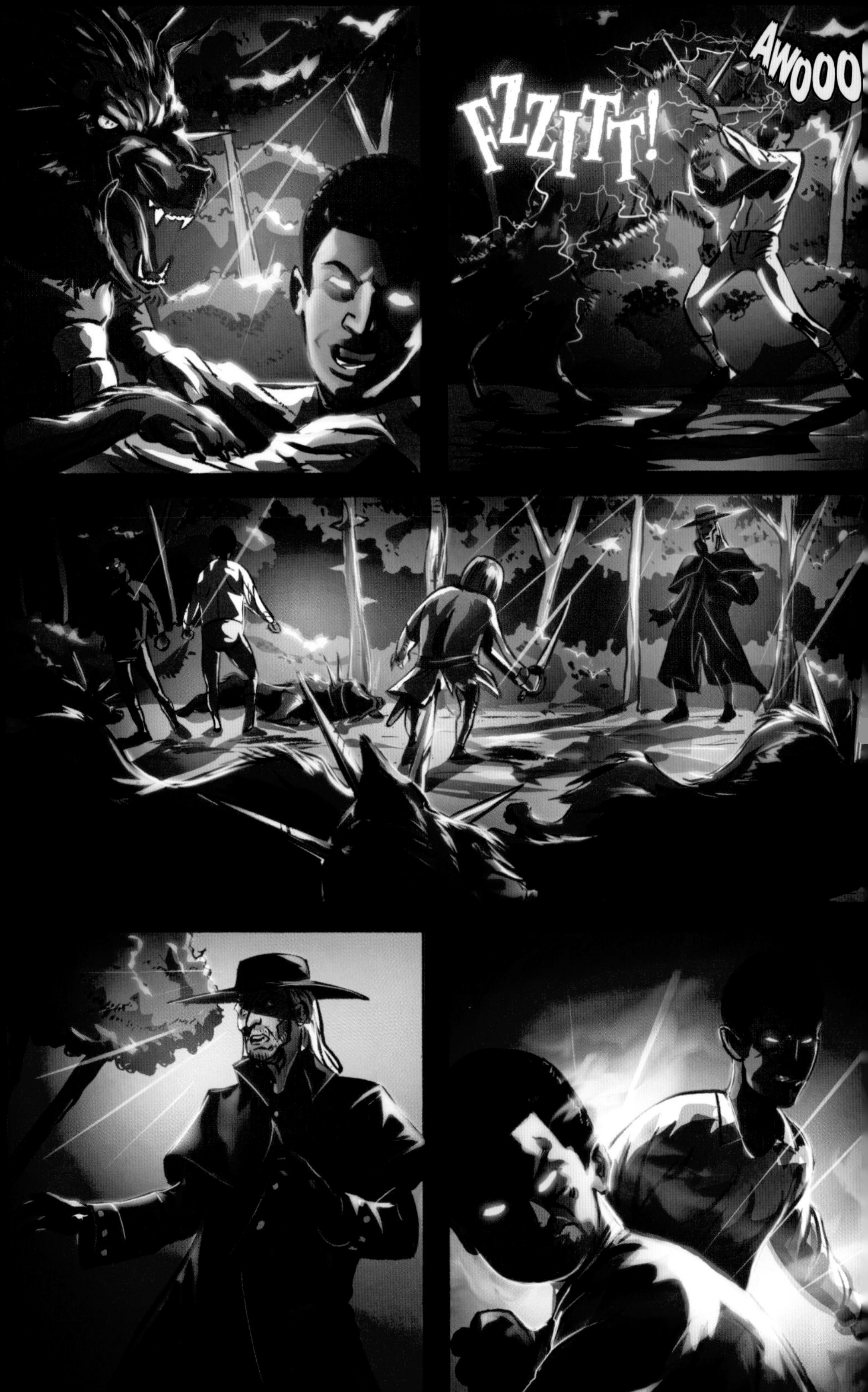
FZZITT!
AWOOO!

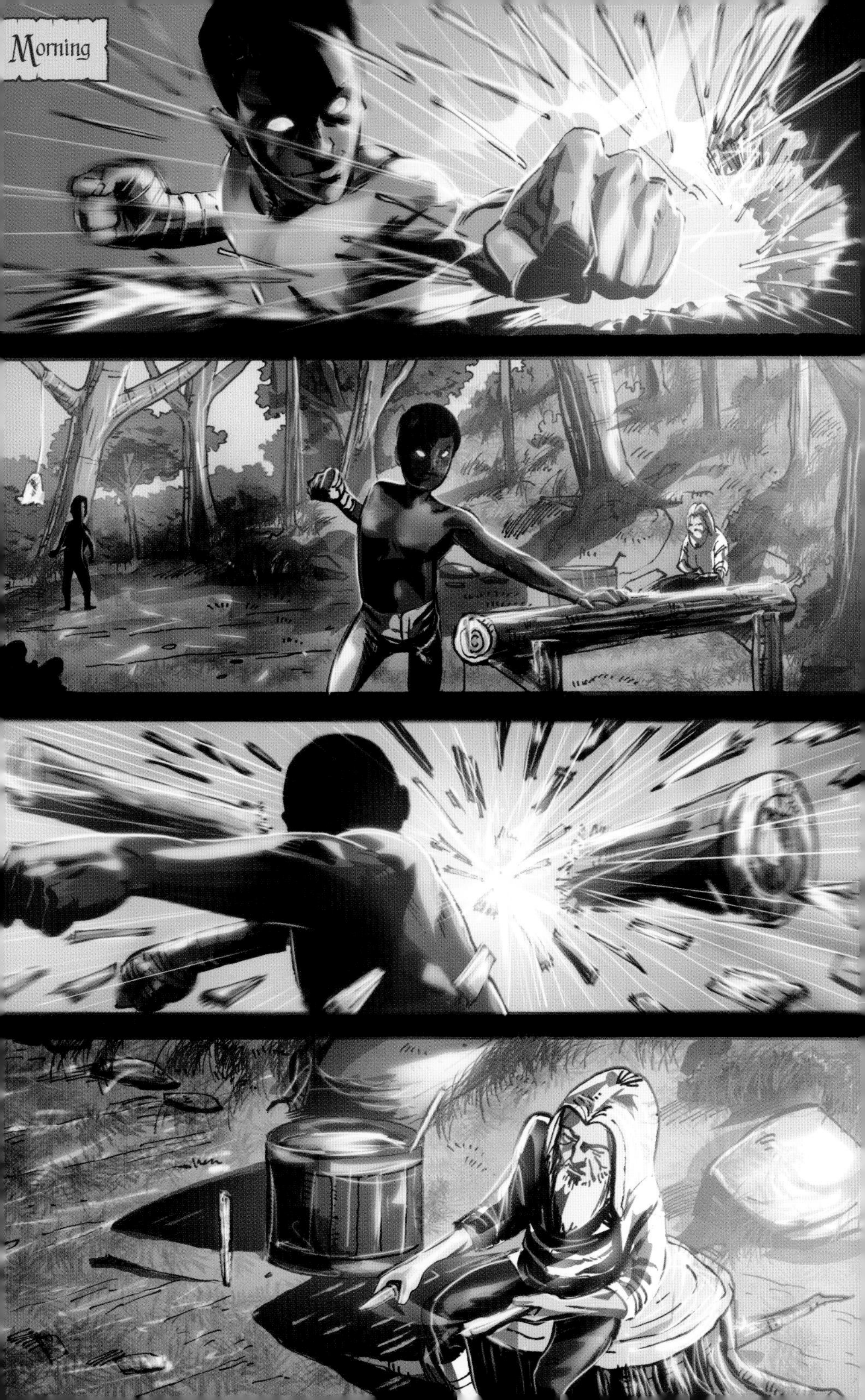
Morning

DR. FRANKLIN SAYS THAT A SPECIAL ABILITY, LIKE GOLD COIN, MUST BE KEPT IN A PRIVATE POCKET AND SHOULD NOT BE TAKEN OUT JUST TO SHOW OTHERS YOU HAVE IT.

FRANKLIN IS A GREAT MAN, BRODY. YET GREAT MEN ARE NOT ALWAYS WISE.

FRANKLIN HAS NEVER FELT THE STING OF A BULLWHIP UPON HIS FLESH, NOR THE HEEL OF TYRANNY UPON HIS NECK.

"O SAN KI ENIYAN JA DI IKU JU K'KENIYAN GBE NINU SHEKE-SHEKE."

BUT *WHY* MUST WE LEARN TO FIGHT?

YOUR HANDS ARE TREMBLING.

I HAVE NOT UTTERED THOSE WORDS IN ALMOST SIXTY YEARS. SIXTY LONG YEARS.

"...THAT MUST BE RETURNED TO THEIR RIGHTFUL HEIRS."

YET THERE ARE THINGS, CHILDREN...

Barbados, 1710

" 'TWERE A WEALTHY PURVEYOR OF FURNITURE I BE IN MY YOUTH—

"—BUSINESS BEING MY SO[...] PREOCCUPATION THEN.

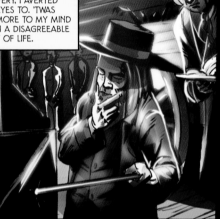

"SLAVERY, I AVERTED MY EYES TO. 'TWAS NO MORE TO MY MIND THAN A DISAGREEABLE FACT OF LIFE.

"BUT MY INDIFFERENCE TO THE ABOMINATION WOUL[...] CHANGE QUICKLY ONE WARM SEPTEMBER MORNING[...]

" 'TWAS NO MORE THAN A WOMAN'S SCREAM THAT DREW MY ATTENTION AWAY FROM MY TRADE AND WHOLLY TRANSFIXED MY EYES FOREVERMORE.

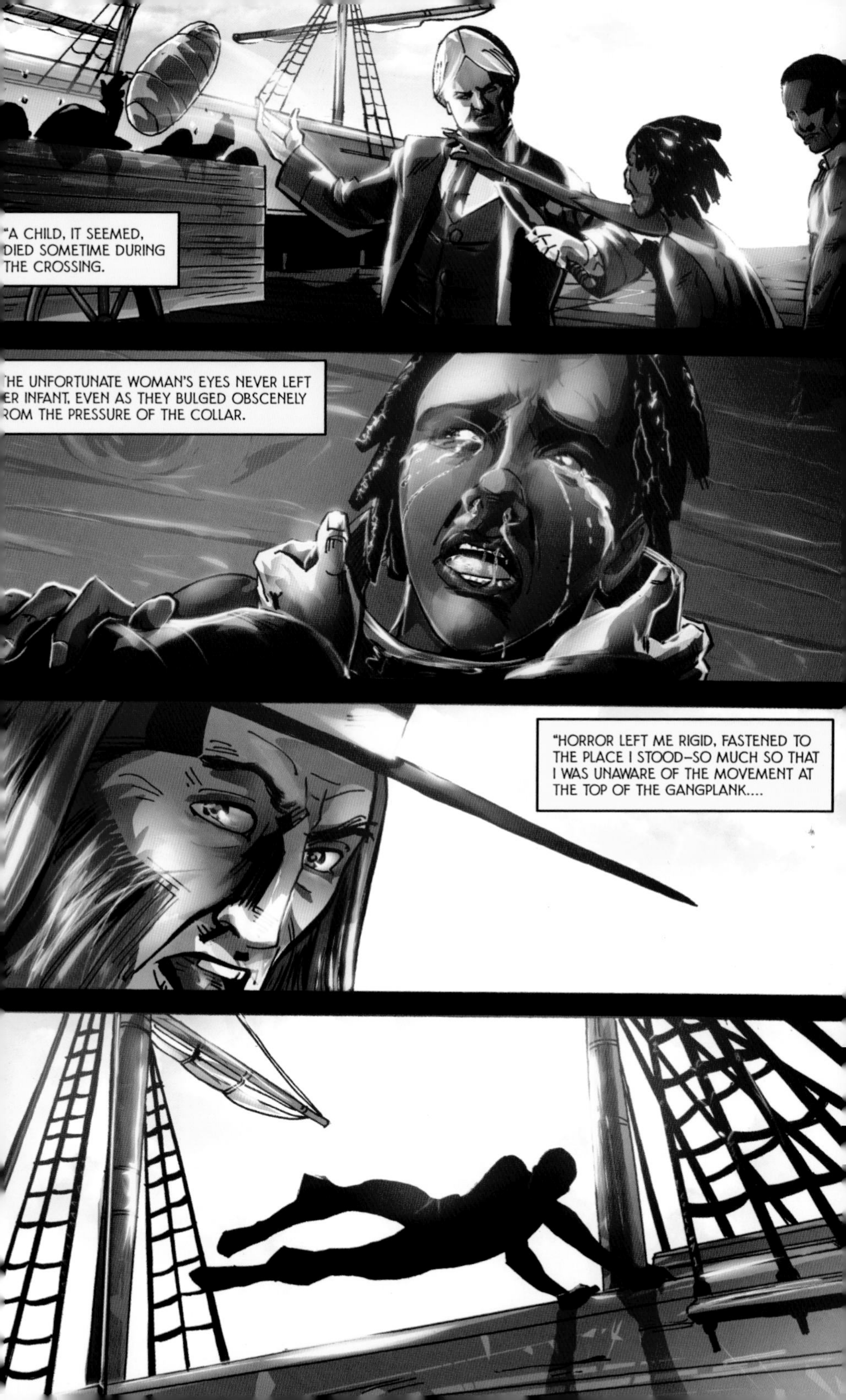
"A CHILD, IT SEEMED, DIED SOMETIME DURING THE CROSSING.
HE UNFORTUNATE WOMAN'S EYES NEVER LEFT ER INFANT, EVEN AS THEY BULGED OBSCENELY ROM THE PRESSURE OF THE COLLAR.
"HORROR LEFT ME RIGID, FASTENED TO THE PLACE I STOOD—SO MUCH SO THAT I WAS UNAWARE OF THE MOVEMENT AT THE TOP OF THE GANGPLANK....

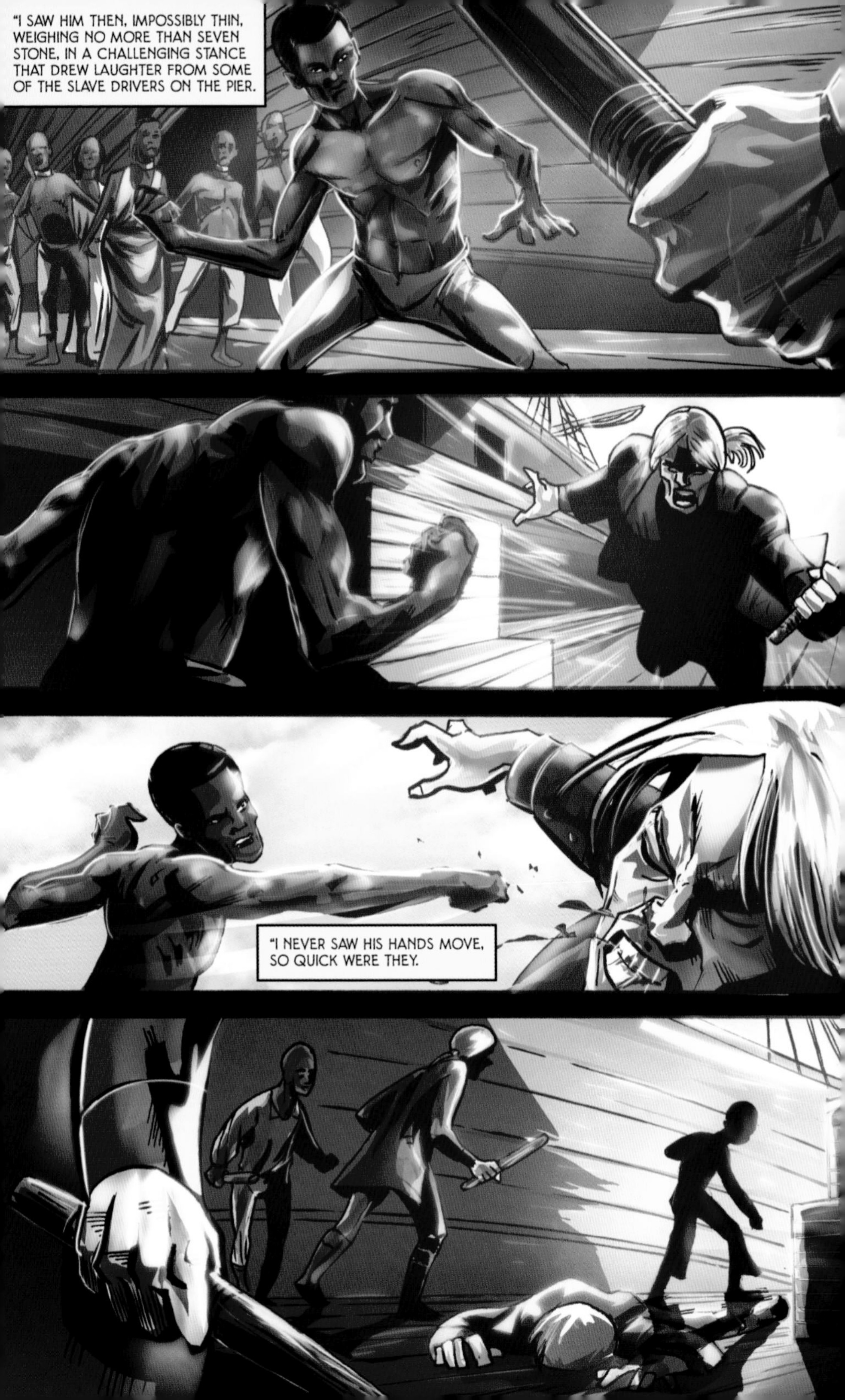
"I SAW HIM THEN, IMPOSSIBLY THIN, WEIGHING NO MORE THAN SEVEN STONE, IN A CHALLENGING STANCE THAT DREW LAUGHTER FROM SOME OF THE SLAVE DRIVERS ON THE PIER.
"I NEVER SAW HIS HANDS MOVE, SO QUICK WERE THEY.

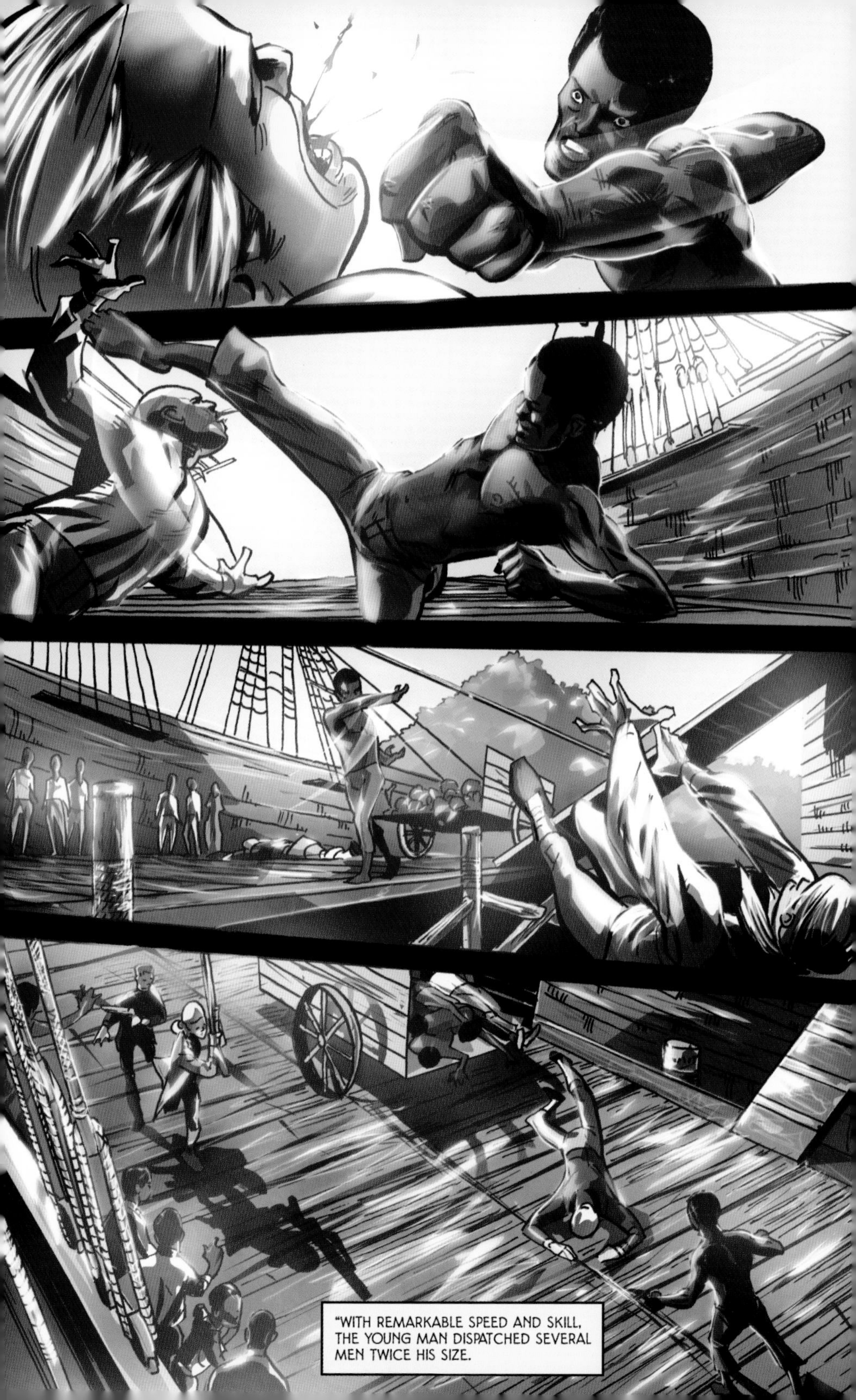
"WITH REMARKABLE SPEED AND SKILL, THE YOUNG MAN DISPATCHED SEVERAL MEN TWICE HIS SIZE.

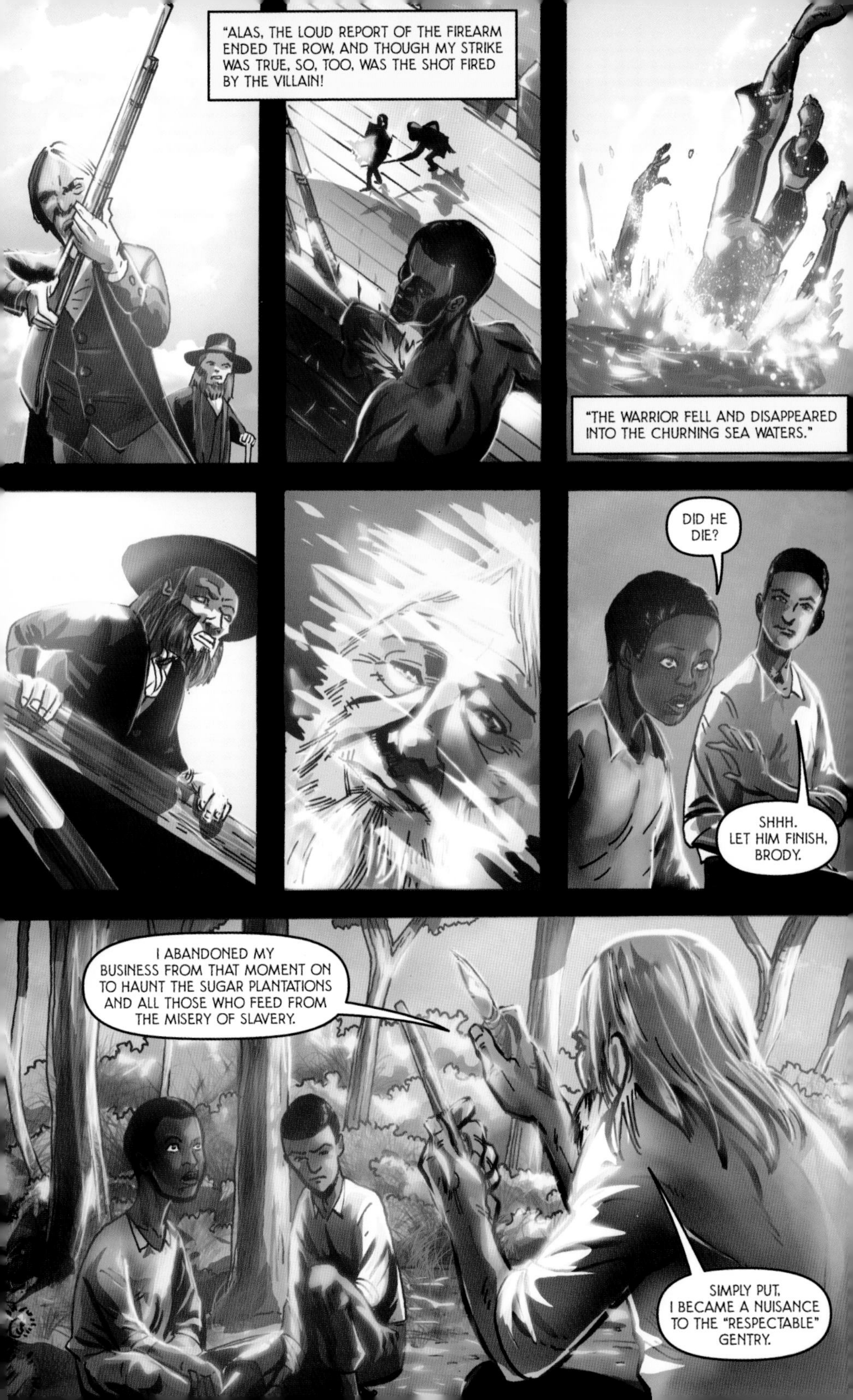
"ALAS, THE LOUD REPORT OF THE FIREARM ENDED THE ROW, AND THOUGH MY STRIKE WAS TRUE, SO, TOO, WAS THE SHOT FIRED BY THE VILLAIN!
"THE WARRIOR FELL AND DISAPPEARED INTO THE CHURNING SEA WATERS."
DID HE DIE?
SHHH. LET HIM FINISH, BRODY.
I ABANDONED MY BUSINESS FROM THAT MOMENT ON TO HAUNT THE SUGAR PLANTATIONS AND ALL THOSE WHO FEED FROM THE MISERY OF SLAVERY.
SIMPLY PUT, I BECAME A NUISANCE TO THE "RESPECTABLE" GENTRY.

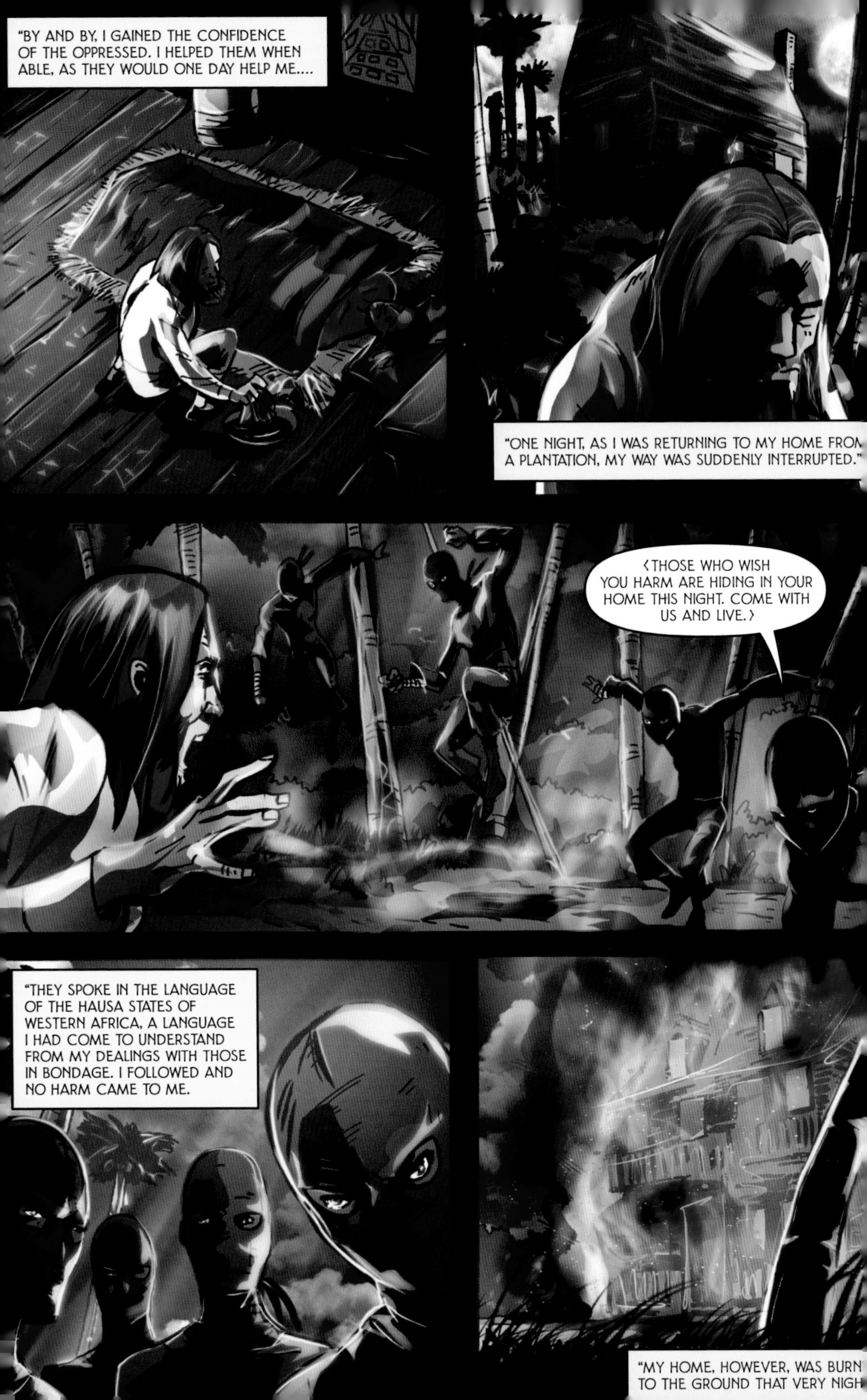
"BY AND BY, I GAINED THE CONFIDENCE OF THE OPPRESSED. I HELPED THEM WHEN ABLE, AS THEY WOULD ONE DAY HELP ME....
"ONE NIGHT, AS I WAS RETURNING TO MY HOME FROM A PLANTATION, MY WAY WAS SUDDENLY INTERRUPTED."
‹THOSE WHO WISH YOU HARM ARE HIDING IN YOUR HOME THIS NIGHT. COME WITH US AND LIVE.›
"THEY SPOKE IN THE LANGUAGE OF THE HAUSA STATES OF WESTERN AFRICA, A LANGUAGE I HAD COME TO UNDERSTAND FROM MY DEALINGS WITH THOSE IN BONDAGE. I FOLLOWED AND NO HARM CAME TO ME.
"MY HOME, HOWEVER, WAS BURN TO THE GROUND THAT VERY NIGH

THE FOUR DARKLY CLAD MEN BROUGHT ME BEFORE THEIR WARRIOR CHIEF.

"OLOGUN.

TO MY SURPRISE, THE SAME WARRIOR FROM THE PIER—THE ONE I HAD THOUGHT TO BE DEAD!

"HE EXPLAINED THAT HE HAD BEEN INJURED BY THE SHOT BUT HAD MANAGED TO ESCAPE TO THIS PLACE.

"OLOGUN HAD GATHERED THESE FOUR MEN OF STOUT HEART TO TRAIN AND MASTER AN ANCIENT ART OF HAND-TO-HAND COMBAT HE CALLED *DAMBE*.

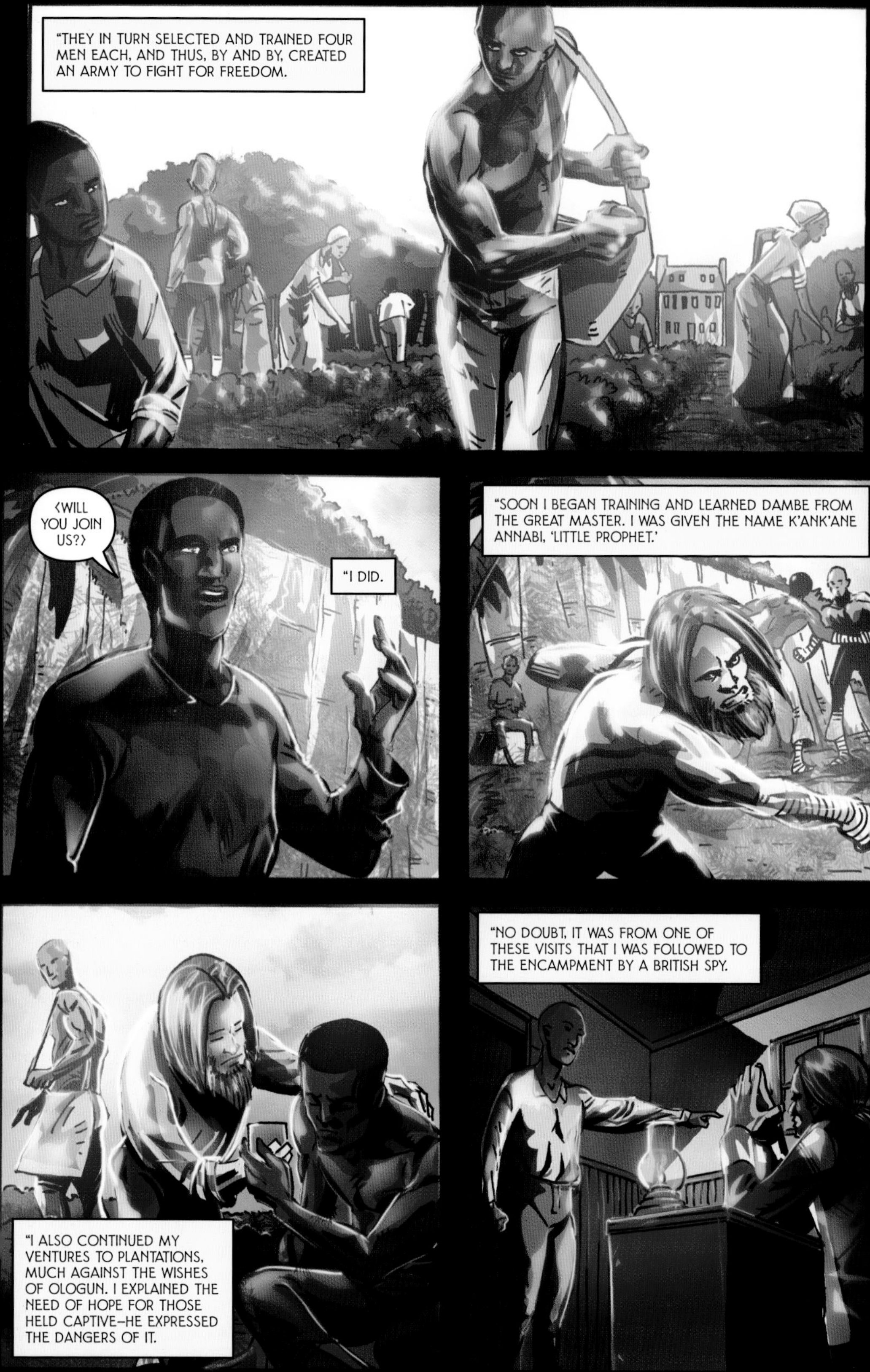
"THEY IN TURN SELECTED AND TRAINED FOUR MEN EACH, AND THUS, BY AND BY, CREATED AN ARMY TO FIGHT FOR FREEDOM.
<WILL YOU JOIN US?>
"I DID.
"SOON I BEGAN TRAINING AND LEARNED DAMBE FROM THE GREAT MASTER. I WAS GIVEN THE NAME K'ANK'ANE ANNABI, 'LITTLE PROPHET.'
"I ALSO CONTINUED MY VENTURES TO PLANTATIONS, MUCH AGAINST THE WISHES OF OLOGUN. I EXPLAINED THE NEED OF HOPE FOR THOSE HELD CAPTIVE—HE EXPRESSED THE DANGERS OF IT.
"NO DOUBT, IT WAS FROM ONE OF THESE VISITS THAT I WAS FOLLOWED TO THE ENCAMPMENT BY A BRITISH SPY.

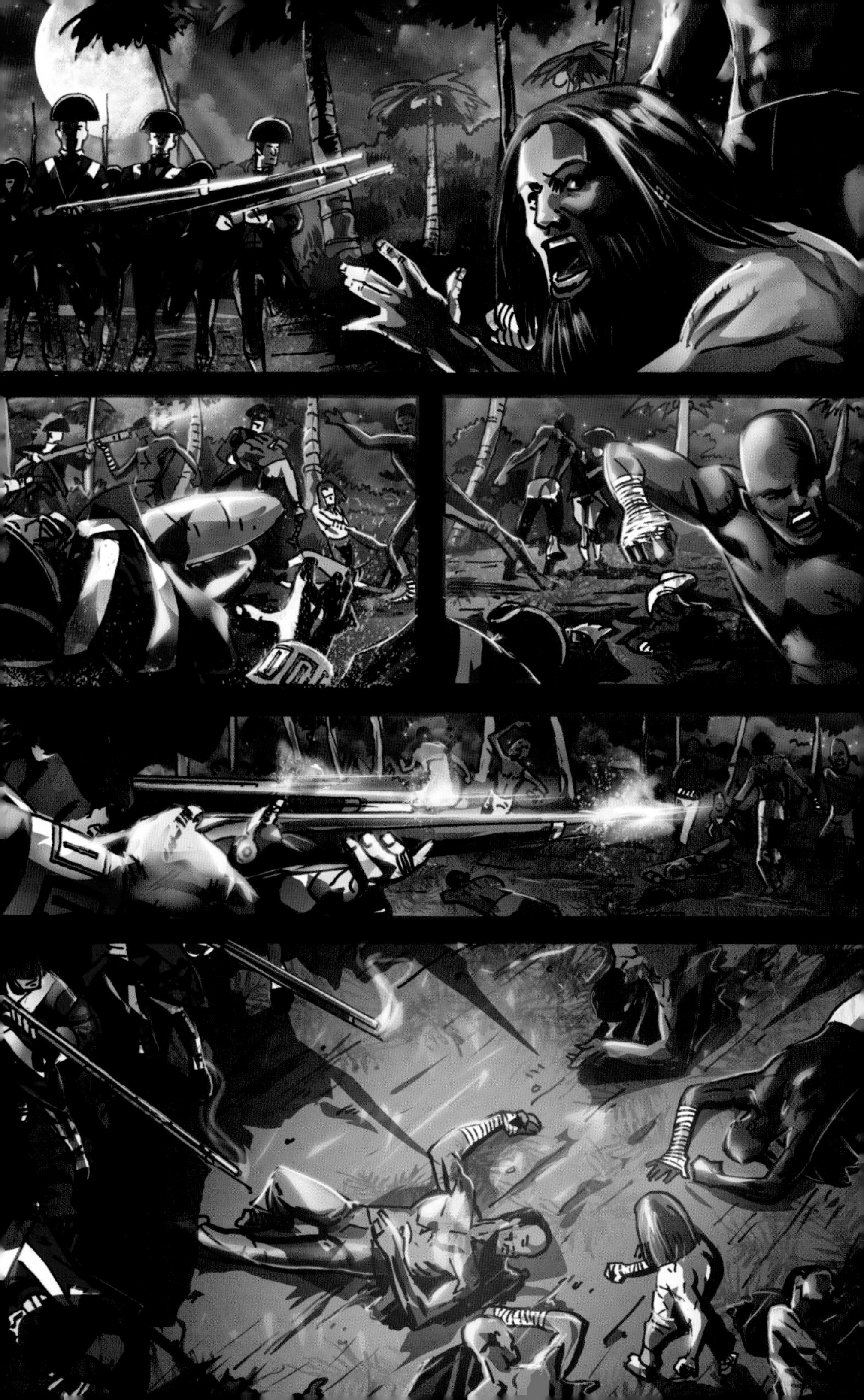

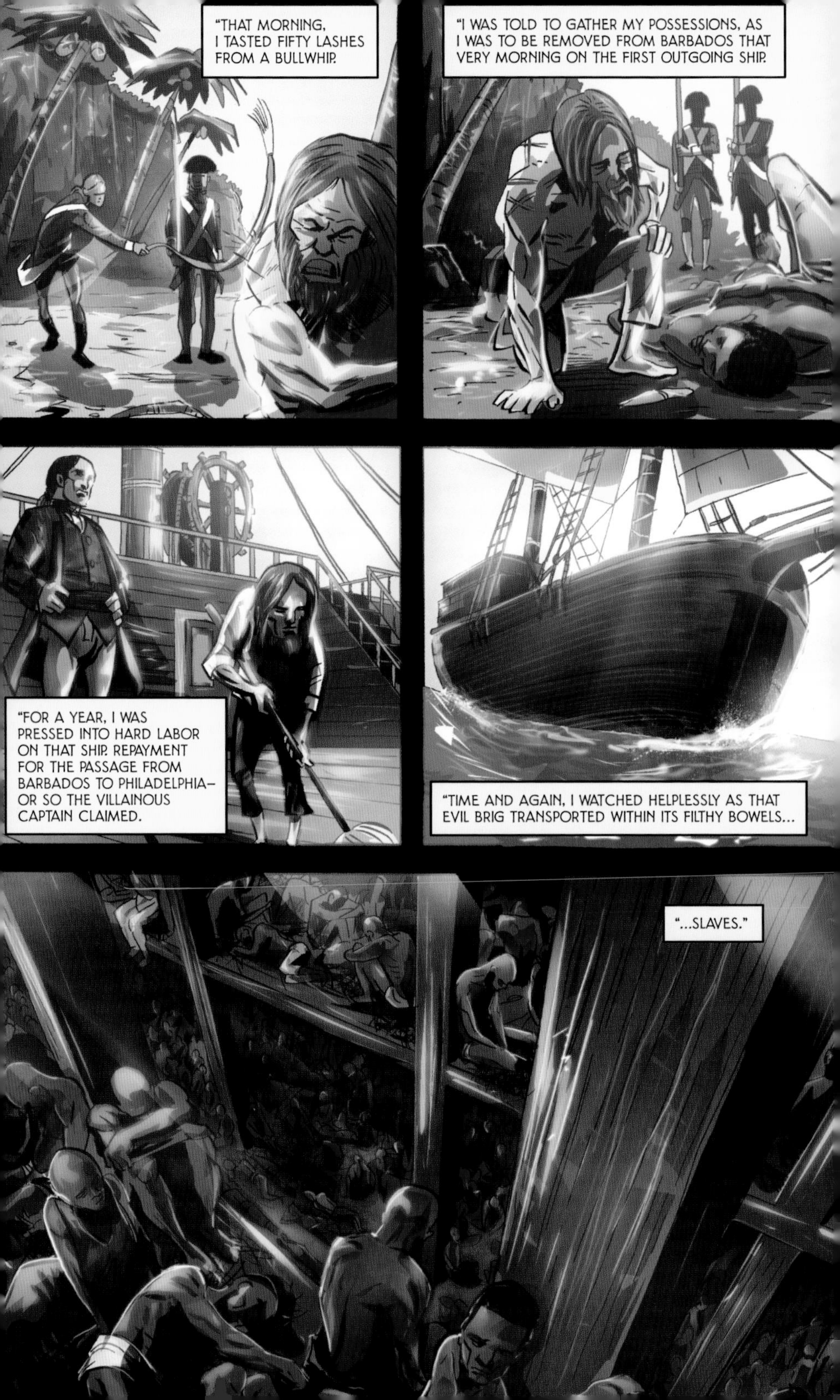
"THAT MORNING, I TASTED FIFTY LASHES FROM A BULLWHIP.
"I WAS TOLD TO GATHER MY POSSESSIONS, AS I WAS TO BE REMOVED FROM BARBADOS THAT VERY MORNING ON THE FIRST OUTGOING SHIP.
"FOR A YEAR, I WAS PRESSED INTO HARD LABOR ON THAT SHIP. REPAYMENT FOR THE PASSAGE FROM BARBADOS TO PHILADELPHIA– OR SO THE VILLAINOUS CAPTAIN CLAIMED.
"TIME AND AGAIN, I WATCHED HELPLESSLY AS THAT EVIL BRIG TRANSPORTED WITHIN ITS FILTHY BOWELS...
"...SLAVES."

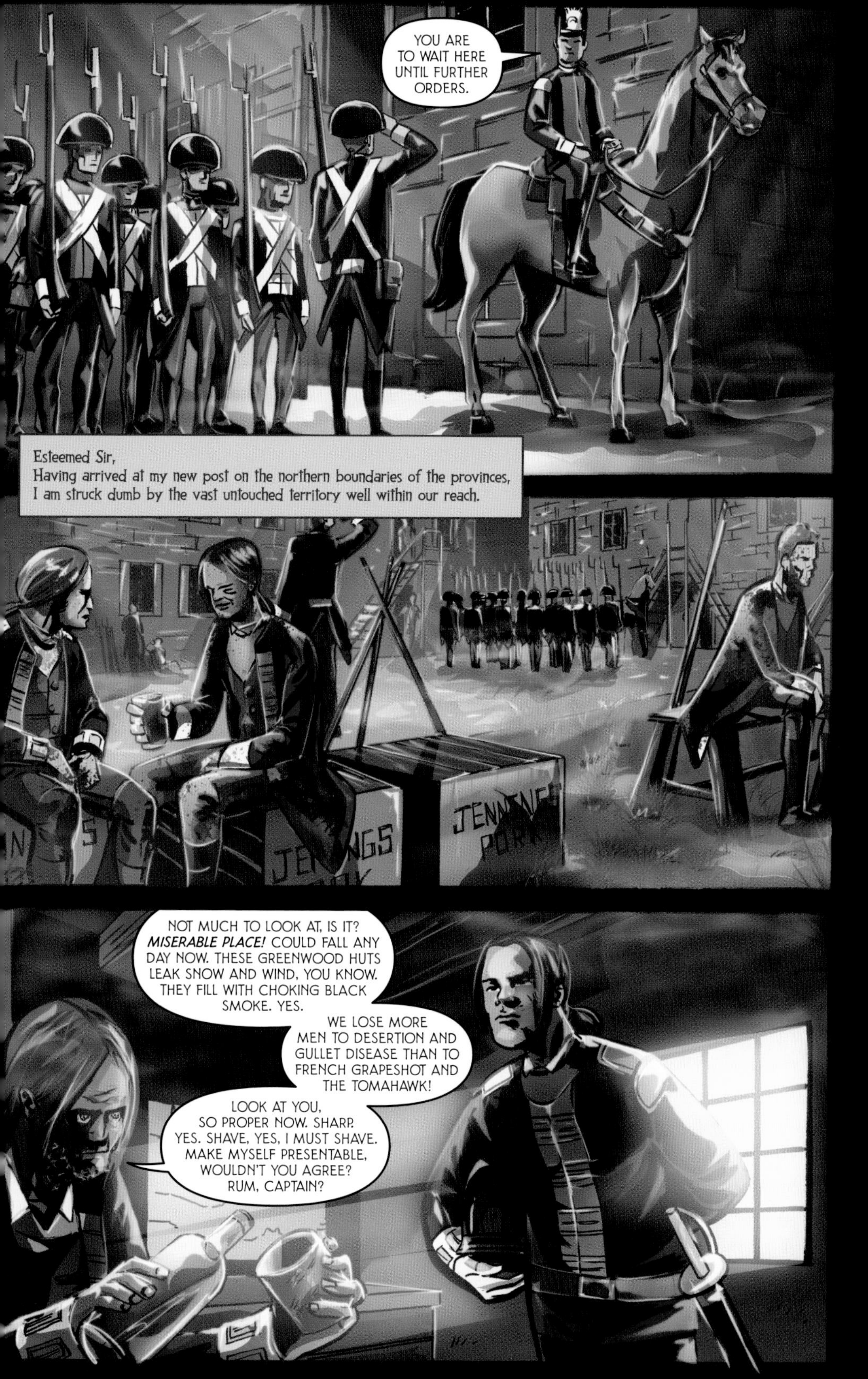
YOU ARE TO WAIT HERE UNTIL FURTHER ORDERS.
Esteemed Sir,
Having arrived at my new post on the northern boundaries of the provinces, I am struck dumb by the vast untouched territory well within our reach.
NOT MUCH TO LOOK AT, IS IT? *MISERABLE PLACE!* COULD FALL ANY DAY NOW. THESE GREENWOOD HUTS LEAK SNOW AND WIND, YOU KNOW. THEY FILL WITH CHOKING BLACK SMOKE. YES.
WE LOSE MORE MEN TO DESERTION AND GULLET DISEASE THAN TO FRENCH GRAPESHOT AND THE TOMAHAWK!
LOOK AT YOU, SO PROPER NOW. SHARP. YES. SHAVE, YES, I MUST SHAVE. MAKE MYSELF PRESENTABLE, WOULDN'T YOU AGREE? RUM, CAPTAIN?

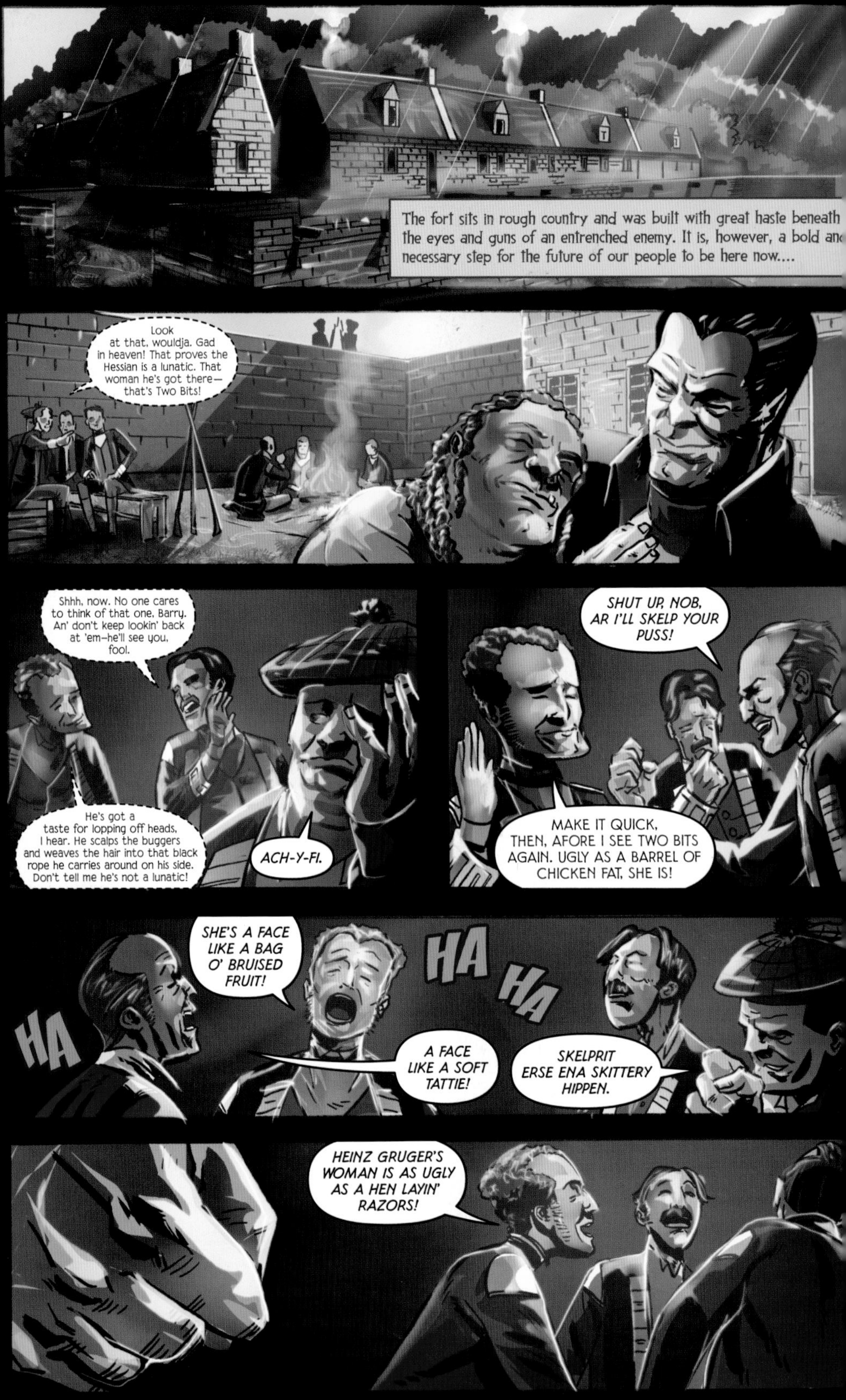

The fort sits in rough country and was built with great haste beneath the eyes and guns of an entrenched enemy. It is, however, a bold and necessary step for the future of our people to be here now....
Look at that, wouldja. Gad in heaven! That proves the Hessian is a lunatic. That woman he's got there— that's Two Bits!
Shhh, now. No one cares to think of that one, Barry. An' don't keep lookin' back at 'em—he'll see you, fool.
He's got a taste for lopping off heads, I hear. He scalps the buggers and weaves the hair into that black rope he carries around on his side. Don't tell me he's not a lunatic!
ACH-Y-FI.
SHUT UP, NOB, AR I'LL SKELP YOUR PUSS!
MAKE IT QUICK, THEN, AFORE I SEE TWO BITS AGAIN. UGLY AS A BARREL OF CHICKEN FAT, SHE IS!
SHE'S A FACE LIKE A BAG O' BRUISED FRUIT!
HA
HA
HA
A FACE LIKE A SOFT TATTIE!
SKELPRIT ERSE ENA SKITTERY HIPPEN.
HEINZ GRUGER'S WOMAN IS AS UGLY AS A HEN LAYIN' RAZORS!

HHHHAAAAA?!

Sie mögen also wie Gruger Sie anfasst, ja? Ich werde Ihnen die Haare ausreißen und Sie in meinen Gürtel einfädeln. Dann werde ich Ihre Knochen zu Staub zermürben!

RRRRIIIIIWW

PLEASE, NO, GRUGAHHHHHHHHHHHHH!

TAKE YOUR HANDS OFF THAT MAN IMMEDIATELY!

DO YOU NOT UNDERSTAND THE KING'S ENGLISH, IMBECILE?

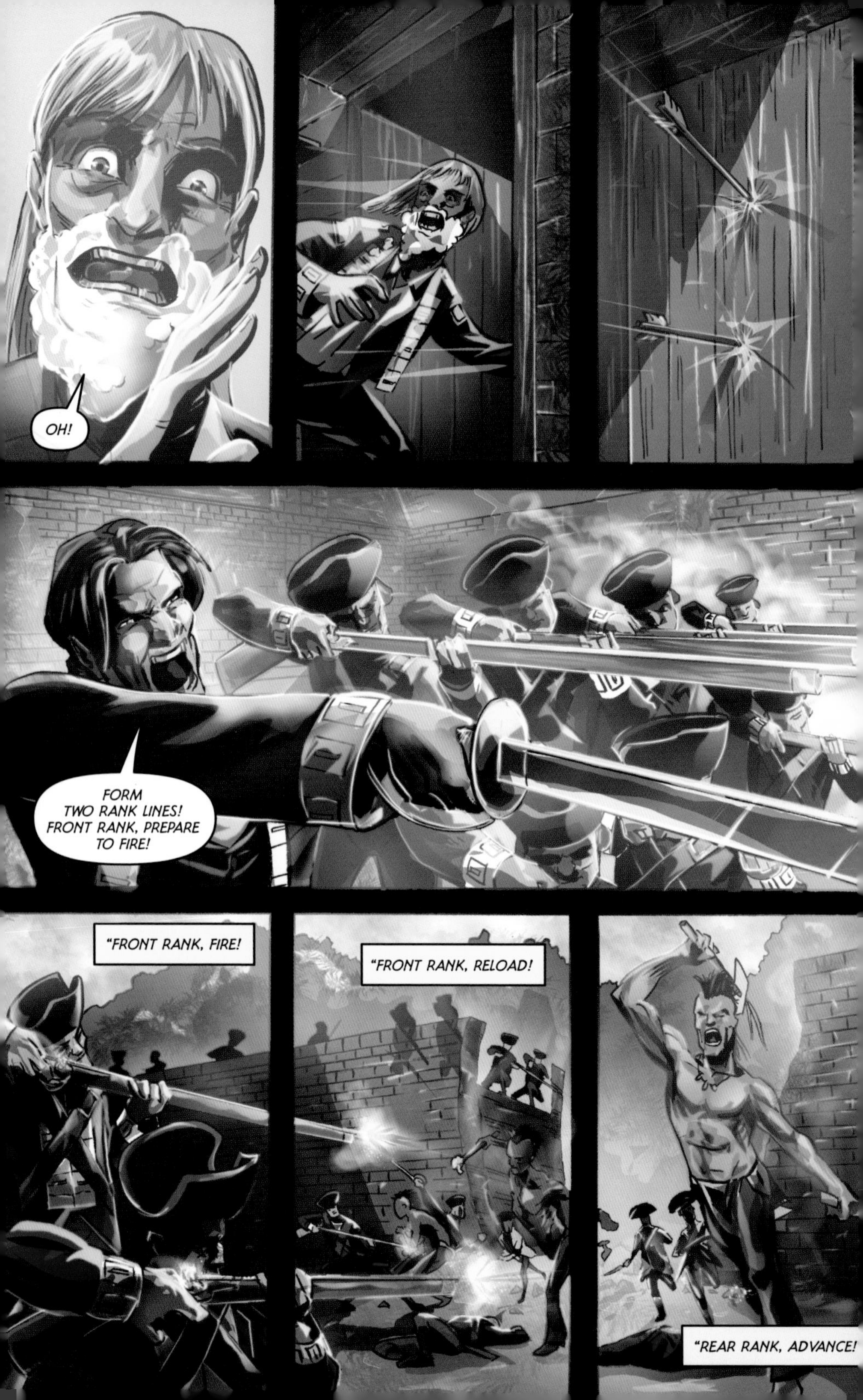
OH!
FORM TWO RANK LINES! FRONT RANK, PREPARE TO FIRE!
"FRONT RANK, FIRE!
"FRONT RANK, RELOAD!
"REAR RANK, ADVANCE!

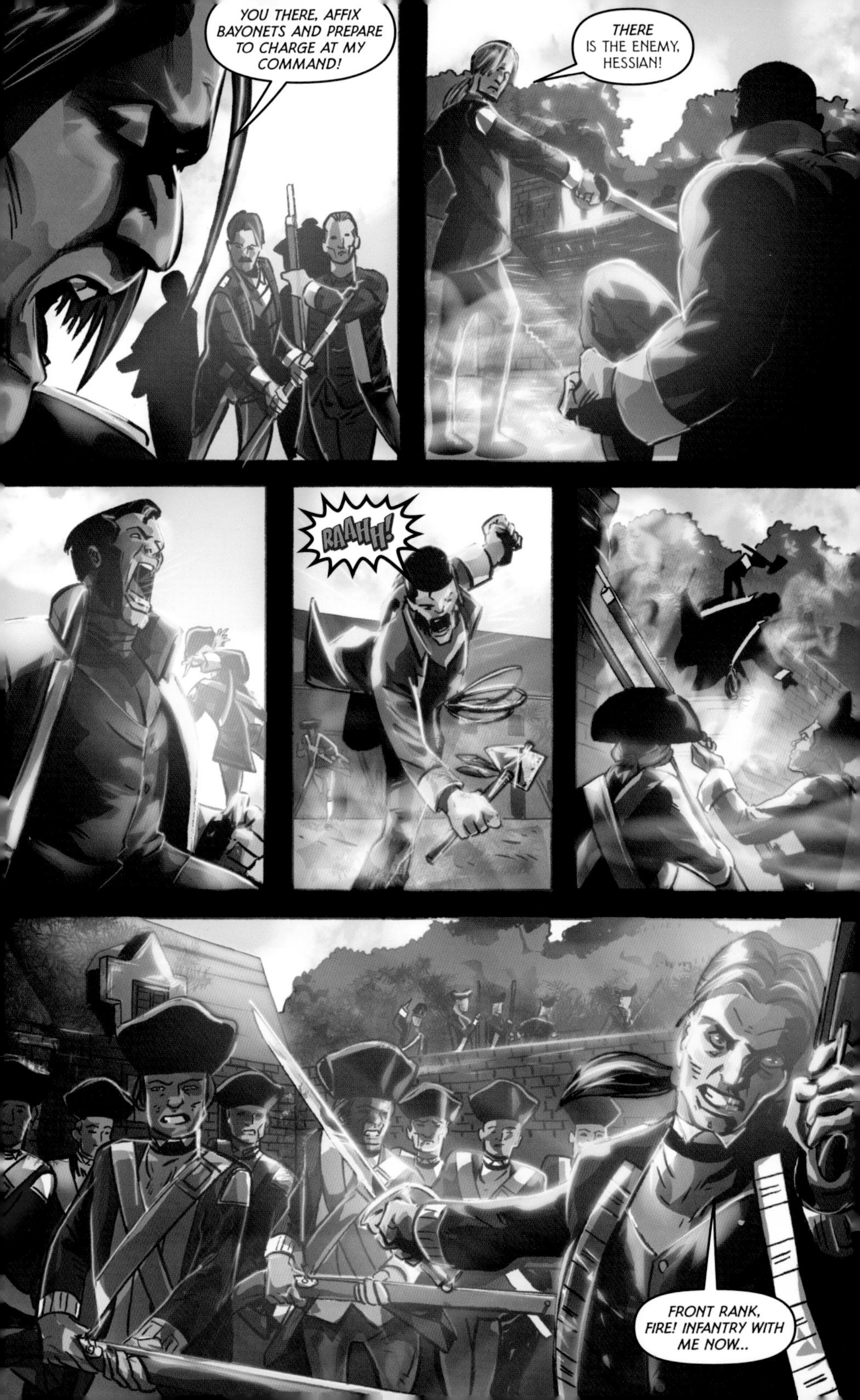
YOU THERE, AFFIX BAYONETS AND PREPARE TO CHARGE AT MY COMMAND!
THERE IS THE ENEMY, HESSIAN!
RAAHH!
FRONT RANK, FIRE! INFANTRY WITH ME NOW...

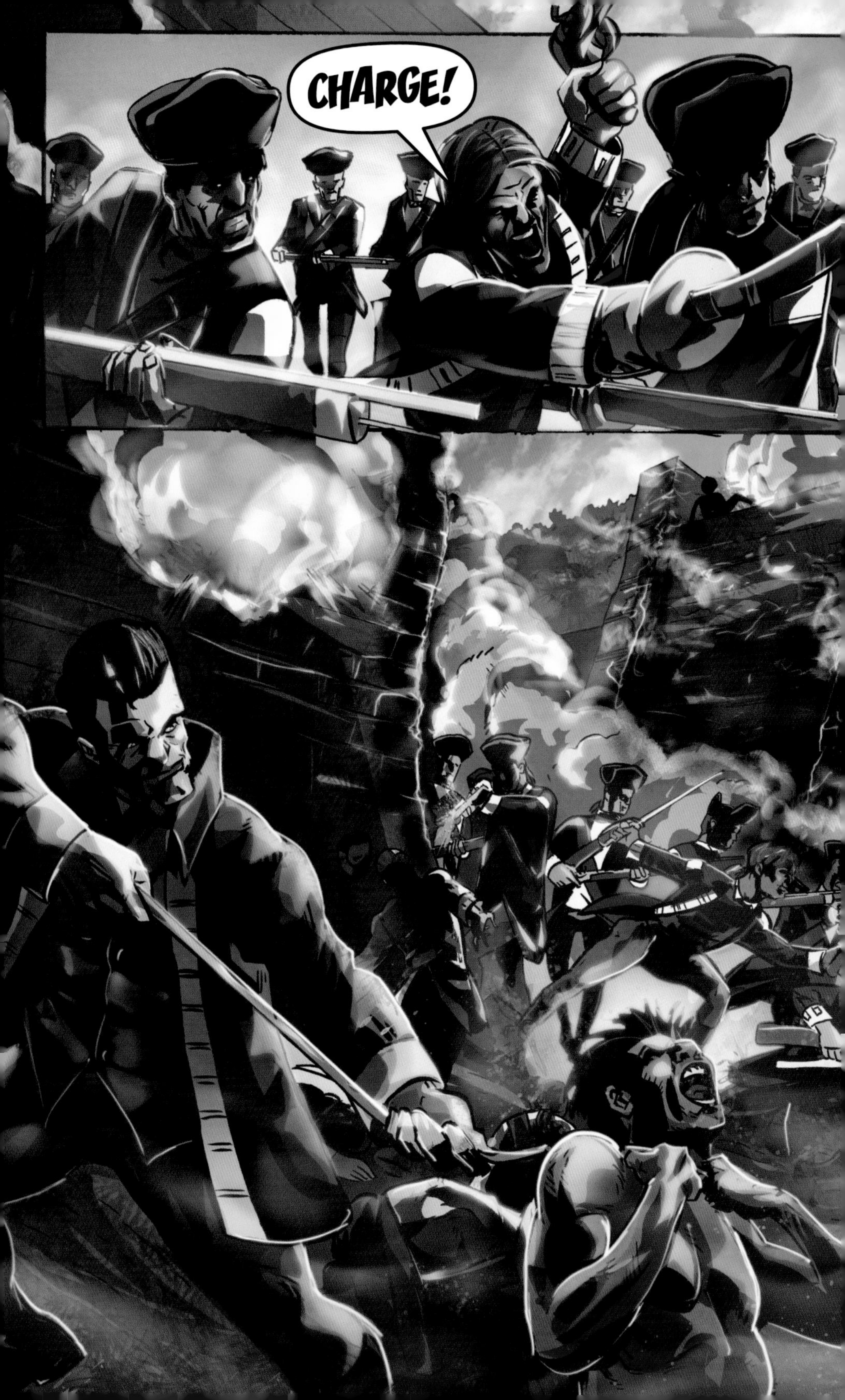
CHARGE!

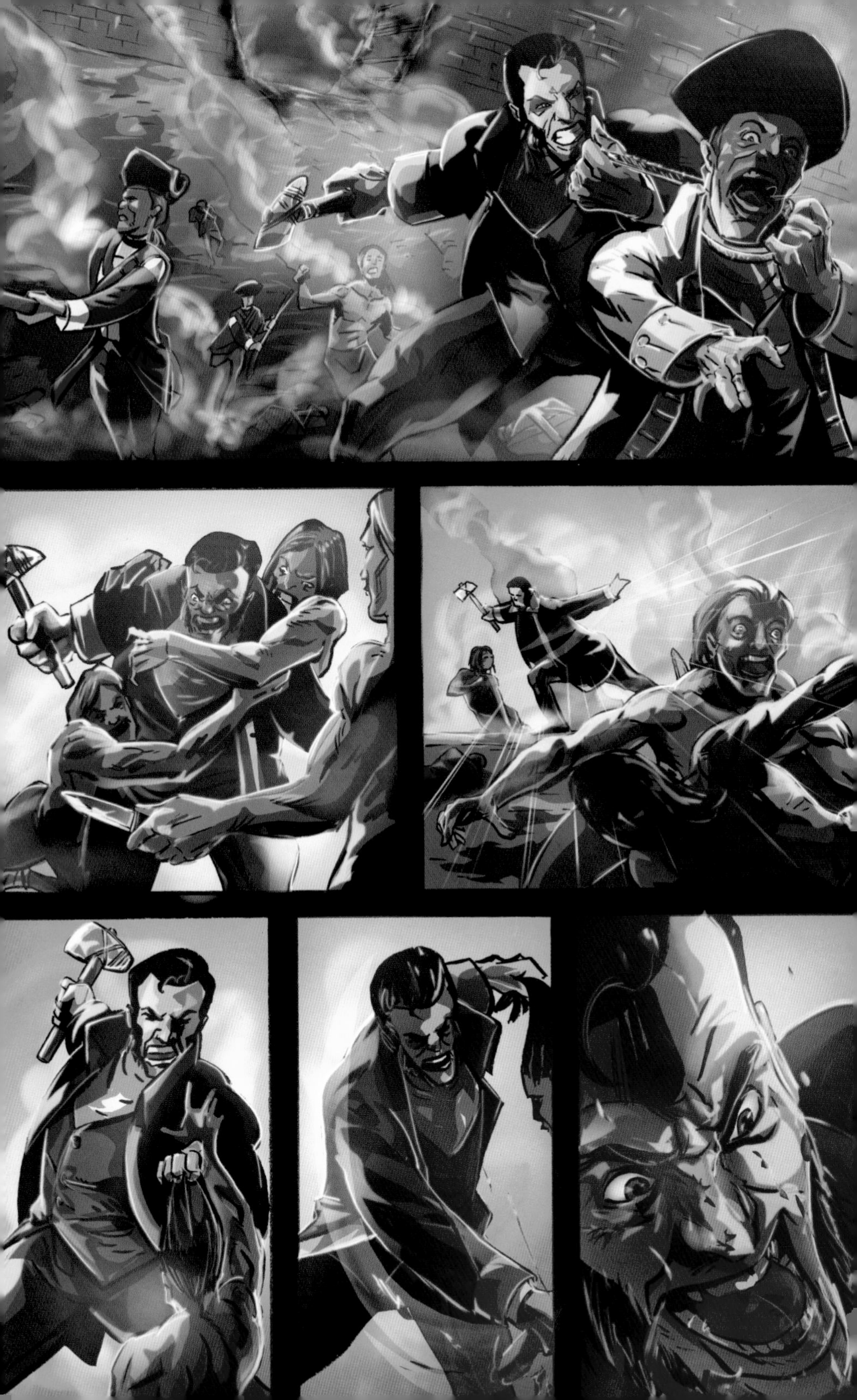

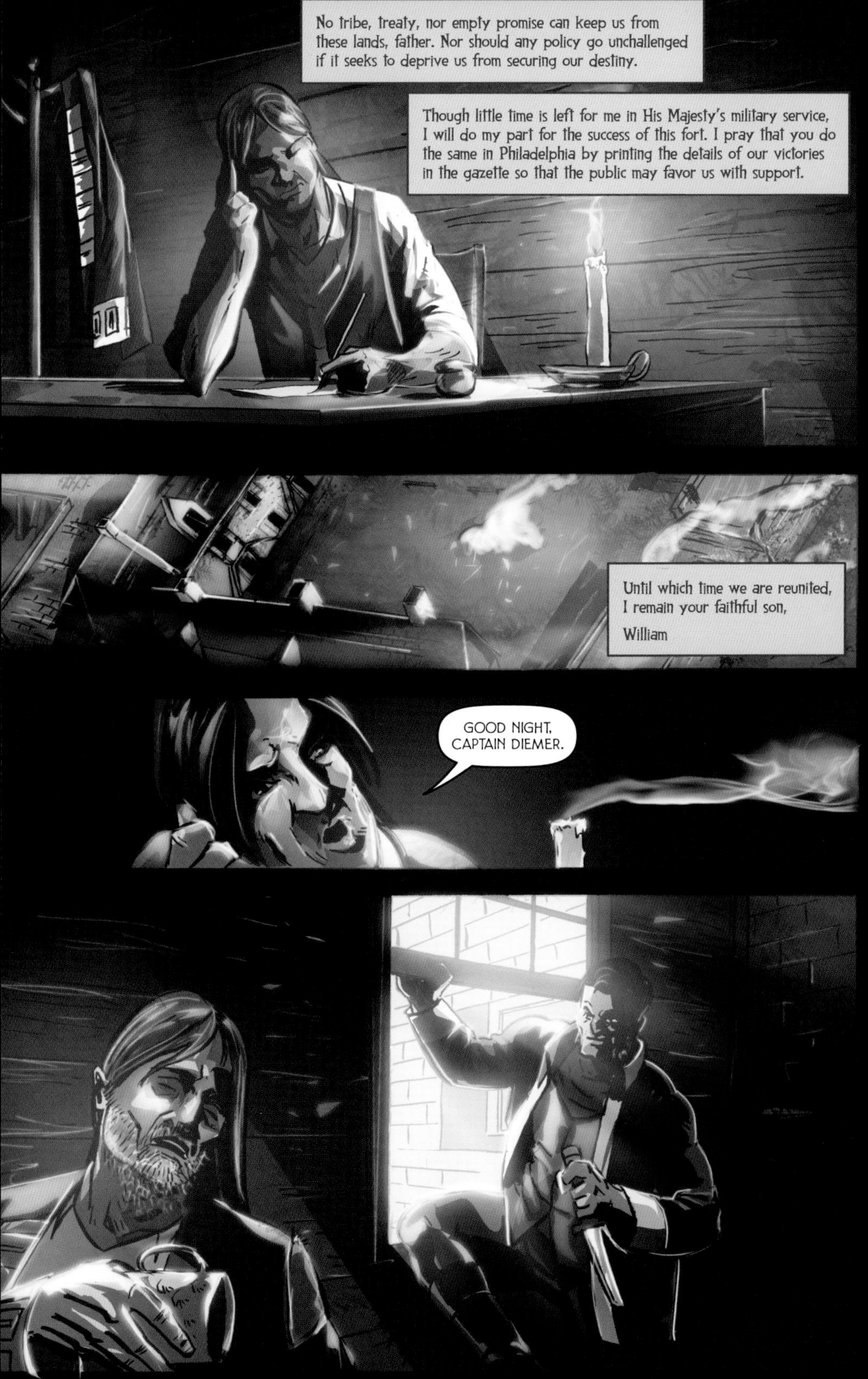
No tribe, treaty, nor empty promise can keep us from these lands, father. Nor should any policy go unchallenged if it seeks to deprive us from securing our destiny.
Though little time is left for me in His Majesty's military service, I will do my part for the success of this fort. I pray that you do the same in Philadelphia by printing the details of our victories in the gazette so that the public may favor us with support.
Until which time we are reunited, I remain your faithful son,
William
GOOD NIGHT, CAPTAIN DIEMER.

BE SURE TO SHOW THEM THE RULES, EZRA.

WULES. GLUG-GLUG-GLUG-GLUG.

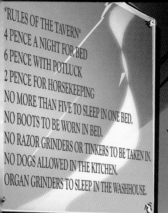

RULES OF THE TAVERN
4 PENCE A NIGHT FOR BED
6 PENCE WITH POTLUCK
2 PENCE FOR HORSEKEEPING
NO MORE THAN FIVE TO SLEEP IN ONE BED.
NO BOOTS TO BE WORN IN BED.
NO RAZOR GRINDERS OR TINKERS TO BE TAKEN IN.
NO DOGS ALLOWED IN THE KITCHEN.
ORGAN GRINDERS TO SLEEP IN THE WASHHOUSE.

I KNOW YOU'RE WORKING FOR THAT PWINT THOP, BUT IF YOU HELP ME AWOUND HERE WITH MY WORK, TOO, I'LL PAY YOU EACH THREE PENTH A WEEK.

DO A LOT OF SHIPS' CAPTAINS STAY HERE?

CAPTHINS, THAILORS, AN' EVWEE TWADE THERE ITH.

BRODY AND I WILL HELP IN ANY WAY WE CAN, MR. JONES.

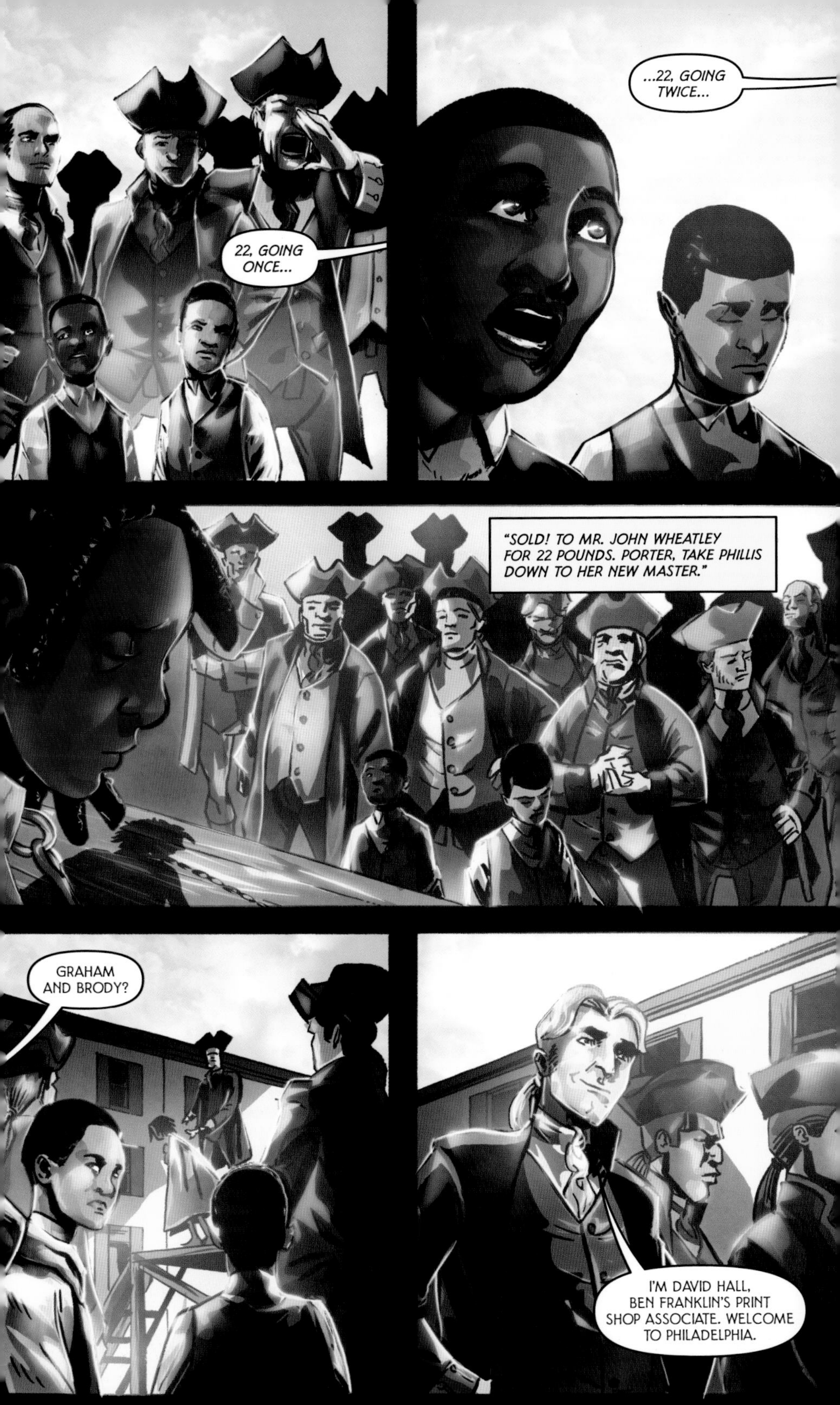
22, GOING ONCE...
...22, GOING TWICE...
"SOLD! TO MR. JOHN WHEATLEY FOR 22 POUNDS. PORTER, TAKE PHILLIS DOWN TO HER NEW MASTER."
GRAHAM AND BRODY?
I'M DAVID HALL, BEN FRANKLIN'S PRINT SHOP ASSOCIATE. WELCOME TO PHILADELPHIA.

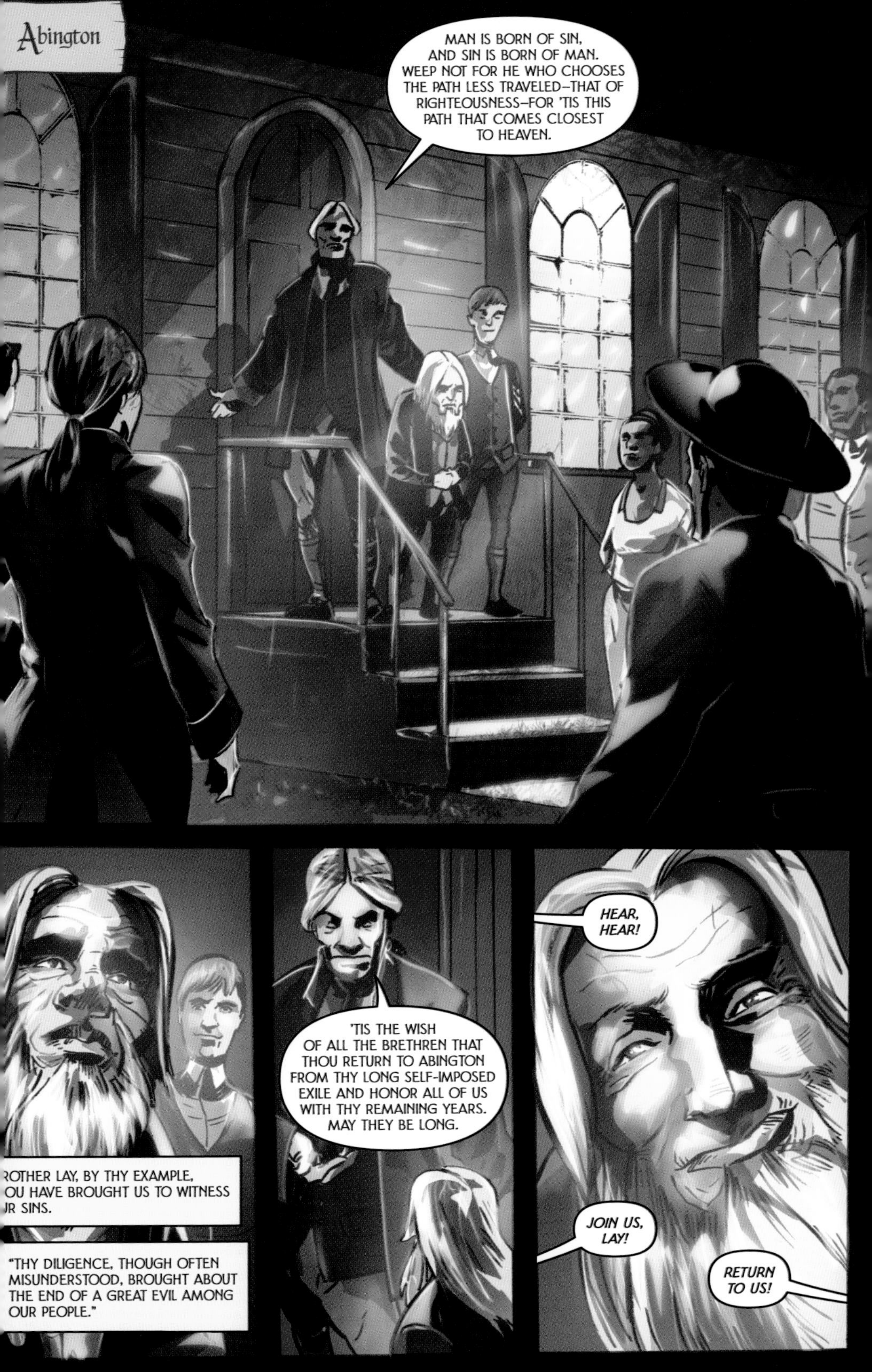

Abington
MAN IS BORN OF SIN, AND SIN IS BORN OF MAN. WEEP NOT FOR HE WHO CHOOSES THE PATH LESS TRAVELED—THAT OF RIGHTEOUSNESS—FOR 'TIS THIS PATH THAT COMES CLOSEST TO HEAVEN.
ROTHER LAY, BY THY EXAMPLE, OU HAVE BROUGHT US TO WITNESS R SINS.
"THY DILIGENCE, THOUGH OFTEN MISUNDERSTOOD, BROUGHT ABOUT THE END OF A GREAT EVIL AMONG OUR PEOPLE."
'TIS THE WISH OF ALL THE BRETHREN THAT THOU RETURN TO ABINGTON FROM THY LONG SELF-IMPOSED EXILE AND HONOR ALL OF US WITH THY REMAINING YEARS. MAY THEY BE LONG.
HEAR, HEAR!
JOIN US, LAY!
RETURN TO US!

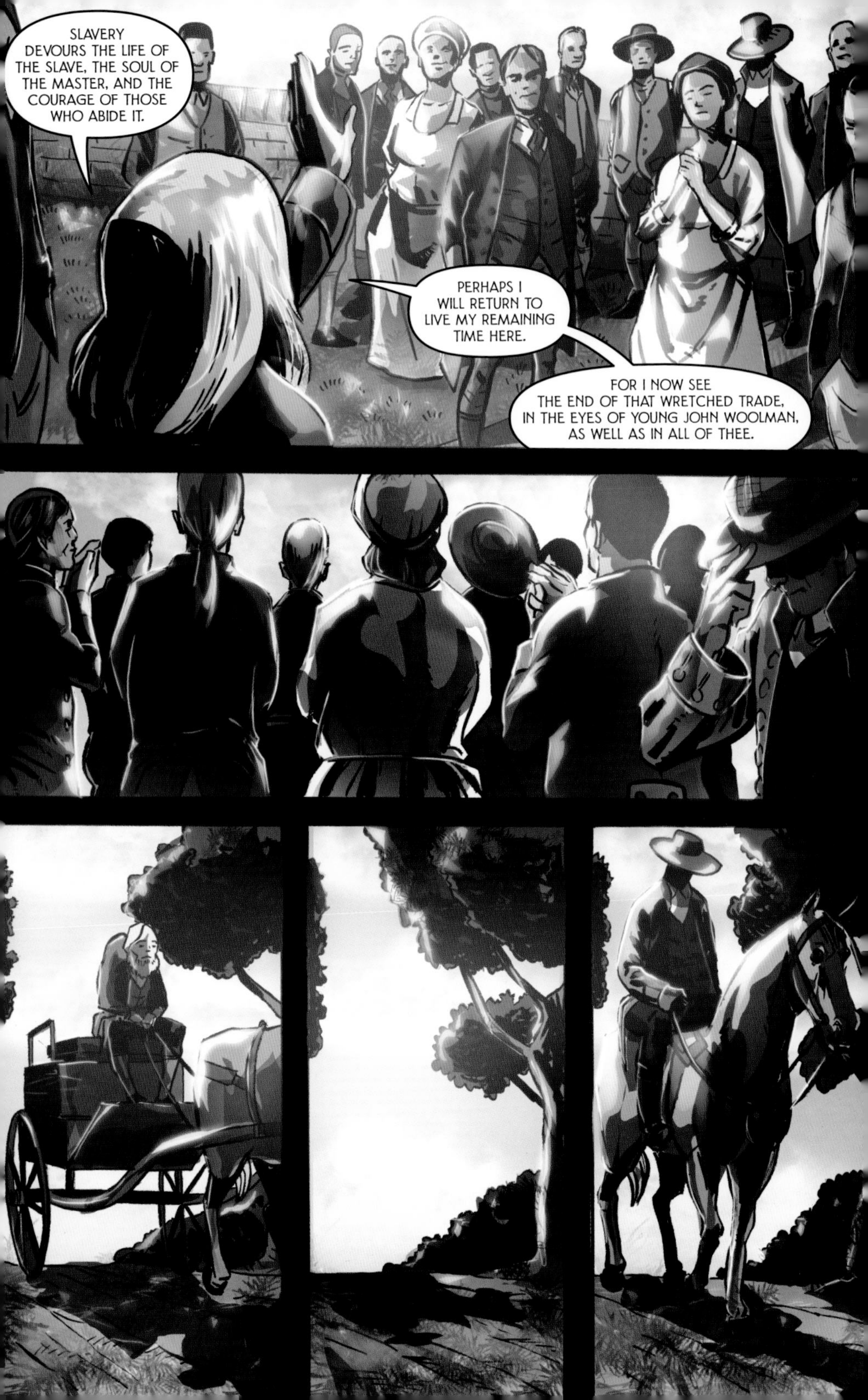
SLAVERY DEVOURS THE LIFE OF THE SLAVE, THE SOUL OF THE MASTER, AND THE COURAGE OF THOSE WHO ABIDE IT.
PERHAPS I WILL RETURN TO LIVE MY REMAINING TIME HERE.
FOR I NOW SEE THE END OF THAT WRETCHED TRADE, IN THE EYES OF YOUNG JOHN WOOLMAN, AS WELL AS IN ALL OF THEE.

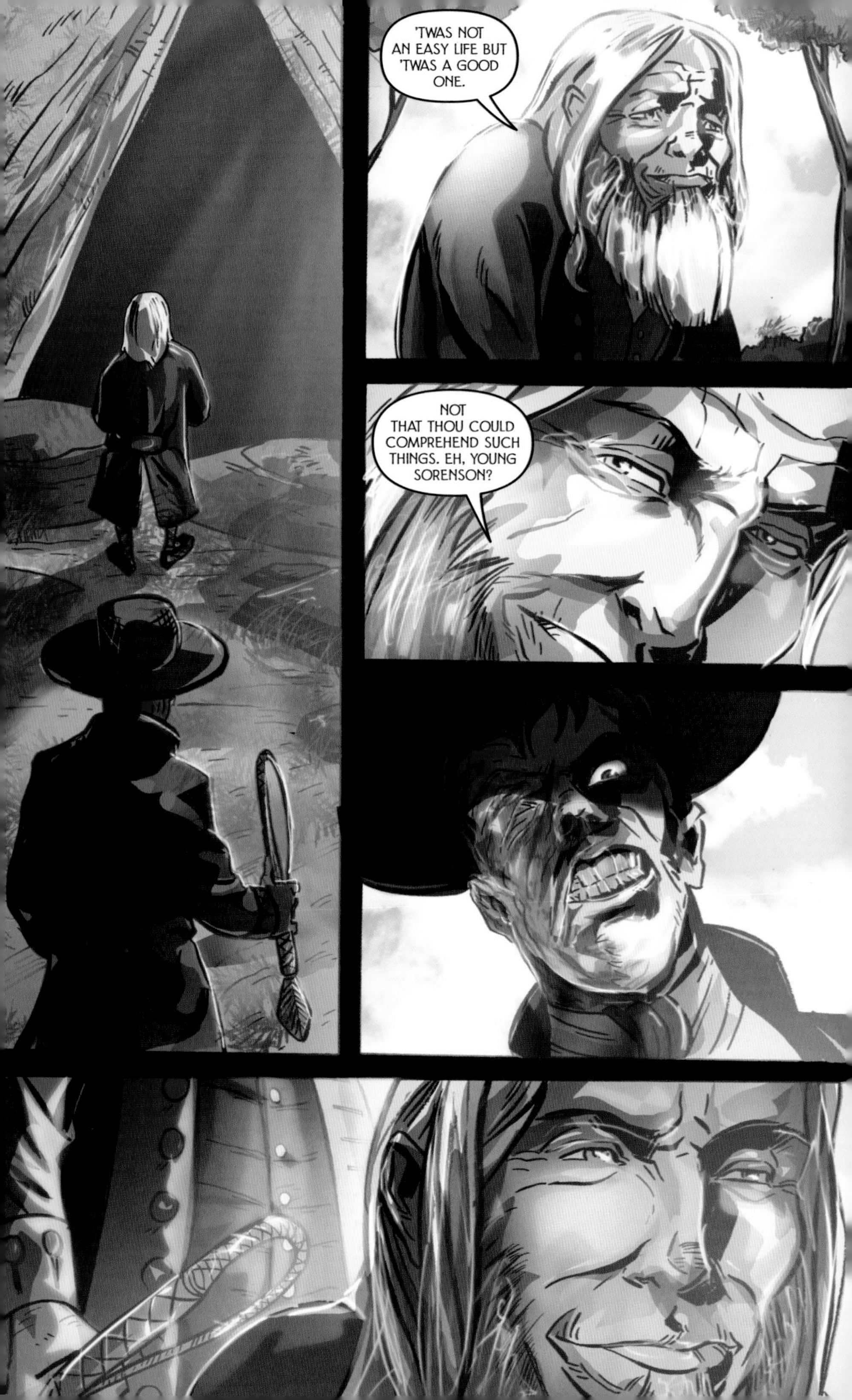
'TWAS NOT AN EASY LIFE BUT 'TWAS A GOOD ONE.
NOT THAT THOU COULD COMPREHEND SUCH THINGS. EH, YOUNG SORENSON?

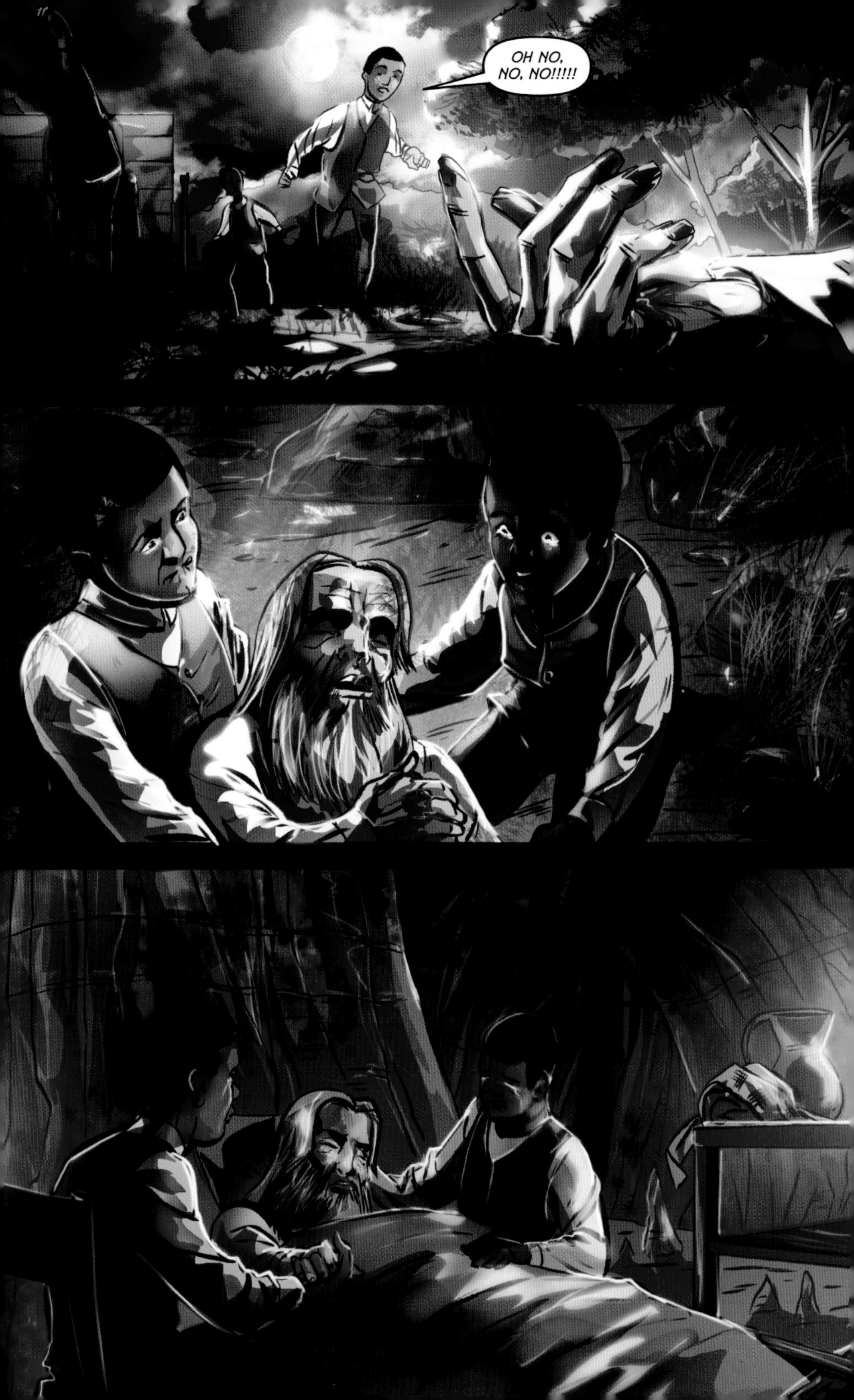
OH NO, NO, NO!!!!!

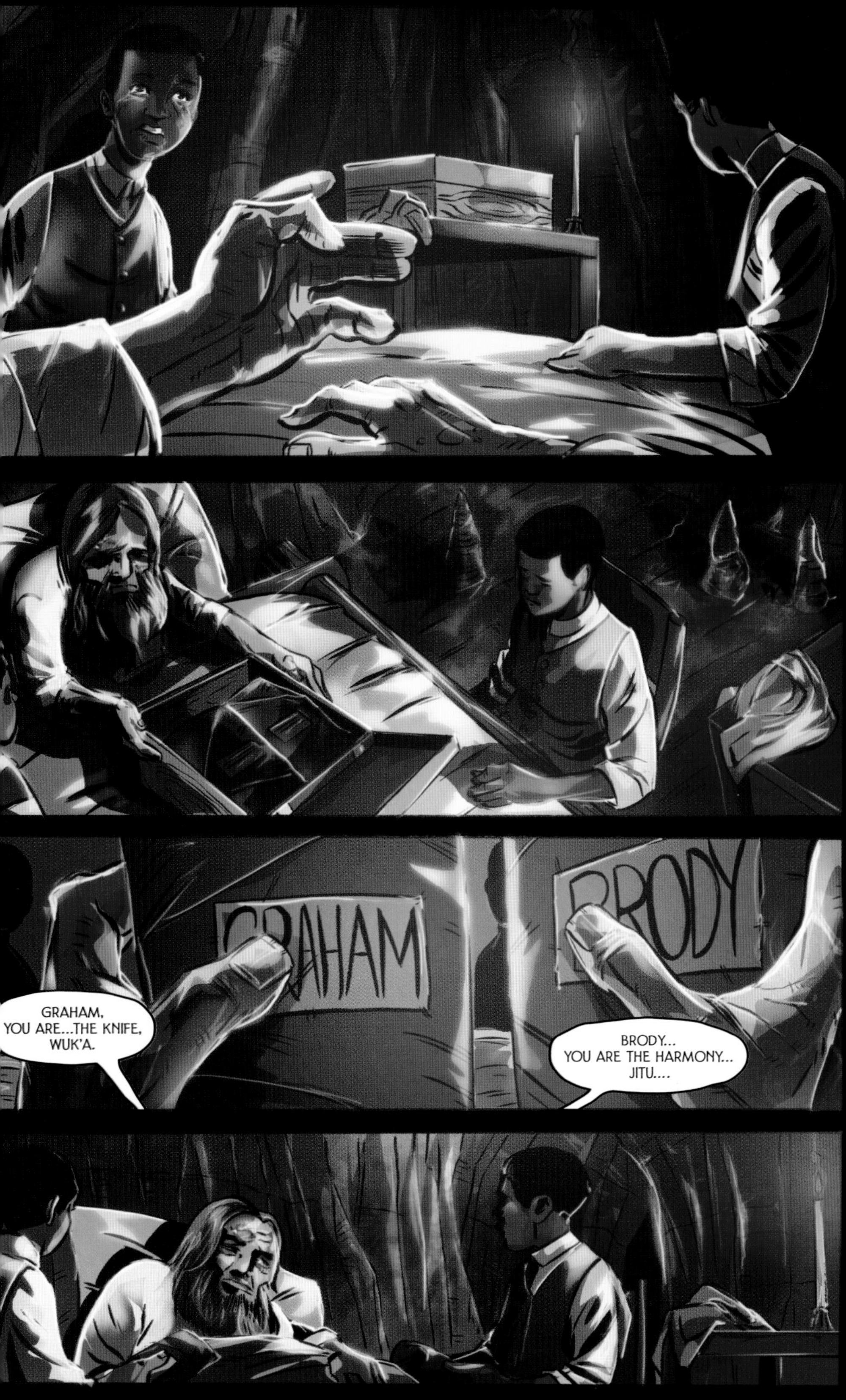
GRAHAM
BRODY
GRAHAM, YOU ARE...THE KNIFE, WUK'A.
BRODY... YOU ARE THE HARMONY... JITU....

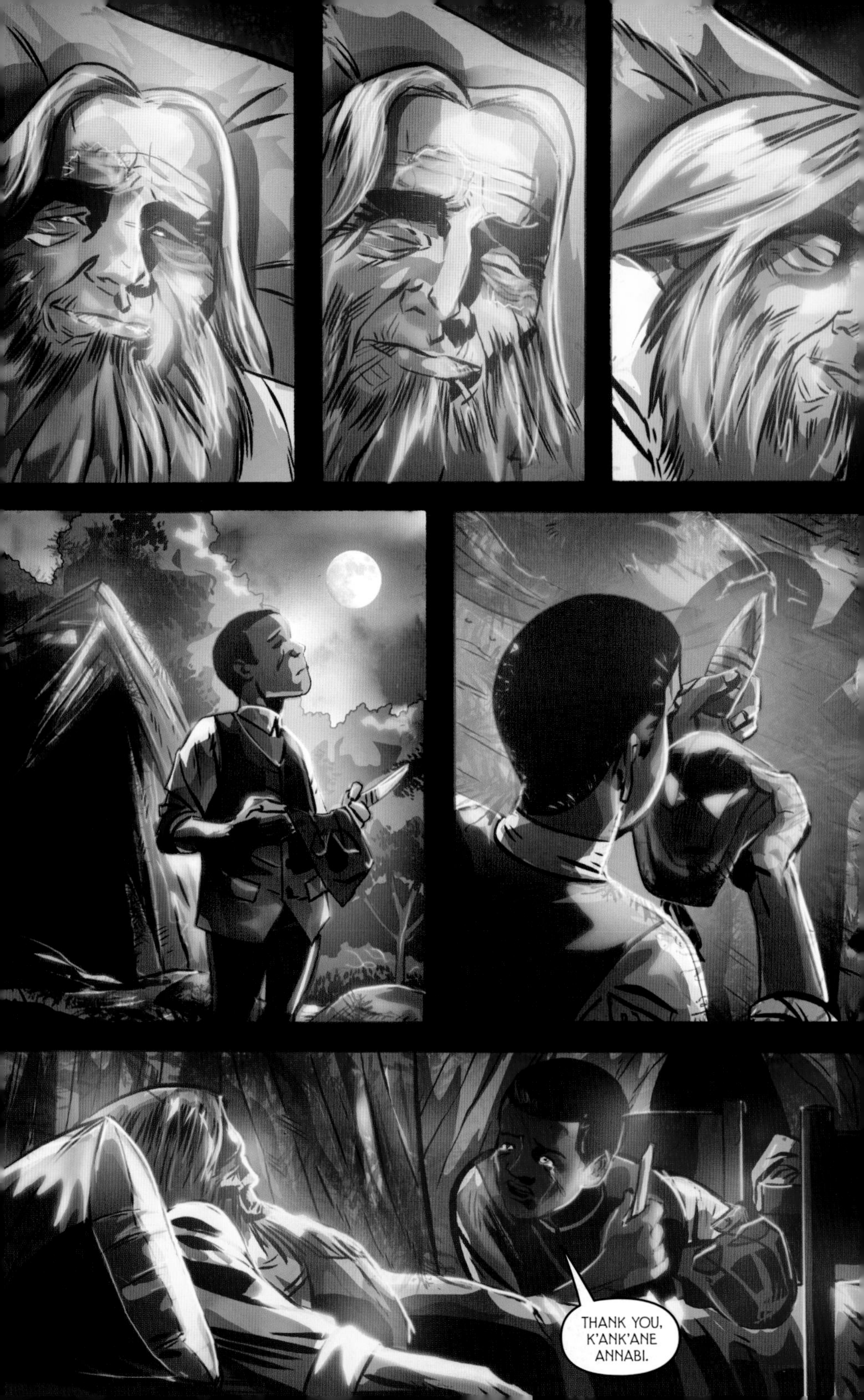
THANK YOU, K'ANK'ANE ANNABI.

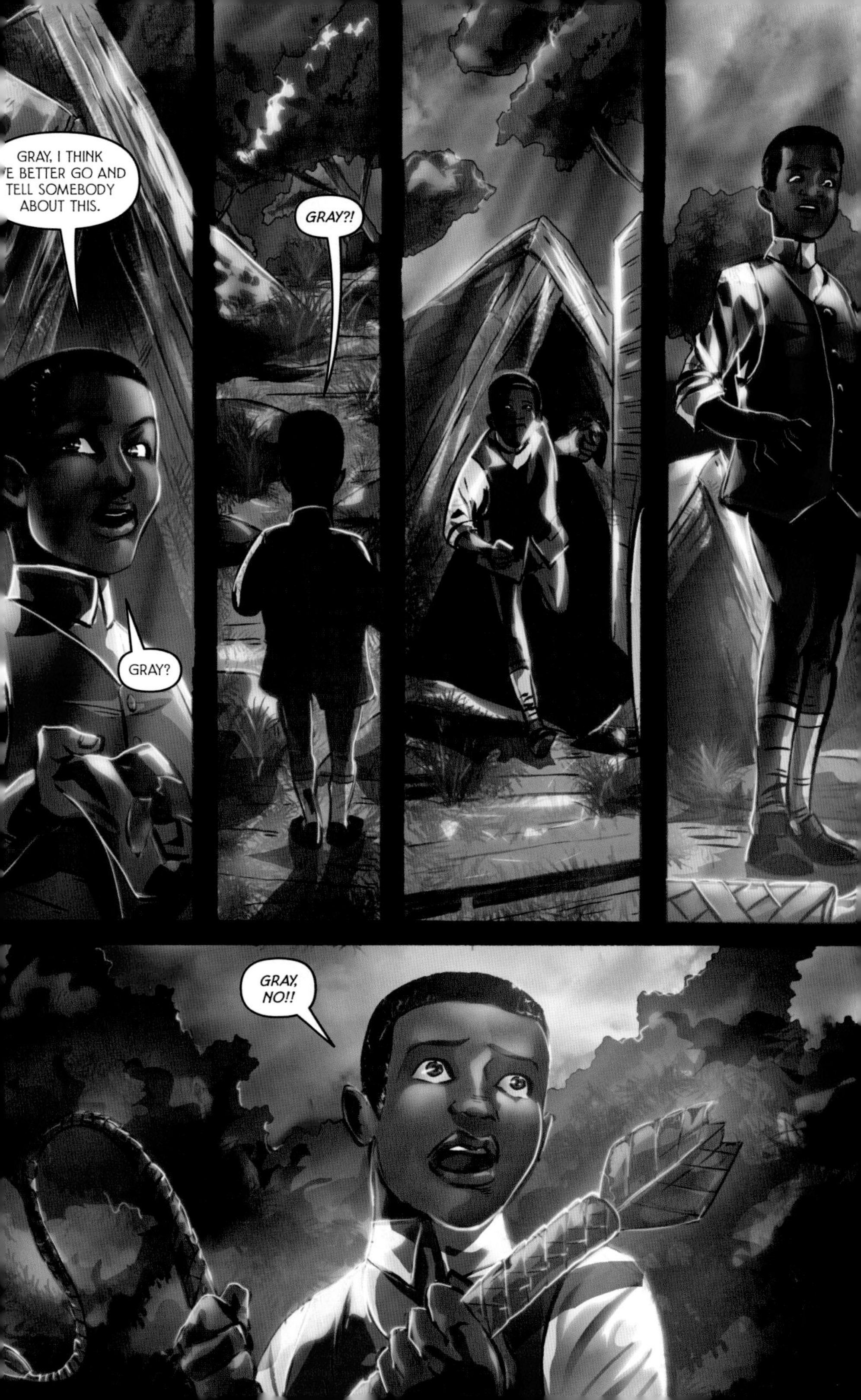
GRAY, I THINK
'E BETTER GO AND
TELL SOMEBODY
ABOUT THIS.
GRAY?
GRAY?!
GRAY,
NO!!

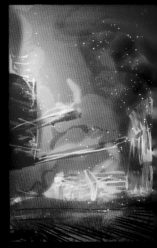

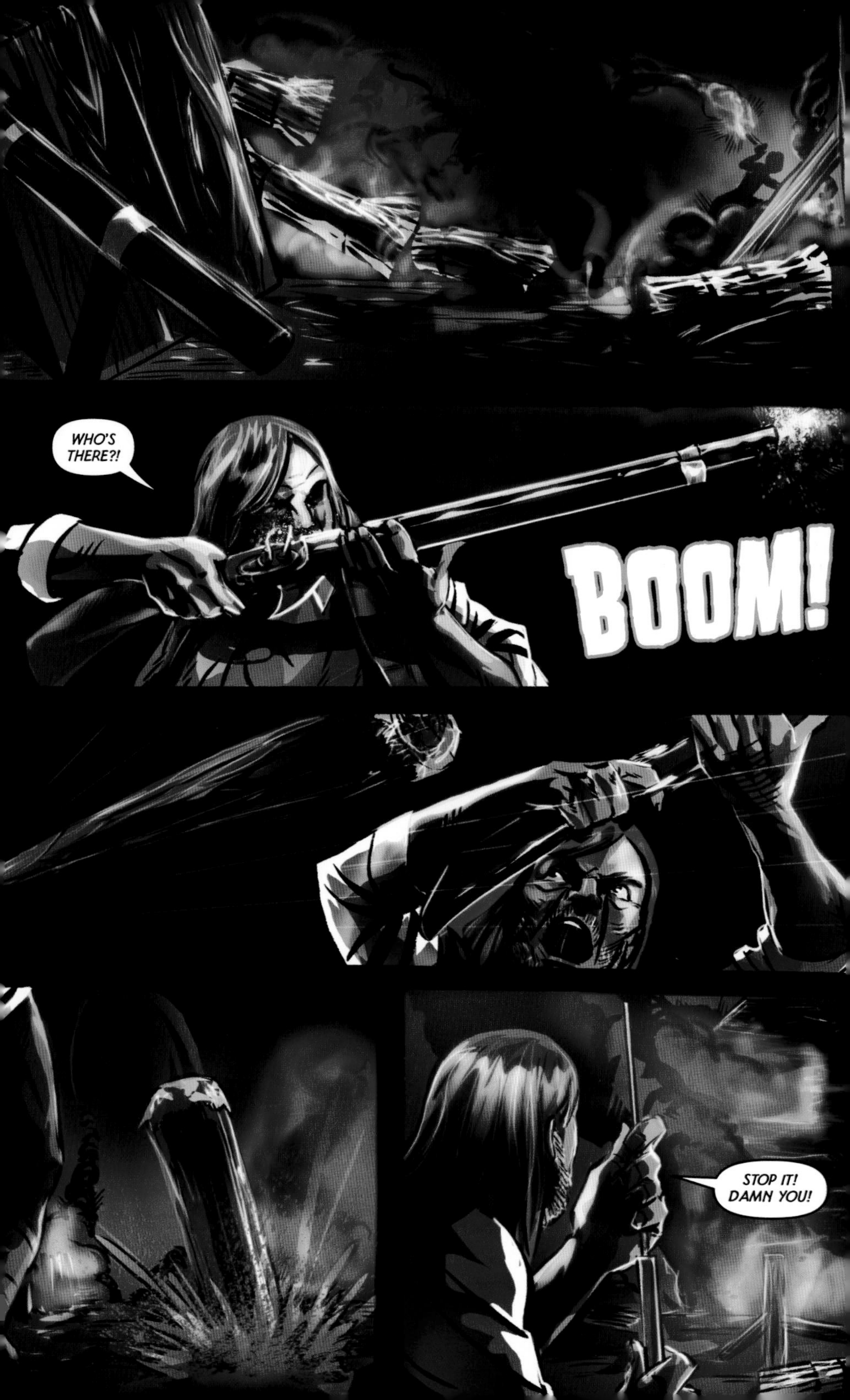
WHO'S THERE?!
BOOM!
STOP IT! DAMN YOU!

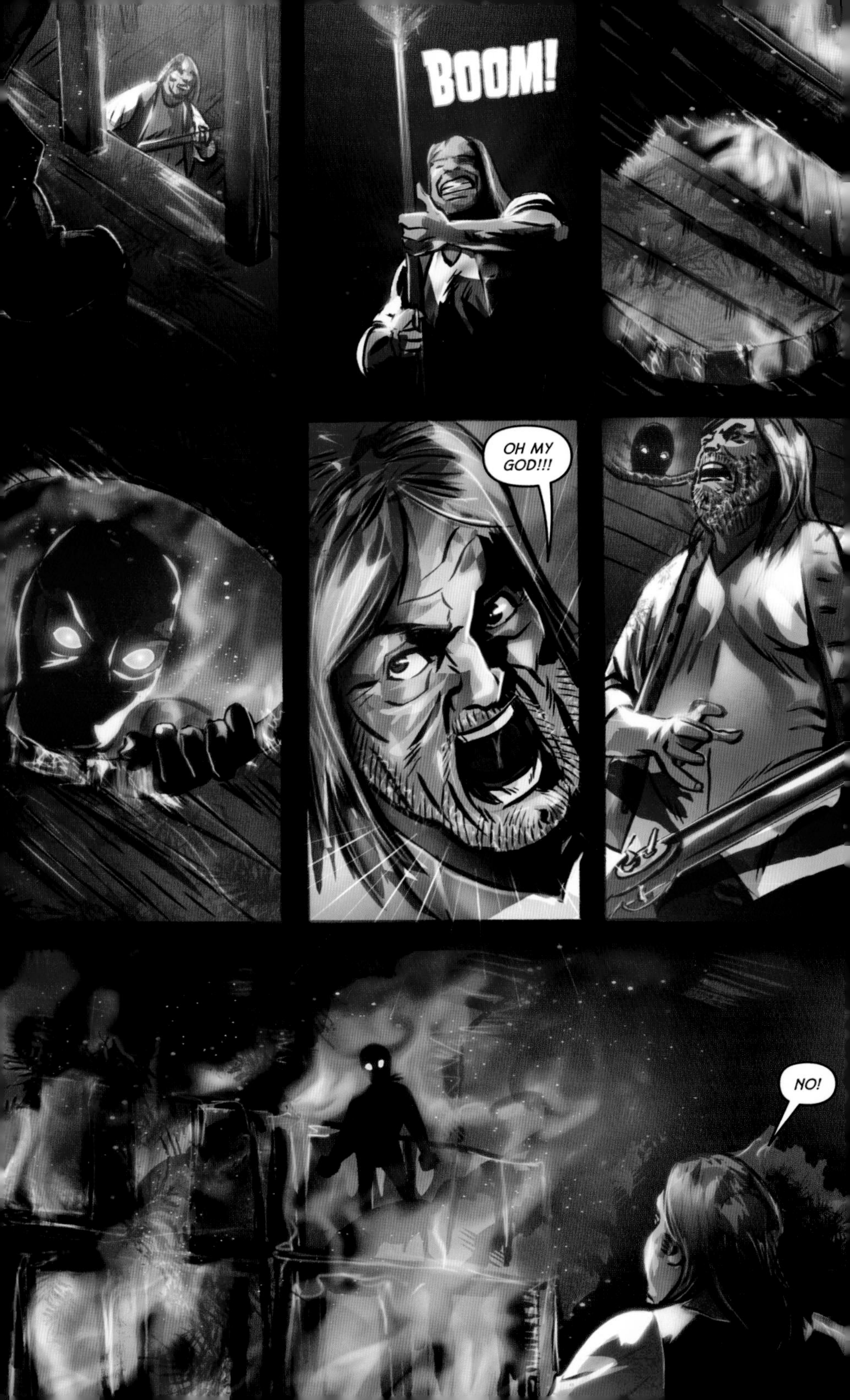
BOOM!
OH MY GOD!!!
NO!

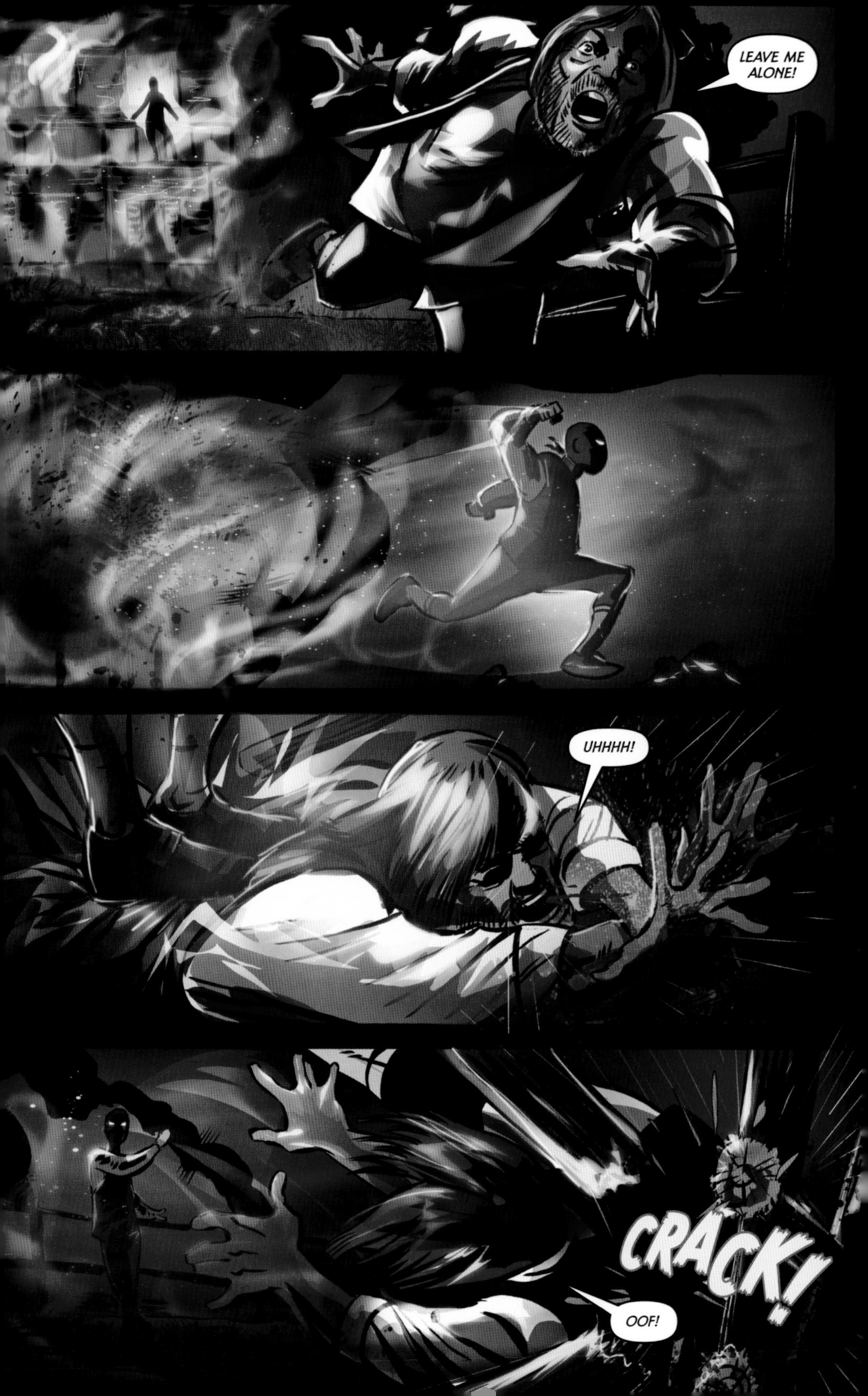
LEAVE ME ALONE!
UHHHH!
CRACK!
OOF!

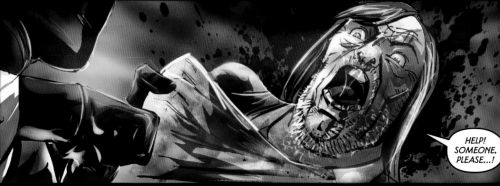

HELP!
SOMEONE,
PLEASE...!

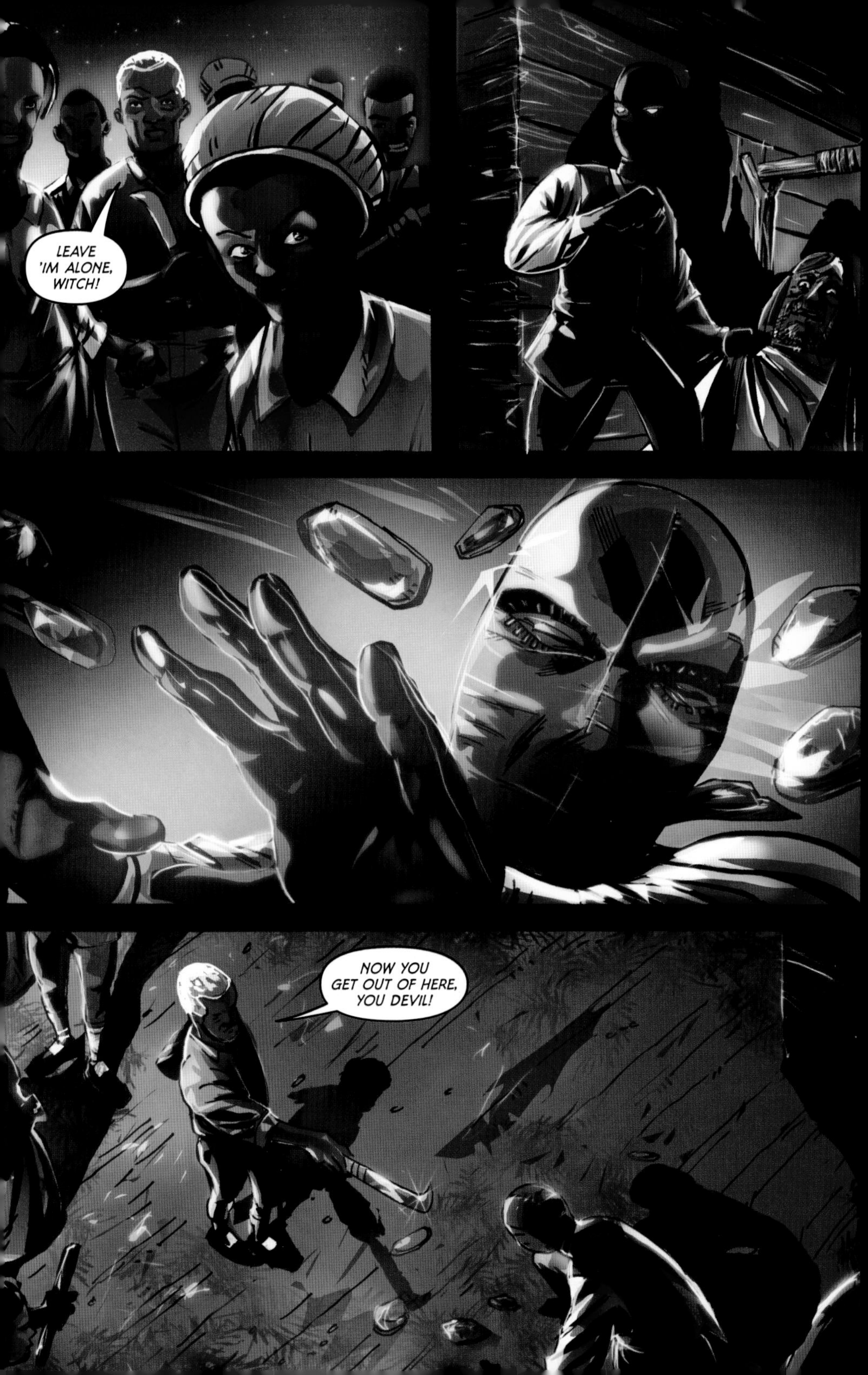
LEAVE 'IM ALONE, WITCH!
NOW YOU GET OUT OF HERE, YOU DEVIL!

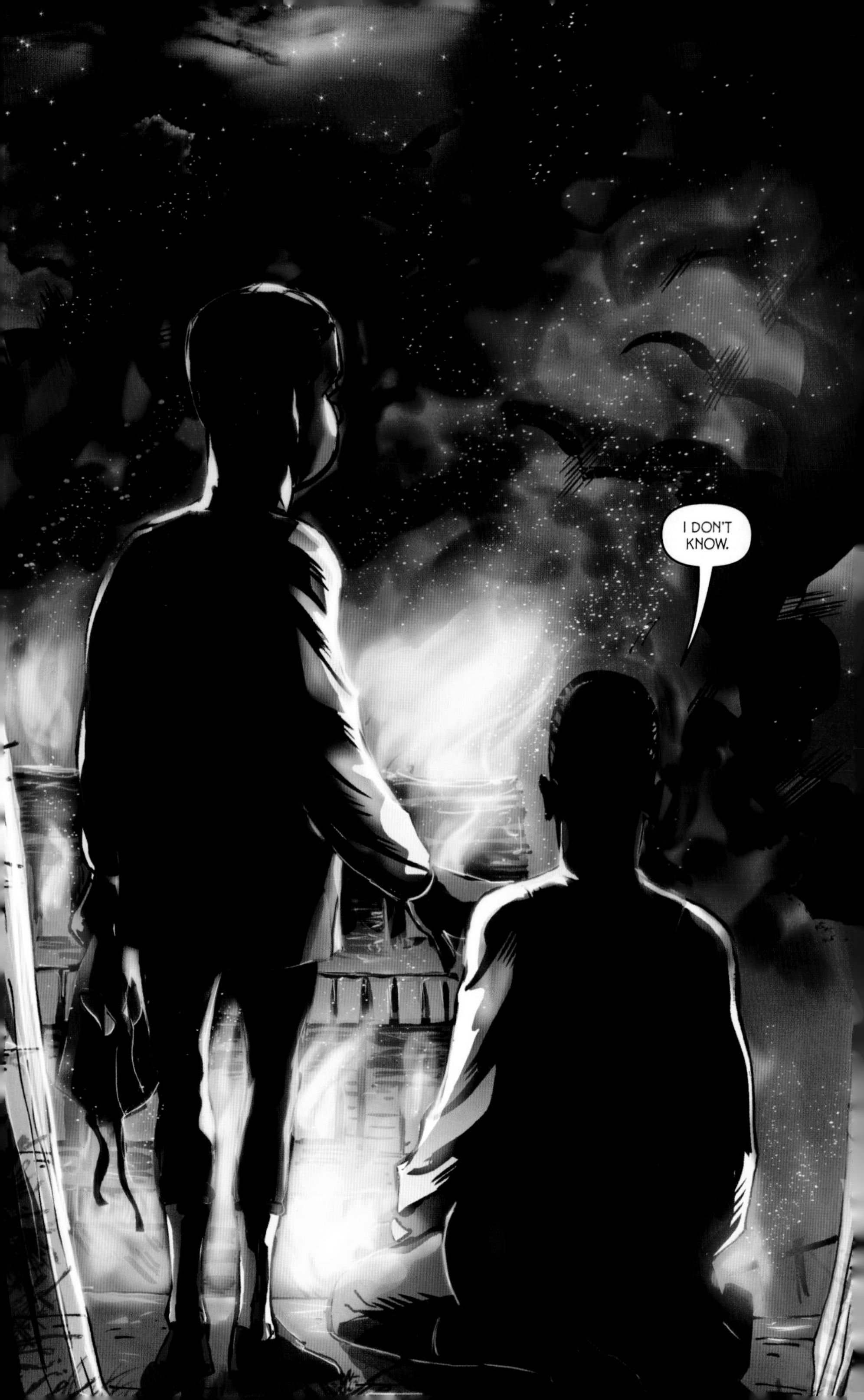
I DON'T KNOW.

EPILOGUE

"Anyone may steer a ship in a calm sea, my brothers....

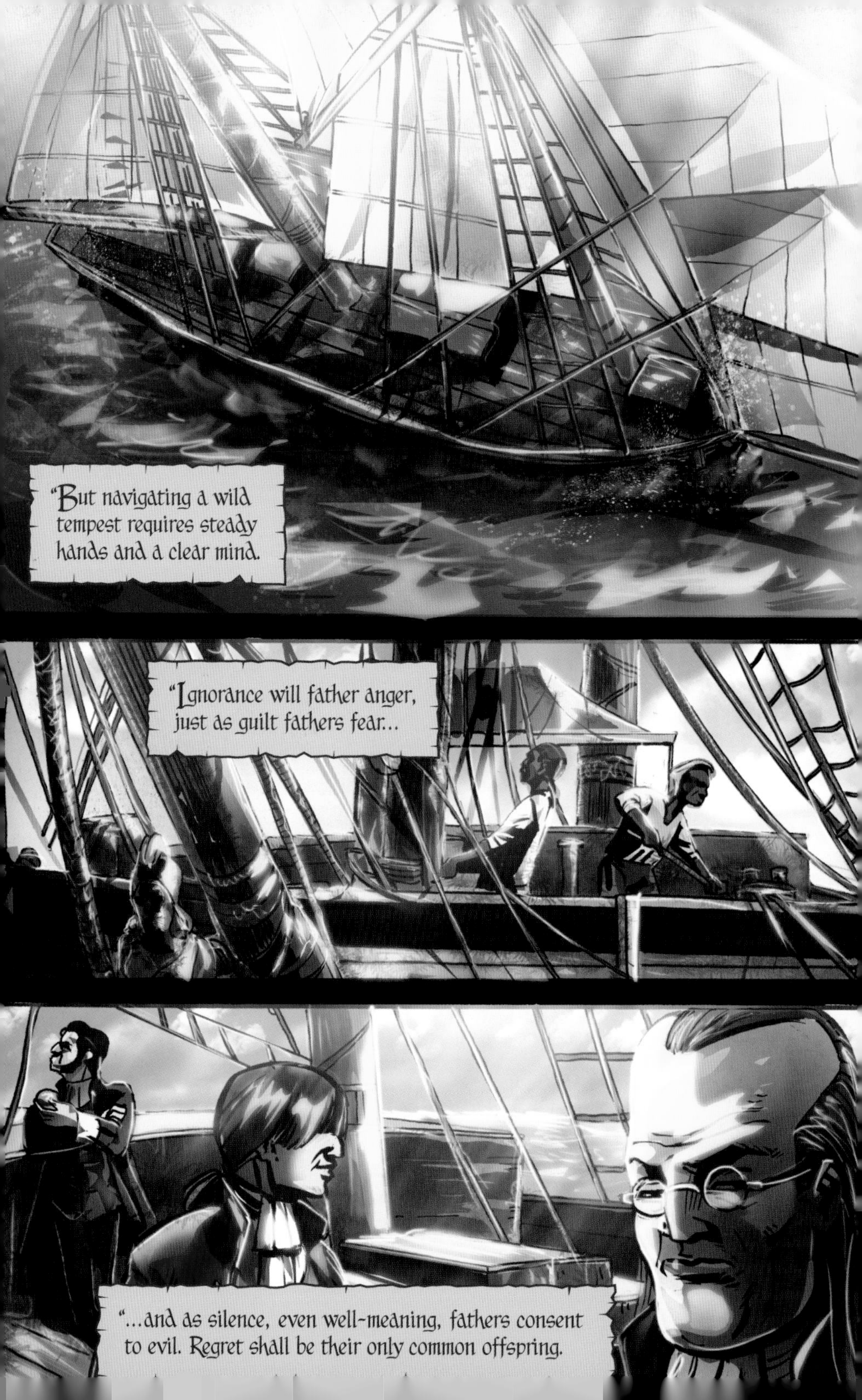
"But navigating a wild tempest requires steady hands and a clear mind.
"Ignorance will father anger, just as guilt fathers fear...
"...and as silence, even well-meaning, fathers consent to evil. Regret shall be their only common offspring.

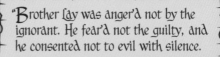
"Brother Lay was anger'd not by the ignorant. He fear'd not the guilty, and he consented not to evil with silence.

"His ship has prevailed over the storms of life to find safe harbor in heaven.

"Will we?"

AUTHORS' NOTE

While some settings, characters, and events in this book are drawn from history, we have taken extensive liberties in the interest of crafting an exciting story. To learn more about the book's facts, fictions, and conjectures—and much more behind-the-scenes information—visit www.thesonsoflibertybooks.com.

ACKNOWLEDGMENTS

The Lagos brothers wish to thank the following for their support, including many who have given their friendship and love over the years: Mr. Cal Hunter and the Grand Design, Wes Reid, Jill Grinberg and her team, Steve Walker, Oren Kramek, Chris Dickey, Nicholas Eliopulos, Heather Palisi, Ellice Lee, the Random House copyediting and production teams, Bruce Brooks, David Graham, Melanie Wellner, Jason Michalski, Carlos Yu, Jamal Igle, Tom Simon, Susan Halmy, Frank Morabito, Aleisha Niehaus, Marilyn Ducksworth, Mitzi Sisk, Matt Johnson, Jody Allen, Will Smith, Darrell Weaver, Neil Surgi of Bookland, Dr. Don Tucker, Michael Harrison, the nuns of St. Anthony of Padua, Glen Ackerman, and Jefferson Lima Jr.

And to our loved ones: Alexander's wife, Cristi Lee, and son, Attis Quinn; Joseph's wife, Laura, daughter, Sophie, and sons, Alex and Liam; Marisa and Mark Tucker; Carson Tucker; Jennifer and Cody Tackett; and, most importantly, Mamá y Papá.

Steve Walker thanks the following: My family, especially Dad, Mom, and Bernadette, for being so supportive; my friends, especially Jamal, Keith, and Steve, for sharing their time, knowledge, and opinions when I needed them; my collaborators on this project; and, of course, Holly, who is my everything.

Oren Kramek dedicates his work on this book to his family and friends.

This book is dedicated to
YOU.
Live free, wherever you may be.

This is a work of fiction. All incidents and dialogue, and all characters with the exception of some well-known historical and public figures, are products of the authors' imagination and are not to be construed as real. Where real-life historical or public figures appear, the situations, incidents, and dialogues concerning those persons are fictional and are not intended to depict actual events or to change the fictional nature of the work. In all other respects, any resemblance to persons living or dead is entirely coincidental.

Cover illustration by Steve Walker and Oren Kramek
Title page illustration by Oren Kramek

Visit us on the Web! www.randomhouse.com/teens

Educators and librarians, for a variety of teaching tools, visit us at
www.randomhouse.com/teachers

www.thesonsoflibertybooks.com

Library of Congress Cataloging-in-Publication Data is available upon request.

ISBN 978-0-375-85670-9 (trade)
ISBN 978-0-375-85667-9 (trade pbk.)
ISBN 978-0-375-95667-6 (lib. bdg.)

MANUFACTURED IN CHINA
10 9 8 7 6 5 4 3 2 1
First Edition

Random House Children's Books supports the First Amendment and celebrates the right to read.

[redacted]